GOOD GIRLS GO TO HELL

GOOD GIRLS GO TO HELL
MASQUERADE SERIES
BOOK TWO

LEAH K PLAMM

LEAH K PLAMM

Good Girls Go To Hell
Copyright © 2023 Leah K. Plamm
All Rights Reserved.
Paperback ISBN 978-619-7592-05-4
PDF ISBN 978-619-7592-06-1
e-book ISBN 978-619-7592-07-8

Without limiting the rights under copyright reserved above, no part of this publication may be reproduced, stored in or introduced into a retrieval system, or transmitted, in any form, or by any means (electronic, mechanical, photocopying, recording or otherwise) without the prior written permission of the copyright owner, except in the case of brief quotations embodied in critical reviews and certain other noncommercial uses permitted by copyright law.

This is a work of fiction. Names, characters, places, brands, media, and incidents are either the product of the author's imagination or are used fictitiously. Any resemblance to actual persons, living or dead, events, or locales is entirely coincidental. The author acknowledges the trademarked status and trademark owners of various products referenced in this work of fiction, which have been used without permission. The publication/use of these trademarks is not authorized, associated with, or sponsored by the trademark owners.

Published by: Leah K. Plamm 2023
leahkplamm@gmail.com

To my loved ones and to all the readers who are fighting their demons. You are not alone.

To all the girls that are "too" soft and forgiving. Don't change. We need more kindness in this world.

And lastly, to all the good girls who would rather live in hell than fuck a nice guy. How's that anxiety treating you?

"The path to paradise begins in hell."

— Dante Alighieri

PLAYLIST

"Love Story (Taylor's Version)"—Taylor Swift
"Mary's Song (Oh My My My) (Taylor's Version)"—Taylor Swift
"All These Years"—Camila Cabello
"Two Ghosts"—Harry Styles
"Bruises"—Lewis Capaldi
"Skinny Love"—Birdy
"Nightmares"—Ellise
"Breathe Me"—Sia
"Nightingale"—Demi Lovato
"Heaven"—Julia Michaels
"Lightweight"—Demi Lovato
"Fix You"—Coldplay
"Wolf"—Selena Gomez, Marshmello
"Almost Is Never Enough"—Ariana Grande, Nathan Sykes
"Bang Bang (My Baby Shot Me Down)"—Daniela Andrade
"Stone Cold"—Demi Lovato
"Stronger"—Britney Spears
"Used To Love (With Dean Lewis)"—Martin Garrix, Dean Lewis

"Born To Make You Happy"—Britney Spears
"Under Your Scars"—Godsmack
"Dark Paradise"—Lana Del Rey
"Burn with You"—Lea Michele
"Timeless (Taylor's Version) (From The Vault)"—Taylor Swift
Spotify YouTube

AUTHOR'S NOTE

This book contains some explicit scenes and is intended for an adult audience. The main character deals with an eating disorder, please proceed cautiously if that is a trigger for you. You can find the full list of trigger warnings on my website: http://www.leahkplamm.com

CHAPTER ONE

STELLA

A shiver shakes my core.
It's cold. And dark.
Did I leave the window open?

I try to make a move to get up and close it, but I can't. I'm curled up in a confined space and there's nowhere to move.

What the hell?

My hands won't move, a slicing sting around my wrists. They're tied.

My head hurts like it's going to explode. Have I been…drugged?

I scream as the realization sinks in. This is not my first rodeo. I've been kidnapped again.

"Stella, you need to focus"—the memory of Mamma's voice rings through my head as vivid as it was back then—*"I need you to run very fast for Mamma, okay? Run as far away as possible and don't stop for anything."*

I'm struggling to remember how to slip out of what seems like zip ties around my wrists. Dammit, I should've listened more in self-defense class and ogled the hot instructor less.

The door of a trunk opens, bright light blinding me.

"Bitch is awake." A rough male voice with a Russian accent makes me jerk my head in its direction. His masked face is hidden behind a flashlight.

"Put her to sleep then," a second raspier voice says.

I whisper through my dry throat, "Wait. No. I'll cooperate."

Am I negotiating with terrorists now?

His mask tugs around the corners of his mouth. The bastard is smirking at me while I'm begging for my life.

He winks at me, making a sign to zip my mouth, then leans in, slipping a satin sleep mask over my eyes, which I recognize is from my carry-on bag, and yanks me up by the arm, throwing me out of the trunk. My knees hit the ground with the hissing sound of the tearing of my jeans. Pain registers somewhere far in my mind as I hear him chuckling.

I was at the airport in New York. I got into a taxi. And that's it. It all blurs after that.

Am I still in New York? I can't hear anything from the humming in my ears. How can a city so noisy be so silent all of a sudden?

The man's callused hand grabs my biceps and pulls me off the ground. I trip over my feet, my whole body shaking, shivers rising under his touch. He feels tall next to me.

There's a door creaking. A swift change of the cold air to warmer and the pungent smell of gasoline attacking my nostrils.

"Please, not back in the trunk," I plead and the raspy one grunts.

"Just fucking walk. Before I change my mind and keep you for myself." I feel him sniffing my neck, and bile rises to my throat.

Please, don't sell me as a sex slave. Please, please, please. I prefer death.

The tall guy drags me through the threshold of another door and pushes me forward. I trip and land on my face, my nose meeting the cold tiles as I hear someone drawing in a sharp breath on the other side of the room. *A new person*, my inner voice chirps in hopefully. I scramble to my knees, turn, and sit on my ass, the rusty smell of the blood wetting my nostrils making me sick. I draw my knees to my chest, thankful I didn't wear a dress today and went with jeans.

"A gift," the raspy one of my kidnappers says slyly.

Another door clicks somewhere, followed by footsteps as someone comes deeper into the room.

"Who the fuck are you, and what the fuck is this?" the new person asks matter-of-factly with just a hint of anger.

I hear some shuffling and muttered curse words in Italian.

Yes!

Shoot.

No.

This can't be good. At least my chances of ending up dead instead of raped just skyrocketed. There's not many Italians who'd want to keep me alive. Actually scratch that. There are none.

"This," the tall Russian barks out, like I'm some object, "is the last of the Morelli famiglia. Daddy's hidden princess."

The cold finger of the tall Russian traces my cheek, and I shudder.

"Don't. Touch. Her."

I suck in a sharp breath, choke, and practically spit my lungs out when I hear the voice of the fourth man somewhere behind me. Too familiar. Too Italian. Thicker and angrier than my last memory of it.

So, I am dreaming after all. Or maybe I'm already dead.

My heart seems to slow down, waiting for more proof I've just arrived in heaven. Or hell, for all I know. But in the exact right place.

Heavy footsteps hit the floor behind me. Tall Russian finally backs off, and I gasp for breath as if I've been under water this whole time.

A much stronger presence slips into his place. One I feel everywhere.

It's *him*.

My mind must be playing tricks on me.

"She can't be a Morelli. The whole family passed away," someone states. It sounds so natural like they weren't brutally massacred.

"Damn right she is. We've been tracking her for a long time now," tall Russian explains, but I can sense he's standing at a safe distance from the man next to me. "It's a gift from Federoff. She's yours to kill."

"Although, I'd fuck her first." Raspy Russian puts in his two cents through a cough. "She seems like a naughty little —" Cold fingers touch my skin just before a crunching sound slices the air. Russian curses are spit from the tall one, and a wail from the raspy one tells me he just got what he deserved.

"For touching her, you lose your hand."

No!

It can't be true.

More men invade the room, the clicking sound of loading guns in the air. The Russians go quiet.

Rough fingers glide across my cheek to my temple, eliciting a spark with the power of lightning I haven't felt since I was sixteen.

It can't be…

He slides a finger under the strap of the sleep mask and pulls it up.

"Lucifer!" I gasp, blinking against the most beautiful eyes. Gray as prowling clouds in a thunderstorm. Just as I remember them.

My racing heart skips a beat. Or two.

For a split second they soften, but somebody clears their throat, and just like that they turn cold and sharp as a steel knife. He stands from the ground where he was crouching before me and steps back.

It's then I remember he's dead.

"What?" I want to shout but end up barely whispering.

Lucifer, my first and only love, the ghost haunting me for the last eight years of my life. Always creeping in my first and last thought of each day, breaking my heart with every memory.

He's here. In front of me. Twenty-eight years old, very much alive and more gorgeous than ever.

His dark curly hair is still shoulder-length and shaggy. Where there was a scrawny boy, now there's a big, strong man with broad shoulders and tattoos starting at his knuckles and disappearing under the rolled-up sleeves of his gray shirt. He's grown since the last time I saw him when he was twenty and I was sixteen. He must be six foot six.

Dangerous, delicious, and so, so Italian. My favorite combination.

The only thing that hasn't changed is the look in his stormy eyes he could never hide from me. The same one that's earned him a thousand punishments from my father every time we got too close.

Oh, just how close we were...

A soft "Lou" falls out of my lips.

"You taking the bitch or what?" the raspy Russian growls, like a cold shower to my heated thoughts.

I didn't realize he's holding his limp hand like it's broken, still standing tall and proud even though three guns are pointing at him, just a lot angrier. I remember that stance. Mafia soldiers. Never broken, they don't have a heart. I should know, I grew up around them.

Lucifer's slicing him with a stare. I swear, for a moment I think he could kill him. But that's not my Lou. He's not a monster.

"What do you want me to do, boss?" The other guy takes a few steps in our direction. I want to see his face, but I can't concentrate on anything else other than my not-so-dead ex-lover.

"For insulting her." Lucifer takes a gun with a silencer out of the other man's arm and in two swift shots the Russians are falling to the ground. "You lose your head."

My scream is buried somewhere so deep I can't reach it. The love of my life just killed someone. He killed two people. For me.

Could it all be a bad dream? Then why do I still feel the zip ties cutting into my wounded flesh?

How can Lucifer be alive when he was killed with my family? And why is this man calling him boss?

Ha! Maybe the insomnia finally got me.

Lucifer bends down, stretching his arms out to me. The static electricity from his touch zips through my skin, and I crawl back with a little squeal. His brows furrow, and his lush lips press into a thin line. He closes his eyelids, taking a breath, and when he opens them, there's not a trace of emotion left.

He flipped it off like a switch.

Pushing his arms beneath me, he lifts me up against his chest. If I'm not already dead, I'm pretty sure my heart just stopped.

I can't hold it anymore. As much as I try to stay awake, my eyes act on their own accord and close shut.

I'm sorry, Mamma.

"Find out who knows of her." The last thing I hear is Lucifer's steps as he takes us out of the room and then the words I never thought would come out from his mouth. "Kill them all."

CHAPTER TWO

LUCIFER

Moonlight grazes Stella's olive skin. An angel. Living proof that God exists.

A test I've once again failed.

Damien Black picks up at the third ring. "You're ruining my engagement night."

The only thing I've ever liked about Black is the thought of his pretty face smashed underneath my Italian loafers.

"Congratu-fucking-lations," I grit out. "They found her."

"What the hell, Visconti? I thought we had a deal!"

Trying to keep myself from driving a fist through the mirror, I grip the dressing table, my knuckles turning white. "We did and you didn't carry out your part to protect her. Consider me sparing your miserable life my wedding gift."

Black and his huge-ass ego have the nerve to chuckle. "You have as much fault as I do since you were the one that was supposed to keep them away. Where is she? I'm coming to get her."

Fuck.

I know it's wrong but I can't stop myself. I'm signing my suicide note with her name on it.

"Stella's staying where she should've been all along. With me."

"If the other families find out about her, she's dead. Not on my watch," he hisses low.

"This is not a negotiation. You had your shot and you blew it. She's in better hands now."

"Lucifer…" he warns.

"I'll leave you to your celebration. Goodbye, Black."

"This isn't over, Visconti."

I disconnect the call.

"Lou," a soft feminine voice whispers. Goose bumps break out all over my body.

That. Fucking. Nickname.

I turn around to find her on the bed still sleeping, back turned to me.

Fuck me.

I'm not prepared for this. For her.

Like a siren's song, a soft moan compels me to go closer. Admire her. Caress her cheek.

Stella jerks awake at the touch, her big curious eyes widening.

Il mar azzurro di Sicilia. The Sicilian sea lives in her eyes. Sunshine and aqua-blue perfection.

I brush a fallen golden strand from her face. Her lips part like she wants to say something but stops.

"Hi, princess." The nickname I gave her rolls off my tongue with ease as if time has rewound back eight years.

The whole spectrum of emotions passes through her face until she settles for a soft smile that doesn't match the tears rolling over her blushing cheeks. Her hand sneaks up on me, a burning grasp on my wrist, and I can see the fear in her eyes vanishing as she realizes I'm here in blood and flesh.

"Lou," she repeats, as if her touch isn't hurting me enough. "How?"

It takes all my strength to rip her hand off my wrist and put it back. "The doctor will be here soon to check on you."

"What are you talking about? What doctor?" She sits up and draws her knees to her chest as the tears keep falling with the speed of her questions. "How are you alive? Why?"

I hate seeing women cry. I despise seeing *her* cry. As much as I want to pull her into my arms and promise her everything will be all right, I can't. I'm not the boy she knew. So much has changed in eight years.

"Stella"—it cuts me open to see her shudder under my cold, rehearsed tone—"clean yourself up and use the bell. Your maid will send the doctor to you."

I leave her there, shivering and bawling on the satin sheets, and make my exit before I change my mind, turn around, and beg for her forgiveness on my knees.

CHAPTER THREE

STELLA

I stare at the closed door, confused. Where, in God's name, am I?

Nothing is familiar.

A soft pink wallpaper. White couch with pink fluffy pillows by the windows. My feet land on the plush carpet and take me to the closed heavy curtains. I take a breath and find myself squeezing my eyes shut as I grip the fabric in my fists. Nostalgia wraps around my fragile heart preparing me for…a French window and an unfamiliar garden behind it.

I don't know what I expected to see. Maybe my old home? I feel like I'm going insane.

I stare at the garden but all I see are memories replaying on the glass like a movie screen.

A five-year-old girl sits at the balcony, awaiting her father. The growl of an engine announces his return, and she jumps out the chair, running down the lavish staircase to welcome him. After stumbling out to the courtyard, she stops dead in her tracks in front of a boy. A very confused and lonely boy with the saddest, most beautiful eyes she's ever seen.

My father, Giovanni Morelli, brought Lucifer home a few days after my mother's funeral. Il Diavolo, my father called him. He said the fury in his eyes reminded him of hell's fire, silver like the ashes of the sinners.

My father was a very religious man. Funny, considering what he did for a living.

I didn't understand it. All I saw in Lou was a hurt and abused nine-year-old boy with olive skin and dark curls falling in front of his face. He was beautiful even then.

Now that I think about it, I fell for him at that first glance. Long before I realized it at thirteen.

I take a few steps back until my back hits the wall, and I slide down to the ground like the tears on my cheeks.

How is this possible?

My chest hurts with the quiet sobs. Was he alive this whole time while I was mourning him? Maybe he didn't know I survived. Maybe he thought I died in the massacre.

It can't be anything else, he wouldn't do that to me.

Or maybe I'm still naïve.

Our manor was so big it was like a village. It had its own church, vineyard, houses for all the staff, and a beach coast. Believe it or not, for a long time I thought this was the whole country. My father never let me out of the estate after what happened to my mother. Locked me in his gilded castle and let me believe this was all the world had to offer. At the time I was happy with it; I didn't know any other.

Very few people came in and out of Morelli's manor, and the staff were wary of their kids being in my presence, so that left me with one option—Lou.

First, he was my friend. Then he became my knight in dirty armor. And on my sixteenth birthday, he became my lover, which made him my everything.

A few months before the massacre, something in the

atmosphere changed. My father was on edge, my stepmother was insufferable, and Lucifer often ran off to somewhere. That's when I realized there might be a whole other world outside of these high walls in Sicily.

The day my father came to my room and told me to pack my luggage for a trip I was so excited my scream must've shaken the foundations of the mansion. Lou was nowhere to be found when I searched to tell him Giovanni finally let me out of my cage. I didn't know there was a "no return policy" in the deal.

We traveled through unknown and beautiful lands on an airplane I've only seen in the movies. I was so fascinated with the people on the streets, the colorful buildings, and crowded beaches. I landed in Rosehill, Florida where my godmother Melanie Black lived with her children. Melanie's mansion was a lot smaller than mine. She had neighbors with even smaller houses, and they weren't her servants. I always thought people lived in closed communities like ours.

In my defense I didn't know my father was the head of the Sicilian mafia. I wasn't allowed to watch TV, and the only movies I had were chosen by my nannies. I thought Giovanni was a businessman who often traveled abroad to new lands. Until the news came.

A violent shudder shakes my body, ceasing my trip down memory lane. I peel myself off the floor to go to the bathroom.

Dio mio.

I look like I've been chewed and spit out by death. Smell like it too. Bruised nose, bloody mouth. My clothes are torn and dirty. God, what if my kidnappers threw away my luggage?

I return to the room only to find my suitcase is sitting half-opened on the floor in the corner where I didn't notice it before. If I was kidnapped in the taxi and Lucifer killed the Russians it would make sense that he found my luggage in their car. I rummage through it. Everything safe except for my sleeping eye mask is here. However, there's no sight of my purse. No phone, no watch, no documents or money. I have no idea what time it is. I was supposed to be at Ivy and Damien's engagement party. They're probably worried sick.

I grab a towel and rush to the shower. Not even the sting of the water on my wounds can rip my eyes off the bloodied water on the white tiles. Flashbacks keep coming at me and I hug my middle, leaning against the wall.

I was sitting in the Blacks' living room, playing a game on the newest PlayStation with Damien, when I heard the voice of the reporter from the TV in the other room.

"The infamous head of the Sicilian mafia, Giovanni Morelli, has died in a mass shooting late last evening, along with his wife, his children, and everyone that lived in the sprawling Morelli property, most of which has burned down in a fire. The war between the Sicilian mafia families has gone to new levels, resulting in more than one hundred victims. The exact number is uncertain at the moment. The police are still searching through the premises for any survivors..."

They found none.

All the sounds around me meshed into background noise. Somewhere along that statement, I had moved from one room to the other and somehow ended up on the floor on my knees staring at the big flat screen TV, watching the lady reporter stand in front of the walls of my burning home, tears streaming down my cheeks, and the only thing that passed through my mind was one word.

Lou.

Then the sobs came with another word. *Orphan.*

Damien held me in his arms as I broke apart, trying to find the answer. Was this another bad dream? Like the ones I was constantly having. But I couldn't. My legs were numb, and my body was limp. I'll never forget Aunt Melanie's face when she ran home to find me.

My father, my stepbrothers, my friends. They were all dead.

Lucifer's death was never confirmed. I had hope for nearly three years after the massacre that somehow he got out alive. But I knew whatever had happened during the days, he would always come home in the evening to sneak into my room and kiss me goodnight. I knew he would've been at the manor that night, probably on my balcony. And when I didn't hear from him for three years I knew I had to move on.

Yet here we are, eight years later, I'm twenty-four and more confused than ever. All the hurt I've felt for the last eight years is replaced by conflicting feelings of anger, betrayal, hope and happiness.

As the drops of the hot water beat on me like a whip, I close my eyes for a second and allow myself a small smile. Lucifer is alive. It's time to get the answers to almost a decade of questions.

CHAPTER FOUR

STELLA

"Come in," Lucifer's thick voice commands on the other side of the closed dark door, and the butterflies in my stomach take flight as if I'm sixteen again.

I push open the heavy door to find Lucifer illuminated under a desk lamp, settled behind a mahogany desk with piles of papers and a laptop on it. Wood and leather seem to be the theme of the interior of this apartment or house or whatever it is.

"Did you get examined by the doctor?" he asks, not even lifting his head.

"Yes." I step in further, excitement putting a bounce to my step. "He said all the symptoms lead to drug poisoning. I have a minor concussion and some bruises but I'll be fine."

"Good." He continues, not a trace of emotion in his voice. Under the sparse lighting, his dark and sharp features give him a devilish look. My Lou was more of an angel. "Is there anything else?"

Something isn't right, and I don't wait for an invitation to find out what it is. I sashay my way to the brown leather armchair.

My Lou.

It still feels like a dream seeing him a few feet away from me. In the same gray clothes, showing off all his muscled, tattooed sexiness.

Oh, screw this.

I rush forward, forgetting all about manners, and push his chair back. His eyes widen for a second before his whole body goes stiff as I wrap my arms around him.

"I've missed you so much. I can't even tell you what I've been through." My tears start involuntarily, but I don't try to suppress them. I just burrow my head in his hot chest and let all my feelings out. "When I lost you, Lou...I thought the pain was going to kill me. Why did you do this to me? I never loved another..." My words get cut short when he puts me on the ground. "What are you doing?" I object, but it doesn't really matter because he's a giant, and I'm barely five foot four on a good day.

His eyes are stone-cold, lips pressed into a thin line as he backs away from me and redirects me to the armchair.

"Sit, Stella. We have some matters to discuss." A shiver runs through me at the coolness of his tone.

Okay, that's new. Lucifer would never talk to me in that manner. It's like I'm seeing a stranger.

What did you think? He was alive the whole time and he let you suffer.

He doesn't seem surprised by me being alive. He must've known. Maybe...maybe he never loved me.

Silence spreads as I sit down.

"How?" The loudest question in my head pops out before he speaks.

He takes in a breath and settles in his chair. "I'd advise you to lay off the questions."

Who does he think he is? I might've loved him once upon

a time and maybe I never stopped but I refuse to be talked to like a child. I deserve to know the answers. My fists hit the surface of the desk. "You can't just show up after I've mourned you for eight years and ask this of me!"

He rises from his seat, shadowing over me. "You shouldn't have. Men like me are not for you. Now sit your ass down and listen to me."

I stagger back, shaken by this stranger who looks an awful lot like my Lucifer, but it can't be him. Lou would never order me around this way. The back of my knees hit the chair, and I sit on the edge once again.

"Why was I kidnapped?"

"Because of your last name." He scratched at his five o'clock shadow.

"Who were these Russian people? Did you get in trouble with the mafia?"

"You're asking too many questions."

"How did they make the connection to you?"

He stays silent as my hands start shaking even more. He clearly never cared enough to let me know he was alive. Why would he care now to answer my questions? I'm just an inconvenience to him.

He presses two fingers on his temples and closes his eyes. "You have to trust me on this one."

"Trust you? You're not acting like yourself, Lou. You would've never..." *What*? Keep me in the dark? Kill two people in front of me? Lie about his death? Clearly, he has no scruples.

"The situation you've put yourself in endangers your life."

"That *I* have put myself in?" I can't hide the hurt in my voice. He knows what the first kidnapping did to my mental state. "*I* was going to my friend's engagement party. *You* and whoever your *buddies* are, put me here."

I throw a glance at the large library behind him. It would be the perfect place to spend my time if I was staying. Fortunately, I'm not.

"I want to leave. Immediately." Yet, a part of me wants to stay with him. Find out what really happened. Why?

I've never realized I needed closure. I had it. They were dead. But now...

"You'll be staying with me until I figure out a way to resolve the problem."

"The hell I am! I have a life, Lucifer." He looks as bored as ever. "I have people that love me. They will be looking for me." The press of his mouth is enough to tell me he got the accusation in my tone. Damien's probably organizing a search party for me. I don't even know how much time I've been gone.

"You're staying here, you're laying low, and that's the end of this conversation!" he growls.

I narrow my eyes. "Why didn't you just let them kill me? Or better yet, do it yourself. I can see you've skipped the mourning."

Is there a part of my Lou behind this stranger?

He closes his eyes, and when he opens them again, there's anger bubbling inside, redness staining his cheeks and clenched jaw.

That's good, I convince myself. I'd take angry over the indifferent any day. Emotion. Whatever emotion I can provoke so I don't have to stare at these lifeless gray eyes.

"Where's my phone?"

"Stored somewhere safe. Your friends have been let known that your plane was delayed, you got robbed and you're staying with a friend."

"They'll never believe these lies."

The corner of his mouth lifts. "They will if they know what's good for them."

"Is that a threat?" I can't believe his audacity. "Are you a mobster too?" Nothing else makes sense.

"Watch your mouth." He says like I'm a naughty child. "I'm a respectable businessman in construction. You got into the wrong hands and you'll be free when this situation is resolved."

"Do you owe them money or something?"

"I didn't want it to come to this, but if I have to, I'll lock you up, princess."

My lips part and my left eyebrow tics.

For the second time in two days my world has been turned upside down.

I can't believe Lucifer used the pet name he gave me and my father's favorite threat in the same sentence. He even used the same exact words as him.

"You mispronounced Stellina." I hiss and get up. That's what my father used to call me right before he locked me in my room to cry and beg.

But I'm not that little scared girl anymore.

"I demand my phone back with my documents."

"You can't have it."

"Damien wouldn't believe a second of this. He'll send you back to the land of the unliving."

A ghost of a smile appears on his face. He raises an eyebrow. "Try me."

I force all my energy to produce the most sugary smile I have. "I would but the man I loved died a long time ago."

His cocky face falls. I can feel the room chilling as he turns to a stranger once again, but I'm not having a second more of this meaningless conversation. It's clear the man I used to love stayed buried under the ruins of my legacy.

The princess isn't saved by the beast. She needs to save herself.

I turn around and leave the door open as I exit, strutting through the wooden hallways of this huge place all the way to the bedroom.

The sun is starting to rise when I throw myself onto the bed, and I spend the next seemingly thousand hours silently crying, tossing and turning, trying to find a way out of this hellhole. Who needs sleep when your labyrinth nightmares have become your reality?

CHAPTER FIVE

STELLA

"The Russians now consider her a threat, and they want her dead." The voice of the man I barely remember from that night sounds uncharacteristically casual for a statement like that.

My ear is pulsing so hard that it's seconds away from knocking on the door it's pressed against. Some might judge me for eavesdropping, but I should know if I'm going to die soon, right? Lucifer sure as hell won't tell me. He didn't even stop by my room yesterday. And so far I've come up with no solutions to my problem of being trapped here.

"You killed two of their people," the voice argues.

"They shouldn't have touched her."

"I agree, however…"

Lucifer doesn't let him finish. "They won't do anything while she's here."

"But they expect you to. We're in bad enough relations as it is. You don't want to…" His words die as I hear footsteps inside the room.

The door I'm leaning against flies open, and I fall forward right into Lucifer's arms. Naked, sweaty, strong arms. *Oh,*

Dio mio. Save me from my misery. I steal a look behind his shoulder. A training room with a punching bag in the middle. The other man is looking our way, and he doesn't seem one bit happy.

Lucifer pushes me off him, and I stagger back. He instantly grabs me by the shoulders to steady me. My mouth fills with saliva as I gape at his semi-naked, tattooed body dressed only in red boxing shorts. The light reflects the millions drops of sweat trickling down his abs, and I've never felt that kind of jealousy.

"Can I help you?" He raises an eyebrow with a smirk that tells me he finds joy in the way I'm left speechless as I shamelessly ogle him.

"I… I…"

Boy, did he grow up. I've never seen such handsome splendor in my life. Jaw so chiseled under his five o'clock shadow it could cut stone. He kept the shoulder-length of his tousled dark curls, and part of me wonders if it's because he knows how much I loved them. It gives him that kind of boyish but I'll-fuck-you-to-death look. It'll be a marvelous death.

Danger. Abort mission. Danger.

Oh, so now my brain has decided to switch on. Too late, I'm already hypnotized. This sight will give me something to think about during sleepless nights.

There's a hint of a smile under his impassive mask. "I'm going to pretend that didn't happen. Now go back to your room." His voice is decadently dark.

Stella! What's the matter with you? You want out of here, not in.

I've never had thoughts like this. But I can't help it.

"Um… I can't stay there anymore." *Good job, Stella, now peel your eyes off him and demand what you came for.*

His lips press in a thin line. "I heard. Your constant pacing through the hallways is giving me a headache."

"I have to work, Lucifer. I'll lose my clients. Let me go to work and I'll come back in the evenings."

I didn't say it was a great plan. But I'd already researched every corner of this floor. There are security cameras at every exit, bodyguards everywhere and the windows are too high.

"I told you already, this is non-negotiable."

"I'm losing it, Lou," I try my back-up plan, looking deep into his eyes, searching for the Lou I know. There must be some compassion left in him. People can only change so much, right? "I can't sleep. I can't eat. I need to go out or I'll go mad."

He averts his gaze, sighing as his hands fall from my shoulders, and he gestures for me to enter.

Yes! Success!

I didn't expect this to work at all, seeing as he ignored my banging on his office door all day yesterday.

Inside the huge gray and blue room smells like sweat and testosterone. There are all kinds of exercise equipment and a punching bag.

The only odd thing is the man in a three-piece, designer burgundy suit. Now that I can see him better, he looks strangely familiar.

"Have you ever been to Sicily?"

The corners of his mouth curl upward. "A couple of times." There's a spark in his blue eyes that I'm sure I've seen before.

"Okay, now"—Lucifer steps between us and as my gaze falls on his hard chest, I almost forget what I came in for—"Marcel will help you shop online for whatever you need."

"Why do I have to be the babysitter?" Marcel snorts.

"Online shopping? What am I, a bored housewife? The

least you could do is let me see New York if you're going to force me to stay in this—"

"Your safety isn't debatable." Lucifer cuts me off with a hard stare. "Make sure you get everything you need to feel good here because this is your new home, and you're not going to leave it until I say so."

"I hate you." I sneer, crossing my arms on my chest. He might not let me leave but I'll find a way out.

A little smile appears on his face, but he quickly masks it. "Be smart, go get dressed, and take this chance while I'm giving it to you."

"What are you talking about? I'm dressed." I look down at my white Daisy Dukes, blue crop-top, and Tory Burch sandals.

Okay, I may have dressed in the skimpiest clothes I could find in my suitcase. And I may have been pacing the hallway in hopes he'd see me, realize what he's missing and take me away so I won't have to climb out the third floor. And maybe my plan wasn't that sharp. But I had to try something. He acts like eleven years of us never even happened. Like I'm just another stranger in his new life.

Marcel tries to suppress a laugh, but it comes out as a snort.

"What?" I ask, feigning innocence.

For the first time since I got here, Lucifer's eyes drift to my body. "God help me," he murmurs, shaking his head. "You're not walking these hallways looking like that."

I raise my eyebrows and cock a hand on my hip. "And what exactly would *that* be?" He looks down at my naked midriff, and suddenly all the confidence I've gathered through years of hard work vanishes to thin air.

Last he saw me I weighed a lot less. Not that I'm overweight by any measure, but now I've got curves and a lot more meat on my bones.

I perk my chin up, "I'm sorry. You're not the only one who's changed. This"—I gesture from my head to my toes—"is who I am now. Marcel, I'm ready whenever you are." I stomp out of the room, not giving Lucifer another chance to jab at my insecurities. I don't have that luxury.

Marcel follows swiftly behind me. "Gotta get something from the car first."

I let excitement wash over me as we wait for the elevator. This is my chance. A little part of me wants to see the house. Who Lucifer grew up to be. Is he a slob or a clean freak? Is he a minimalist or a bohemian-style type of guy? But I don't have that luxury, I need to be fast.

"After you." Marcel gestures when the elevator arrives. The ride is short and uncomfortably silent. The doors slide open, revealing a big garage housing three vehicles: a red Ferrari, a black town car, and a big black SUV Cadillac, all of them with tinted windows.

As the smell of gasoline fills my nostrils, the memories from my terrifying encounter come back. I'm pretty sure that's where we entered after the Russians blindfolded me. Rest in peace; they won't be missed.

Marcel opens the back door of the SUV and looks at me over his shoulder. A distant flashback hits me like a brick on the head—a little boy with light brown hair and blue eyes staring at me, hiding behind the grape vines of the manor.

"Giovanni brought you to the manor, didn't he?"

He freezes, his eyes concentrated on mine. He kind of reminds me of my father, same deep ocean-blue gaze, a bit lighter hair.

I got my features from my mom. Aqua eyes, natural sun-kissed skin and golden hair, and fluffy cheeks that show embarrassment way too fast. She was beautiful from the little memories I have of her.

"I was wondering when you'd remember, *Stellina*." He winks at me.

My left eyebrow tics. I hate that nickname. "You used to come every Sunday for the service at our church two summers in a row, and we played so much. Lucifer hated you."

His booming laughter echoes off the white garage walls. "He did, yes."

"Is that why you stopped coming?"

His laughter dies as he produces something from the back seat and then locks the door. "No."

The conversation died as fast as it started. I realized I got distracted and missed my window. What were the chances that the garage door was unlocked?

Following behind Marcel, I look around for any escape chances. There's a window in the hallway leading to the street where the sun is shining on a good August day, and nothing in sight is familiar.

I need to create a distraction.

"So, how did you end up here? And where exactly is this here?"

"New York," he offers with a mocking tone.

"Ha-ha. I guessed that by the cloud of dust in the sky and the heartless buildings."

"New York might be a lot of things but it's not heartless. It has a pulse and an opinion, and I'm sure if you would just give it a chance, it will suck you right in like you've always belonged."

What I do know is this city is Lucifer's new home. A home that he didn't feel the need to share with me. A home that he probably shared with lots of other women. Women with tall legs and tanned bodies who dress like supermodels and walk the streets freely like it's their runway and they're the stars of the show. Or so I imagine.

"We're in the Upper East Side," Marcel says.

"You didn't answer my first question," I say, still staring at the reflection of the beautiful building.

Marcel tugs me ever so slightly in the direction of the elevator. "Lucifer helped me in a hard time. I owe him my life."

Hmm, that's interesting. *Not your business, Stella,* my inner voice pipes in. *Stop being so nosy, start being more smart.*

I look out another window that faces the inner side of the building where the garden is. "I can't spend another minute in my room. Please?" I beg him as we wait for the elevator, puppy eyes and all.

His mouth tugs at the corners, but he remains stoic. "Garden it is. Through here." He shows me the way to the back door. "Fair warning, it's scorching hot out there. I'll bring the laptop."

He disappears into the elevator leaving me alone in the silent hallway. My eyes land on a golden-framed mirror on the wall. Like a spell, I freeze in front of it.

"Here's your vegetables, no pasta for you. Look at you, your last summer jeans barely fit you." My stepmother's evil laughter echoes in my mind.

I look down at my thighs. I'm beautiful. I am. I have to believe it. But I swear it feels like they're getting bigger with every second I look at them. *Stop it, Stella. Stop it!*

Escape.

Right. That's where I was heading. The past is the past. It's going to stay dead as it should.

I grab the windowsill and hoist myself up. Thank God for

Ivy's non-stop pestering about workouts. I manage to open the window. It's small, it barely fits me. I wiggle myself through it, almost tasting the freedom when a hand grabs my calf.

"Where do you think you're going?" Marcel pulls me back down and I land with an elbow in his mouth.

His brows furrow but he pins me to the wall. "And here I was thinking you'd be sunbathing."

"Let go of me," I say through gritted teeth.

"Will you behave or do I need to tell Lucifer that you disobeyed him the second you got the chance?"

"I'm sure that'll go well." I smirk. "What will your boss say when he learns you let me out of your sight?"

He pushes me toward the garden. "You want to work or no?" He gestures with the laptop. "I could leave you to rot in that bedroom or you can cooperate and make this easier for yourself. I'm not exactly fond of babysitting, the other guys even less so. I can send one of them to tame you."

I mutter a couple of suggestions of where he can put those guys.

"What was that?" He smirks.

"Fine." I push through the door and enter the garden.

"What do you do for work anyway?" he asks.

"I'm a fashion designer." I sit at a picnic table in the shade. "I need top-of-the-notch sewing machines and fabrics. I'll give you a contact for the fabrics." I know their number by memory.

He rolls his eyes, settling on a bench. "Is that all, your highness?"

"Yeah." I think for a second. "Actually, can we get some groceries so I can cook?"

"Sure, I'll introduce you to the chef."

CHAPTER SIX

LUCIFER

"I believe you'll do the right thing. Don't forget Federoff hates you, but he hates the alliance more. You need to get on his good side or at least not be his target." Enzo Rossi, my consigliere, flicks his cigarette on my wooden flooring, making me cringe inside. A thousand-dollar pinstriped suit, long black overcoat, a custom fedora hat, and a face that doesn't look a day over fifty despite his sixty-four years of life. That's Enzo Rossi for you. A walking, talking prototype of every dapper Don's movie cliché. I've never seen him wear anything that John Gotti wouldn't wear.

I, on the other hand, prefer a more laid-down style. I don't feel the need to shout to the world that I'm the capo of one of the biggest crime families every time I step out.

"I trust your opinion on the matter, sir, but I'm not my father. I won't kill an innocent girl because someone is afraid of her. She's barely a hundred and twenty pounds, for fuck's sake."

"Language, boy!" he scolds me.

I harden my stare. "I'm no boy, Enzo, and I don't hurt women."

"I know you're still holding on to your soul, but you can't save them all. We're not the good guys here, Lucifer." He shrugs, taking one slow step at a time.

"Tell me about it," I mumble under my breath.

The old man's laughter booms through the hallway, and he pats me on the back. "I know it's not your life path by choice, but it's your destiny. You can't change it. Better save yourself some trouble and figure out a way to get rid of her."

It rubs me the wrong way how he's talking about his former capo's daughter. I know Enzo Rossi, and his loyalties lie with the winning side. His job is to give me guidance but still... Stella's an angel. She grew up before his eyes. He says that every year at this "job" takes away a part of your soul, and I can tell it's been a long time since he lost sleep over his conscience. Unlike me, hence the constant sour mood.

"The Carters still don't know she's alive." His blunt statement as usual has a lot more written in between. "Neither do the other families."

"I'll deal with them."

He grins like he knows something I don't and shakes his head. His secretive smiles usually don't bother me, but there's something wrong in this one.

"What's that smell?" He scrunches his nose at the delicious smell that's been swirling in the air all evening.

"That would probably be her."

His forehead furrows. "You're keeping her here? Are you insane?"

"Watch your tongue, old man. How am I supposed to protect her if she's out there? The house is the best sanctuary."

He shakes his head. "You'll never change, boy. Always her knight in bloody armor. Always."

"It's time for you to go. I'll walk you out." I don't want him "accidentally" passing through the kitchen.

But as my luck is, we meet Stella on the second-floor's hallway, making her way from the bathroom to the kitchen.

"Stellina!" She and I freeze on the spot, and her left eyebrow tics as she turns to us. She's always hated the nickname her father gave her. She only ever liked mine.

The idiot in me smirks, but I keep my straight face on.

"Enzo?" She blinks, mouth agape.

"Bellissima." He pulls her into a hug. "You look marvelous, my child."

You fucking hypocrite, I want to scream. He was just telling me to get rid of her, and now she's *his* child.

She stands there still frozen, staring at me with a million questions in her eyes.

Enzo finally lets her go and turns to me with a devilish smile. He could probably read my thoughts. After all, he's the closest to a father figure I've had since I was nine, except for Giovanni. The old man somehow figures out all my dirty secrets. Being in love with the blonde for almost two decades being the dirtiest of them all.

"How? What? Why?" she asks the questions, never once looking at him, keeping those doe eyes focused on my face.

"I'm visiting an old friend, bella," Enzo explains when I don't answer. His smirk grows to a full-blown smile as he sees I'm seconds away from ripping off the hand he has on her shoulder. "I have to get going. I hope I can see you sometime, Stellina. Ciao." He kisses her cheek as her eyebrow tics again. I press the elevator button, and he steps inside. "You better go eat, Lucifer. You don't want her dish to turn cold."

I grit my teeth at another one of his ambiguous statements, and the doors of the elevator close.

I can feel the energy shifting as we walk back, just the two of us.

"What the hell am I doing here Lucifer?" she mumbles, staring at the hallway where Enzo was.

"I told you already. Stop asking questions. It's for your own safety."

"Safety, huh?" Her narrowed gaze tells me there's nothing but questions coming. "I'll give you an easier one. Why did you kill my kidnappers?"

I grumble, starting to walk out, but she catches my arm. Her eyes are telling me she's not letting this go.

"Because they hurt you."

"You are hurting me right now. Should I kill you?"

I take the knife from the counter and pass it to her, the blade pointing at me. "You can try."

She sticks her nose up in the air. "No, thank you. I am not a murderer."

"Well, princess, you better get on with the program because you'll be spending a long while under the roof of the murderer who saved you."

"Why?"

"Let's eat," I offer, trying to get her attention on anything else.

"Mm-hmm," she murmurs, stomping her foot. "At least tell me how long I'm going to be here?"

I press her back to the counter, caging her in. "As long as I say. One more question and you're losing your work rights. Am I understood?"

She nods, her throat bobbing.

I follow after her as she makes her way to the stove, the smell of garlic, basil, and tomatoes making my stomach growl.

"What the hell happened here?" There's flour scattered all

over the place, and I swear there's some on the ceiling. There are four cooked dishes somewhere between all this mess, and I see another one baking in the oven.

"I cooked." She blushes.

"I can see that."

Stella always cooks when she's nervous. It was her hobby at the manor, whenever she wasn't sewing something. I've got no idea why she did it when she never ate the food she cooked, and she was the best of all three chefs her father had.

"There's Pasta alla Norma," she says, like it's some kind of a peace offering.

"You know me well." I close my eyes and inhale the aroma of my favorite pasta.

I'm hyperaware as Stella moves through the kitchen to come behind my back. Her radiating heat makes every hair on my neck stand on end. The air swooshes in my ears as she brushes her golden hair away. I turn around, and my heart skips a beat when I meet her aqua eyes. She looks too pale for a Florida girl, and she's sporting rather large eye bags, but still she's the most beautiful creature I've ever seen. I don't know how God does it, but he put a lot of effort in this one.

I grip the counter behind me and draw back, trying to keep myself off her. I'm a strong man, but even I have my limits. And she's always pushing them. It'll only take one for the rest to fall down like dominoes. I can't afford that. She can't afford that if she wants to live.

"The cake's ready." She leans toward me, and my knuckles turn white clenching the wooden countertop. A rose color creeps up on her cheeks as she's actively trying to avoid my gaze. Her lush lips part, making way for more air, forcing me to think of all the dirty things I could do to that mouth.

"Would you be so kind as to step away, Lucifer?" She tries to sound unaffected, but I can hear her panting.

I feel her presence in my every nerve. Have been since the first day I took a step on her land. A five-year-old girl with stars in her eyes and blonde curls falling around her face. She took my hand and placed it on her heart with the words, "Here, take mine. You'll feel better." She had just lost her mother, but she offered *me* consolation. She had the grace of a princess and a heart of gold even then. And I, in true Visconti fashion, took it and locked it away in my hollow chest so I could feel whatever she's feeling. Mine was damaged anyway. It's only ever been Stella's heart that beats inside me. She gave me a part of herself, and for that I'll always belong to her and only her.

"Huh?" I recover as the retrospection flies away and there she is. The same girl yet more beautiful. Under those layers of fatigue lies a starry-eyed girl with a bubbly personality and a curious, witty mind.

"I said, would you please move your butt from the oven? My cake is going to get burned." She pouts, and visions of me biting those cherry lips dance in my head.

"Sure." I move to the side, careful not to touch any part of her and sit at the counter. "What's all this? Are we having guests over?" I snort out, trying to lighten the heavy mood.

She lets out a little chuckle, and my tense body relaxes a bit. I can do this. I can be around her without the constant pressure of my dick against my pants as I remember the moans she's sealed in my ears.

"Tonight we have a selection of Focaccia Barese appetizer, Balsamic Green Bean salad, your favorite aubergines and ricotta pasta, and some cannoli." She gestures to all the delicious-looking dishes. I haven't felt this eager to try anything since…ever.

Stella is the best Italian food chef. I kid you not. The first time I ate her lasagna, I cried like a grown man should never.

"The chocolate cake is for the soul." She winks at me, and I can't hold my smile anymore. I stretch it out to my ears and dive into the most anticipated meal.

"I see what you're doing." I moan in between bites. "Are you trying to lure me into letting you go with food?"

"Maybe," she says shyly. "Is it working?"

I level her with a stare. *Good try.* "Why aren't you eating?"

"Oh, I had a sandwich earlier. I'm still not hungry." She looks down at the empty counter space while talking.

She's all grown up now, a woman with curves in all the right places. Not like the skeleton in the manor where her mother forced her to eat like a mouse and throw up.

She puts one cannoli on a plate and takes a little bite. *Come on, princess, you can do better than that.*

I take another bite of this deliciousness, close my eyes, and blurt out, "I've missed your pasta so much."

I hear her fork clunk against the porcelain dish, and next thing I know two hands wrap around my neck. Just at the touch of her skin on mine goose bumps arise, and my dick jumps up, sending testosterone to my blurred brain. Afraid if I touch her, I might never let her go again, I stay frozen in place.

She buries her head in my shoulder. "I thought I lost you, Lou," she whimpers, her body shaking. "I'm a horrible person. I didn't even miss my family as much as I missed you."

I can't move or say a word. Something inside me rattles. *No. I can't.*

I clench the wooden chair with one of my hands and untangle hers from my neck with the other. I've hardened my broken, fucked-up heart countless times since the day I was born. When my mother died before I even knew her. When my father hated me because she gave her life for mine. When I was taken away from my family. Every fucking time I had to order someone's head off. Every time I ended someone's life. Mostly, when I had to leave the love of my life to protect her from my world.

But nothing is as hard as letting her go in this moment, when she's unstable and vulnerable, knowing she'll hate me twice as much as she already does.

"Stella." I let go of the chair and push her back. She covers the tears streaming down her cheeks with her hands, making it extremely hard to let go. But I do. I stand and push her palms away from her angelic face. "Look at me, princess. I'm not the same man I used to be. Don't root for me 'cause I'll never be him again."

To my surprise her tears stop, she dabs at her lower lids with a napkin from the table, and she stares me down, "Well, guess what, Lucifer? I'm not the same innocent little girl anymore, either. You crushed me way too hard." She throws the napkin at my face and disappears through the door.

CHAPTER SEVEN

STELLA

It's been four or five days, and so far I've made no progress on my escape. From what I've gathered by my dubious eavesdropping skills and the murky memories of my kidnapping, some Russians want me dead because I'm a Morelli. Which means they must have known my father and are most likely in the same business as he was. How they knew about my connection to Lucifer is unknown yet.

"Miss Jacobs, there's a call for you," the maid announces on the other side of the closed door of my bedroom.

The first time she called me that, I was taken aback, but I figured Lucifer didn't want to tell her my real surname, so he used my adopted one instead. Few people know I am Giovanni Morelli's daughter because he kept me locked away. When he died and I permanently took residence with the Blacks, my godmother, Melanie, gave me her maiden name and told everyone I was her niece. "Come in, Nina."

The petite, white-haired woman dressed in a black and white uniform enters, carrying a phone in one of her hands and a steaming cup in the other. "It's Raquel again. I brought you some linden tea with homemade honey."

"Thank you." I take the phone out of her hand.

She scoops the multi-colored fabrics hanging from my new desk and places the cup on a coaster. "I'll be right outside, bellissima."

I sigh and give her a thumbs up as she exits. Damn Lucifer and his stupid rules. He won't give me a phone as if I'm a twelve-year-old. I'm a grown woman, for Pete's sake.

"Hey, Raquel. How did the meeting go?"

She clears her throat. "I saw Ivy and Damien yesterday at the mall. She told me you're in New York for a business trip. *I* take *care* of your business, remember? Care to explain why you lied to me?"

Shoot.

"I'm sorry. Truth is…" I can't tell her I got kidnapped and now I'm locked against my will by my dead ex-boyfriend. So, I go with the short version. "I encountered an old friend when I flew in for Masquerade's opening. I'm kind of staying with him, but I…"

"Oh. My. God!"

I often tease Raquel that she's the long-lost sister of Janice from my favorite sitcom *Friends*, only slightly less annoying. She walks like Naomi Campbell, but her style hasn't left the eighties, and she has the voice of a duck on helium.

I pull the phone away before she pierces my ear with her exclamation. "Did you finally get yourself a piece of ass?"

"Raquel! Come on, don't belittle men like that."

"Oh, please, Saint Stella? It's nothing they don't do to us. Now, is he fine? What's his name?"

I switch to the important questions. "How did the meeting go? Tell me you've got good news, please."

She grows silent for a second, and that tells me all I need to know. "Honey, I'm sorry. Marc decided to go with Tiffany

Blazeberg. I fought for you. I really did. But they had already made up their minds."

I swallow the bitter defeat. "It's okay. She's really talented. She deserves it."

"The only thing she's talented in is holding Marc's dick. There's no way she got *that* lucky with her mediocre fast-fashion. You are couture, my darling."

This is why I love her even if she's annoying and bitchy sometimes. She has always believed in me.

"Thank you. We'll just keep working to get the next one."

"Yes. Work hard, play hard, baby. Before you hang up, would you tell me why Mary Poppins answers the phone every time I call you? I know you lost yours, but it's been more than a week. Get a new one."

I hate lying. I hate it so much. "I don't have time with all the orders coming in. I'll get one soon."

"Pfft, orders. Yeah, right. It doesn't have anything to do with that mysterious man of yours?"

My heart skips a beat. "What do you mean?"

"You're probably too busy with your little rendezvous to get to the store."

Yeah, I wish. The only thing he's fucking is fucking avoiding me for the whole fucking week since that fucking kitchen argument. I can feel his presence, but I never see him. Not in the hallways or any of the rooms. Not once. A ghost.

I hang up on her before I lose it.

Rendezvous. *Ha.*

I would laugh if I wasn't dying on the inside.

When I was young, I thought my life was a fairy tale. I likened it to the words written in the books in our library.

A castle of a house, a backyard big enough to host the Olympics. Staff members at every corner taking care of my every need. Riding my white horse, Belle, from the stables to the vineyard at sunset. I named her after the *Beauty and the Beast* story. That is the only book I remember my mother reading to me.

But my favorite story has always been *Romeo and Juliet*. Love flourished from tragedy and vice versa. I used to think it was the most beautiful love.

While the other fairy tales got their happily ever after, Romeo and Juliet had forever. They could've found happiness somewhere else. Or live one life for the both of them. But it takes one heck of a person to sacrifice themselves for another human being. I admired their strength. Their connection.

I thought Lucifer and I had that kind of love. Love flourished from tragedy, only days after the death of my mother. I knew God sent him to me. He wasn't anything like the devil my father made him out to be. He was a fallen angel, guarding me from a cruel, sad world.

He sneaked in through my window, comforting me in the dark and lonely nights just like the stars need the company of the moon to shine more brightly. His lucky star, he called me. We were incomplete without each other.

I thought I'd sacrifice myself for him, but when the day came, I couldn't. I stood in Black's backyard hidden behind the rose bushes, up to my ears in mud, clutching a kitchen knife in my hands, and I couldn't. I wasn't strong enough. I hated myself for it. Punished my body for betraying me.

Rosalie, Melanie's daughter and one of my best friends, noticed the signs a couple of years later. Spots around my mouth, sore knuckles from pushing my fingers into my throat, my puffy face. She'd seen a lot of girls in our private school fighting eating disorders. Losing Lou, losing my whole family and everyone I loved had left a much bigger imprint on me than I had strength for. Three years of the best therapists Melanie could find did nothing.

Then came Barry. He was like a drop of rain in the desert. We met at Sunday mass when I was twenty-one and hit it off immediately. I felt safe with him, like I could open up again. Some strange feeling didn't let me. What would he think when he found out what my last name was, who I was? Then I realized I was no longer that person. My past didn't define me. I finally felt like I could breathe. A few months later he proposed. Like a true hopeless romantic I said yes, even though I knew the hole Lucifer left behind was bigger than my heart. I thought I'd find a way to fill it. One battle at a time.

Damien didn't like Barry and neither did the Blacks. We got into a huge fight, so I left their mansion and moved in with him. One day he came home and blurted out that I was getting fat. For the first time in my life, I had completely stopped binging and throwing up for months. I laughed it off through the pain, but then he repeated it the next day. And slowly it became every meal. I tried to avoid the intrusive thoughts, so I started counting calories. Diets, so many diets. I went back to size zero, and he wasn't happy still. All my progress went to hell.

On our wedding day, he accidentally said my real name. Morelli. I'll never forget the hives that broke out on my skin. I don't know how, but he knew. He thought I was some kind of rich mob princess, and he wanted to marry me for the money. But I didn't have any. I didn't have a dime from my family, and I didn't accept the checks Melanie sent me every month. I wanted to be braver. Independent. How stupid was I? I made some money from sewing tatters as Barry called them for the four customers I had but not enough to support myself without him. I didn't know life. Bills, medicine, food.

They all required lots of money. In my sheltered bubble, there was always someone taking care of these things.

Then he hit me. He punched me hard in the face, and then he did it again and again until I was blue and numb. The minute he left the backroom of the chapel we were getting married in, I ran off without thinking. Puked my guts out on the sidewalk and kept running until I couldn't take it anymore.

That's when God sent me Ivy. My best friend and the person I owe my life to. She gave me a chocolate cookie instead of calling the police when I broke into tears in my wedding dress on the bench next to hers in Rosehill Park. She did have her reasons, though, as she was then a fugitive running from the law. She pitied me and took me with her to her hotel. Then she fed me a big bowl of spaghetti, and she took care of me for the next two years. We found this little old house and it became ours. She helped me stand on my own two feet and pay my bills, stood by my side when I decided to pursue a real career in fashion design.

All this progress and look where I am now. In my father's manor, I was caged but I didn't know it. The princess life was the only one I knew. But I'm not a maiden in distress anymore. Seeing it in retrospect, my life wasn't a fairy tale—more like a nightmare. Now I have real friends and family. I have a career. A whole world ahead of me. And yet again I find myself locked away, this time in Lucifer's Manhattan castle.

The very thought of being confined makes me sick to my stomach. I throw the dress I've been sewing on my new machines for the last four hours and run to the bathroom. All my worst memories are coming back one gag at a time. I can't even look at myself in the mirror as I brush my teeth. I despise my pale face.

I stare at the ceiling, sitting on the bathroom floor, too afraid to go to sleep. The nightmares…I call them labyrinth dreams. Stuck in the same loop over and over again, trying to save the people you love and just when you're about to escape someone hits rewind.

It's been like that ever since I lost my mother. Therapy helped for a while, I managed to sleep almost every night while living with Ivy. If I couldn't, I'd work. It started deteriorating after she moved in with Damien but now all the work I've done has completely gone to hell.

I miss Ivy and Damien so much.

I'm so tired.

I can't keep my eyes open any longer. I've slept next to nothing since I was kidnapped. It's the longest period I've gone with so little sleep. I don't have strength.

I slowly stand up and drag my feet on the floor. My brain is too tired to support the concerns about my relapse. The hell with it. I can't fight anymore. I need to rest.

I slip under the covers, feeling my lids weighing as soon as my head hits the fluffy pillow. But rest is the last thing I find as I feel myself sinking into another labyrinth.

CHAPTER EIGHT

STELLA

*B*ending down to take the strawberry-vanilla cupcakes out of the oven, I wiggle my butt to Taylor Swift. I've been practicing the dance moves Ivy taught me all through the big kitchen, spilling colorful sprinkles out of the bag Marcel got me.

It's a good day! Or so I've convinced myself.

Having an eighteen-hour sleep session and burying my head in work since I woke up helped a lot. Cooking is the cherry on top. I used to sneak into the kitchen when my stepmother wasn't paying attention and learn from the chefs and the kitchen staff. There weren't many entertainment options in the enclosed manor other than sewing clothes with my governess.

A needle and a thread, add some pasta, and that, my friends, is how Stella Morelli is made.

Shimmy-shaking my way back, I stumble at the door.

Dio mio!

Lucifer is exiting one of the rooms on this floor, barefooted in linen white trousers and royal blue shirt with rolled up sleeves, showcasing his tattooed forearms. He swivels around to lock the door, dark curls bouncing around his neck. What a delight for the eyes.

"Hey!" With his back to me, he stiffens at my voice. "Lucifer, you can't keep me locked then pretend I'm not here. At least talk to me."

He exhales and turns around.

Progress. I smile, "I've made cupcakes." I shake the sprinkles box in the air, and his lips twitch. I knew it. There's still a fraction of the boy I knew deep down somewhere in that beast of a man. I pucker my lips. "For old time's sake."

He closes his eyes and sighs. *Yes*! *Yes*! *Victory*!

There are only two ways to make my life less miserable right now. Run away, which I haven't figured out yet with all the security and cameras. Or enjoy it, seeing as I'm stuck here.

I saunter to the fridge.

Lucifer follows. "Your sewing machines are giving me a headache." He frowns. What an asshole.

I shrug, my smile never faltering. "So is the thought of you," I mutter.

"What was that?"

"I don't know what you're talking about." I bat my eyelashes.

"Mm-hmm." He leans next to the sink as I take the strawberries and the whipped cream out. "How's your work going?"

"Oh, you know, the usual. Scratching and kicking my way to the top."

"You know…" he starts, scratching his head where the top part of his hair is tied in a bun. "I can pull a few strings and get you on top like that." He snaps his fingers.

"That is so nice of you, Mr. Big Shot"—I roll my eyes—"but I'd have to decline. I started this because I wanted to build something on my own. If I needed strings pulled, I would've gone to Melanie."

"But you let Melanie do a fashion show for you?" He raises an eyebrow.

Aww, he kept tabs on me.

Wait a minute.

My smile falls. "How do you know that?"

"I researched you when you got…delivered." He seems a little flustered. "For safety reasons," he adds.

Silence falls over us like a rain cloud.

Trying to extend an olive branch, I hip-bump him out of my way to the sink. "Come on, help me finish the cupcakes while you tell me about your job." I pop a strawberry into my mouth with a playful smile. "I mean, the construction business has got to be good if you can afford this lavish home."

His lips press into a thin line. "You're asking questions I can't answer."

"Why? Does it have anything to do with what my father did?"

I've spent an embarrassing amount of time thinking this through. I never found out from where or why Lucifer came to the manor. Father brushed me off, and Lou once told me his parents were dead. But nothing else. Not a home town, not a surname. Just Lucifer.

And now he's here, and he's keeping me hostage, albeit for my safety as he likes to put it. Is it just because he's afraid that those Russian guys who want me dead will finish their job, or is there a personal motive behind it? He said he wasn't in the mafia but I don't believe him.

"You won't like what comes if you keep up the questions." He's moved, looming over me. He realizes it before I can do anything about it and goes back to his spot. If he won't tell me, there's always another way to find out.

I flick my fingers at him, splashing him with drops of water.

"Maybe I will," I mutter. His wet nose and eyes scrunch in the most adorable way, but he pretends as if he hasn't heard me.

The soft tune of music playing in the background and the comfortable silence as I wash strawberries and he steals them brings back old memories.

"So," he starts softly.

"So…" I look at him. I swear there's a million questions in his stormy eyes, but he won't ask.

"Why don't you start by telling me about your job and maybe I'll reconsider."

"What do you want to know?" I try to hide my disappointment by snatching the strawberry off his fingers and taking a bite.

He brushes a fallen strand from his face. "Everything."

I have one of these moments, you know, where angels sing in your ear, as the sunlight shines on his naturally bronzed skin. The edginess that the stubble gives him. He always used to be clean-shaven. Maybe that's why I pictured him as an angel. Aging has changed him into a panty-dropping, devilish-looking fine piece of Sicilian man.

The good girl wants a taste of how it feels to be a woman at the hands of a dangerous man.

"Stella!" And now I want to bite that smirk off his gorgeous face. Oh, he knows what he's doing to me. He knows very well. "Earth to Stella. Stop staring."

"I'm just," I drag out like a possessed being, "exploring."

"Sure, Dora the Explorer." He laughs it off. His eyes are light silver with little craters of pencil graphite like a full moon on a crystal-clear night.

"Your eyes, they're so calm."

"Because I know you're safe here. With me."

"Like when we were little, hiding at the stables with Belle. Laughing and playing and…" I stop as I realize where this conversation is heading. Or more so, *what* happened in the stables.

His lips part, pupils dilating, but he quickly looks down. " Your job, princess?"

I bite my lip. "Oh, yes." I turn off the water I forgot was running and grab the plate of strawberries before he finishes them. "So"—I round the counter and grab the whipped cream —"After I moved in with the Blacks, I was in a dark place, and designing was what kept me afloat. I met some clients through Melanie and Rosalie. I almost lost it when Barry—" I stop. Lucifer is staring at me curiously, but I can't say it. It feels like cheating. "And then I met Ivy, and she encouraged me to pursue a career out of it."

"That's your friend, Damien's wife, right?"

"Fiancée technically. I'm trying to get a deal so I could sell my clothes in stores. I'm making samples for the next company that agrees to meet with Raquel and me."

Raquel is my assistant-slash-everything. My little company is a two women show.

"It won't be long before you get a deal. I've seen some of the designs."

"Unfortunately neither I nor Raquel know much about the business part. I think that's where we're failing."

"Well, you're at the right place 'cause business is my native language. I can help you understand negotiations if you want." My ears perk up. I didn't expect him to offer help.

Suddenly, the countertop seems like the most interesting thing to stare at as I try to calm down my nerves. "Thank you. That would be great. Just let me know when you can spare some time."

"I still think you should take me up on my offer. The fashion industry is nothing if not nepotistic."

I think it through. What would I lose? My pride. The stupidest thing to be standing in the way of success but I need it. I've been lied to, abandoned, kidnapped, kept a prisoner, and sugarcoated all my life. I have one pride and that's my grind.

Though taking the short path to unlimited finances seems so much more appealing right now…

"Do you think love is an illusion?" Lucifer surprises me out of nowhere.

"Love is just the brush. You need the artist to create the painting." He stares at me with a look I can't decipher. "I think we create the illusion of who or what we want. Love is just a means to an end."

"I need to know," he starts, taking a step toward me. "Was it an illusion?"

I freeze. Why does he need to know? What is wrong with him? I gave him an opportunity to listen to my feelings and he threw it away. He sure as hell isn't getting it from me again. Not now.

"Yes," I answer as I blow the package of sprinkles in his face. "Like your expression right now." I giggle at his confused face.

He surprises me by grabbing a fist of rainbow sprinkles and hurling them my way.

"Heyyy!" My giggling turns into laughter as his whole face starts reddening.

"You wanna play?" He grabs a slice of strawberries and throws it my way.

My jaw falls. "Oh no, you did not." I grab the closest thing to me—a can of whipped cream—and I point it his way.

"I dare you. Throw food once more, and I'll make a cupcake out of you."

He shrugs and takes a strawberry from the counter. "You mean like this?" He throws it my way, I fail to dodge it, and it hits me right in the forehead.

"It's so on." I jump at him and spray a good part of his face and clothes with whipped cream before he reacts. I grab the sprinkles box and run to the other side of the counter. He wipes the cream out of his eyes with his shirt, exposing his abs, causing me to forget I'm pouring the sprinkles in my hand, and now they're spilling onto the floor, along with all my dirty thoughts.

It. Is. Not. Fair. Not to womankind, not to mankind, not to my heart.

Suddenly the thought of him being with other women pops into my head. I never actually considered that. In my head he was always mine. But he's not. And it's been eight years.

"Oh, princess. This means war." He startles me. I leap, squeaking when I see him coming at me with the second can of whipped cream. When did he get it out of the fridge?

"Bring it on, bad boy." I stick my tongue out at him, and he starts toward me slowly, like a predator stalking his prey. I take a few steps back and squeal as he rushes toward me. I start running around the countertop. "You'll never—" I yelp as two hands wrap around me from behind, and I feel a sticky, wet, hard body pressing against me.

"Catch you?" He sprays my face with whipped cream and throws some sprinkles at me with his other hand.

"Hey, it's not fair. You're double-attacking me," I scream as I wiggle, trying to get out of his strong grip. "And your feet are bigger." I succeed in pulling one of my hands free and wiping some of the cream from my face. I slap whatever part of him I can reach behind me, smearing the sticky sugar.

"I never said I was fair." Hot lips lock around my middle finger and sharp teeth bite into it. My body trembles as I press harder into his. I feel his dick poking into my waist. Oh my! Memories come rushing in.

A little moan falls out of my lips. He sucks on my finger, and my clit pulsates. I want him. So fucking bad.

"Lou…" But before I finish, he whips me around and faces me.

"Shh." He presses a finger to my lips. I bite it, looking into his clouded eyes. He pulls his finger back and before I manage to react, his mouth is on mine, drinking me in thirstily.

It's not gentle.

It's not slow.

Rough, full lips devouring mine as his tongue dives in, stealing a taste. It's a carnal need.

I bite his lower lip, and he wraps his arms around my butt, lifting me to sit on the counter. There's desperation in his grip on my waist and domination in the way he's swallowing every breath I give him. I thrust my fingers in his hair, pulling his head back, but he licks the cream off my cheek.

I exhale harshly, desperately rubbing my pussy against his pants, probably leaving a wet stain on the white linen, but I couldn't care less.

"I want you. Now." He growls, pressing his body into mine harder.

"You'll never have me." I pant out.

"You don't make the rules, princess." He pulls my shirt up and licks the cream off my chin, making his way to my breasts as I unbutton his shirt. "Fuck," he growls, grabbing the whipped cream and pulling one cup of my pink lace bra down. For a second, he just stares at my puckered nipple with so much hunger I fear he's going to literally eat it. Then he sprays cream all over it and dives in, licking and sucking it for the win.

"Oh God," I plead out, grinding against his hard-as-a-rock cock. He's flicking his tongue and biting, his right hand playing with my other nipple.

"Bellissima, principessa." His raspy voice almost makes me come from foreplay. "I never got to taste if your pussy is as sweet as the rest of you."

"Oh God," I repeat as I feel vibrations pulsating on my clit at the image of him eating me out. We didn't get to this part when we were teens. "I've never…"

"Miss Jacobs, there's a phone call for you." Nina's voice in the hallway startles us as we hear her footsteps coming this way.

"Shit," Lucifer says as he quickly grabs his shirt, covering my back with it before he wraps his big arms around me so no part of my body would be exposed. *Oh, my heart*. And my pussy. They're in serious danger.

Ashamed of what was just about to happen on the kitchen counter Nina eats her dinner at, I don't turn my head around to face her when she walks in and instead bury it in Lucifer's shoulder.

"Oh, sir. Scusi." Her voice wavers. "I didn't know you were busy. There's a call to Miss Jacobs, and I heard noise inside so I thought…"

"Who is it?" His voice is rough and annoyed.

"Don't worry, Nina. Just leave the telephone. I'll bring it back to you later," I say before Lucifer has the chance to send her away.

"It's Mr. Max Perry."

"The fuck?" Lucifer growls out, and I dig my nails into

his abs, trying to give him a hint to shut up and let the woman exit.

"Please just leave it anywhere. Thank you," I say, still facing his shoulder and probably more embarrassed than I've ever felt.

I hear the phone hitting the counter, her rushed steps, and the swish of the closing door. Finally, Lucifer unwraps his arms and steps back, leaving me semi-naked and covered in cupcake decorations, sitting on the sticky mess we made.

"Who is Max Perry?" He sounds angry, staring me down, not even trying to suppress it.

"He's…" Why does he look so mad? "He's an ex."

"Ex what?" He growls. "Boyfriend?"

"Not exactly." I scratch my face, suddenly feeling very itchy covered in all this sugar. "More like a buddy."

"A fuck buddy?" His stormy murderous glare could probably slice me in half. "Why is your ex-fuck buddy calling you here? I said only emergency calls. I doubt he'll come here to emergency-fuck you."

My eyes widen at his harsh, cruel words, and I grab some napkins to wipe whatever I can because I'm feeling dirtier than ever. "It's not like that. We're still friends. He probably got this number from Raquel and called to see how I'm doing."

"Yeah, I'm sure it's not because he wants to fuck your brains out," he grits out as he buttons his shirt.

I throw my napkin on the counter and slap my hand on it. "Someone is projecting. You were just about to do the same."

"Don't get your hopes up." He walks out of the room, leaving me to clean the mess he made.

Not the kitchen. He's got people for that.

CHAPTER NINE

LUCIFER

It's been six hours since I put anything in my mouth. Five days since the kitchen accident. A hundred and twenty-four hours since I tasted the forbidden fruit.

A man's gotta eat. Especially if he spent the last two hours punching the misery out of his system.

All it took was one encounter with Stella to make me flustered. Hard as a stone is an understatement.

I didn't find my common sense in the boxing gym, but a cold shower and some jacking off against the wall proved to be sufficient. For now.

A smell I could never mistake wafts through the cracked door and tries to steal my focus as I'm comparing numbers, trying to concentrate on whether or not we're finally in the clear, and I've fulfilled my purpose. But as it seems I'm losing on both fronts.

Fuck.

What is this kind of torture? I know the devil's already saving me a front row seat. Isn't a fucking eternity enough that he has to send Stella cooking up the magical concoction of my undoing two rooms away?

I close my eyes for a moment and take a deep breath. I shouldn't have come to the second floor's office. Poor judgment: I thought Stella would be gone for longer.

Sighing, I take the folder with this month's profits and stop before opening the door, trying hard not to breathe through my nose.

I won't go in there. Not after what happened last time.

The mere thought of it makes me gag. I'm not proud of the way I ended things. That kind of jealousy? Dangerous territory. I'm never jealous. Just the reminder that someone else held her the way I dreamed of for years and kissed her soft lips that were once moaning my name, and probably fucked her the way only I was supposed to made me lose my mind. She was supposed to be mine. Always and forever.

It fucking hurts, even after all these years. I can't talk to her without endangering her life.

But isn't her life already on the line? You can protect her. The little voice in my head pleads against my case. The fucker.

I shake my head, like that would somehow chase away this absurd thought, and turn the doorknob. Holding my breath, I step out into the devil's den, then carefully close the door behind me. But as I approach the elevator, I hear a sound that guts me from the inside. *Oh, shit.*

Don't do it. Don't fucking do it.

"Stella, is everything okay?" Old habits die hard.

A blonde head pops into the kitchen doorway. She looks shocked, probably because I'm not being an asshole. And the sounds were just what I thought they were.

"Um, yes. No. Y-yes," she stutters, her shiny aqua irises surrounded by dark blood vessels. The lights of the lamps reflect in the wetness on her flushed cheeks. She bites down on her lip and stares at the floor.

"Somehow I don't believe that." I continue the conversation I shouldn't have started. I can't help it. I can't stand the thought of my princess crying.

She's not your anything, you fuckwit. There goes that inner voice again. Apparently there's some rationality left in me but instinct is stronger. And that instinct was always to protect her.

"I... I..."—she sniffs—"I'm okay. I will be. Don't worry." But the pale color of her face and the way her sunflower summer dress hangs loose from her body are telling me otherwise. I've been having some worries regarding her health.

I lean on the entrance arch as she presses deeper into the other corner of the kitchen, never leaving me out of her sight. Smart girl. "You need someone to talk to?"

Her chin dips ever so slightly.

"Sit." I point at the brown leather couch behind the glass doors where the living room is. "I'll be serving tonight."

I can see the internal fight she's having on taking my orders, but she gives up and goes into the living room.

I open the oven, and my stomach roars at the sight of the perfectly baked golden mozzarella. My mouth tries to curve, but I tighten my face muscles to keep my schooled expression on. So what if sometimes I dream of this lasagna? Or fucking the girl who made it on the glass stove while it's cooking in the oven?

I take out the tray and put two slices on plates.

"Talk," I order as I put the plate in front of her on the low coffee table. She trembles as our shoulders brush. I back away before I make another mistake.

"It's not important," she mumbles as she looks down at the steaming piece of art.

I don't have this kind of patience, so I dive in, keeping the conversation going while chewing like a true gentleman. "It doesn't matter if it is. You're sad, and you need to get it out of your system, so you can be the ray of fucking sunshine you always are."

She lifts her gaze to my ill-mannered mouth and wipes the only wet spot left on her left cheek like a shy cat licking her paw. She's so gracious, and I'm such a…pig.

"You remember the meeting I told you about?"

How could I forget the way she waltzed into my office earlier in that dress, looking oh so innocent, demanding a laptop so she could take a meeting for her brand. I had to appoint Marcel to keep an eye on her, of course, to which both of them scoffed and complained until I kicked them out of my office.

I simply nod and she continues, "Well, it was with some businessmen from a retailer store I'm trying to nail down. I totally screwed up. They laughed in my face. I should've waited for Raquel to get back from her vacation. What did I think taking it myself?"

"Hey, hey. Don't be so hard on yourself." I point at her with my fork, trying to contain the murderous feeling in me, wanting to smash the head off whoever dared laugh at my princess. "Look at it this way. It was a learning experience. If they passed on it, I'm sure there's a reason, and it's God protecting you."

"Failure and embarrassment. That's for sure," she murmurs while digging through her food.

"Failure is just another stepping stone to success, princess. And if you fail a task or two on the way, it's because greater things are coming for you. You can't grab onto your biggest dream if your hands are already full."

Her gaping mouth and expression of awe tell me she didn't expect to hear this. It's kind of insulting. I've always been on her team albeit from a distance.

"Look at you all pious." She beams at me.

Damn, her smile could melt Antarctica. "Yeah, yeah… whatever. You know Giovanni always made us go to church and shit…" I scratch my temple when her smile wavers. I need to change the subject, now. "I have to tell you"—I point at the two bites of lasagna left on my plate—"if you keep cooking like this, I'm going to lose these abs."

Her cheeks blush and she looks down at the ground, then the ceiling. "I wouldn't want that to happen." Her gaze slides to her uneaten food, and a dark thought breaks through all the bliss this meal made me experience.

"You know, the chef told me you're cooking every day, for hours. And there's always a lot of food left. Untouched." Until I get my hands on it late at night, at least. "Is there something you want to tell me?" I draw my eyebrows together, uncomfortable silence hanging over us. She's looking down at her bare feet, her head shaking barely noticeable. "Stella?" I push and she slightly winces, still silent.

Shit, shit, shit. Fuck. That's what I was afraid of.

"Princess, it's me." I push her chin up with my index finger so she can look me in the eyes. "You can tell me everything. Anything. I know you well enough to read it on your face."

"It's nothing. You know I cook when I'm nervous." She pulls her head away and hugs her knees to her chest.

"I also learned what bulimia nervosa really is when I went to university. You can't lie to me anymore. I thought you dealt with it."

"I did. I am." She shakes her head. "I haven't had a relapse in three years. But coming here…"

If the devil needs another form of punishment, it's this right here. Knowing I've caused her pain she should've never known in the first place.

"Is it on again?"

Her nose scrunches. "There's no on and off. It's not a TV. I'll be fine, it's just a minor inconvenience…" Her voice wavers, and I just want to hug the shit out of her like I did when we were younger. But we're not kids anymore. And this shit is real.

"I can get you the best psychiatrist as soon as tomorrow. Just let me—"

She puts her hand on mine, and a wave of electricity zips through me.

"Please, don't. I've tried it already, and it doesn't work. What I really need are my best friends. Rosalie, Ivy. Damien."

"That's going to be a problem because going out is not allowed, and you know it. They definitely can't come. But…" I stand up and take the phone out. She's been on a ban since that prick called her. How he got this number is beyond me. "I happen to have this, and I'll give it to you if you promise to use it wisely."

She looks as if she doesn't believe me but she takes the phone anyway. "What's the catch?"

"I need you to start getting some sleep and stop clicking and clacking the machines all night. The whole floor can't sleep."

Not that there's anyone else on the floor. And it's not like I get much sleep with this job either. But she needs to rest more and I don't know how else to make her.

She looks down, and now in the sunset light shining from

the French windows I see the big eye bags under her eyes. "I can't."

She doesn't need to say anything else. We grew up together. We were haunted by the same demons with different faces. Still are.

I offer her a hand, and she looks down at it, untrusting. I can't blame her. I wouldn't trust me either, especially with having her in my hands. But as usual she only sees what little good is left in me, and she puts her small palm into mine. I pull her to me and lay her head on my thighs.

"I'll put off the doctor for now, but I insist on having a coach to keep you healthy. Yoga, meditation, exercises, and whatever other shit there is for the mind."

"Mm-hmm," she purrs as I feel her relaxing and taking off to foreign dreamlands.

"I'll take care of you, princess," I whisper, hoping she doesn't hear the part of me I'm trying to desperately hide from her. From the world. From me.

"Please, Lou." The plea sounds like so much more, but before I can ask her what she means, she's dozed off.

I stay like that, caressing her soft blonde hair and enjoying the way she shivers every time I run my fingers up her cheek while she sleeps calmly in my lap. I don't move. I hardly breathe. I let my guard down for a second, allowing myself the bliss in this moment as it'll pass soon. And like clockwork, sometime in the middle of the night, the phone I gave her buzzes with a text.

Max: I miss you.

That fucking piece of shit. He just won't give up. And the worst part is I get him. I wouldn't either, if the choice wasn't taken out of my hands. Or put in my hands to be exact. I'd suffer a thousand lives without her if I knew that would keep her safe. And I did.

But that motherfucker had his chance, and it's over. Stella's in my house now. And no matter what happens, she'll always be mine. I know it, she knows it, and that poor bastard probably knows it too.

I pull away from her, and she frowns. I slide my hands under her and lift her to my chest. When I return her to her room and put her on the freshly laid satin sheets, I pull away, back into the shadow and watch her steady breathing a little more.

I can feel all the trouble coming my way. She shouldn't be mine, but I won't allow her to be anyone else's. I can't. This will cause one hell of a shitstorm, but she's worth going to war for.

CHAPTER TEN

LUCIFER

"He must've been here at least a year," Kenny, a good friend and the head of my construction supervision says as we both stand on the wet soil of my new construction site, staring at the dismembered body in the massive trench.

Fucking shit. The last thing I need on the day we break ground is that motherfucker lying in the ground.

"So what do we do, boss?" He turns to me, his orange helmet leaning a little to the left on his bald head.

"No one can know about this. The police will start digging, and then reporters will come. They'll shut us down." This is supposed to be our biggest project and the one that can finally legitimize this organization. *My organization.*

"Lucifer, what the fuck is so urgent that I had to ditch poker night?" Uncle Hugo's hoarse, thick Italian accent rings through the dark night. The squishing sound of his shoes hitting the mud tells me he should be behind me right about... "Spill it, boy. Damn Aldo is stealing the capos' money right now."

I look over my shoulder to the short and sturdy man

wearing an Italian three-piece designer suit, unbothered by the drizzle raining over his receding salt and pepper hairline. "Did dressing up take you two fucking hours?"

He points a finger at me, but then his gray eyes divert to the trench behind us. "What is this?"

"That's what I'm asking. I thought we had a deal." My jaw tics as I look at the signature Visconti gray eyes, hardened by a lifetime of violence and washed out by drinking to forget it.

"I know nothing of this." He simply shakes his head twice and takes a puff from the cigarette butt in his hand. "May he rest in peace." He throws it with perfect accuracy on the head of the poor motherfucker. "This is one of your soldier's work. No capo is that stupid."

"So what, boy? You want me to do what? Punish them? Kill them?" He sneers at me. "You and I both know you don't want another death under your belt."

I'm pretty close to testing that statement. "I can't cover up every fucking thing you do, Uncle. What if the police got here before Kenny?" I try to maintain my poker face as the anger inside me bubbles. This stupid mistake could've cost me eight years of tireless work.

He takes out a pack of red Marlboro and lights up another cigarette. "We're the mob, Lucifer. It's what we do."

I grab it out of his mouth and throw it to the ground. "No, it's fucking not. I'm your boss, and everything has to go through me."

"And I'm your fucking uncle, so don't talk to me like that, you little…" The wrinkled face that instills fear in everyone who crosses his path is getting redder by the second. But this alcoholic piece of shit can't make me tremble.

I take a step forward and grab him by the collar of his

crisp white shirt. "I'll only say this once, Hugo. I'm no mobster. I'm a businessman. But don't ever forget we share the Visconti blood. I won't hesitate to remove you and those useless sons of yours if you get in the way of my plans and disobey me again. Is that clear?"

Fire ignites in his eyes, but he spits out behind gritted teeth, "Si, Don Lucifer." He knows I'll do anything to protect my plans.

"I heard interesting rumors about that little home of yours and what you're keeping in there"—his spiteful smile stretches up—"or should I say who?"

There's not enough *fucks* and *shits* in the world I can scream out loud right now. If he knows, that means the news is spreading.

"Shut your fucking mouth before I shut it once and for all."

"Like you did your father's, huh?" He has the audacity to laugh in my face.

Angelo was getting worse every day, killing not only innocent men but women and children. I had to put a stop to it. So, I did what I had to do. I don't appreciate being reminded of it.

I raise my fist to his jaw and press on it. "You're drunk off your shit again, Hugo. If you got something to say, spit it out."

"Um, not to ruin this showdown of power and all, but what do we do with this situation?" Kenny stutters, looking at the car lights that round the corner of the street behind the metal fence of the construction site.

I let go of Hugo and he staggers back. "My uncle and his sons will take care of this. I want it gone in an hour. I don't care what you do as long as it stays buried."

Hugo's jaw tics, but he knows he can't oppose me, so he

simply nods, turns around, and climbs into his vintage Lincoln Continental. As if he couldn't scream mobster any louder.

The only reason Hugo's got any power is because he's an elder Visconti. If it was up to me, I'd finish this whole fucking family without a second thought.

Kenny and I cover the body parts with some nylon, and I leave him to guard it until Hugo and his sons return. The bulletproof town car is waiting at the curb. I prefer to think of myself as financially responsible. I invest my money, instead of flaunting it everywhere I go like my cousins. I live in a townhouse instead of the bloodstained Visconti mansion, and the only times you'll catch me wearing suits and tuxedos is when work requires it. However, it can't be denied that since the day Stella took residence in my home, I've peeked a few times into the closet full of designer shit the family's personal shopper picked out for me. Somehow, I still feel like a fraud wearing them, although my days as the poor orphan soldier for the Morellis are long gone. Even as head of the most powerful Sicilian mafia family after the Morelli famiglia I still feel like an orphan.

I wonder if Stella has figured out I'm actually not.

As soon as I get out of the elevator on our floor and I hear the sewing machine's sound from her bedroom at three forty-five in the morning, I grab my phone and dial my best friend.

"Tiana, I need a favor."

I hear her shushing someone on the other side, and my guess would be Sebastian is somewhere around her, scowling that I'm calling at this hour.

"What's up, L?" She sounds brighter than usual. Definitely with that Federoff offspring.

"You know a lot of people in the fashion industry. Can you do something for me?" I explain to her the whole situation Stella's in without actually mentioning her name, and she's quick to promise me she'll find a way to help.

Now, I only have to convince Stella to take my help. The fashion industry is brutal. It will chew her up and spit her out to the vultures. Over my dead body will a retail manager crush my woman. I'll take care of her, even if she says she doesn't want me to, because that's what I've always done. It's the only thing that comes naturally to me.

CHAPTER ELEVEN

STELLA

"Here." Two hanging garment bags land on the bed beside me as Lucifer's voice comes from behind. "You have a meeting in four hours."

I flip from my belly to my back and find him much closer than he should be. "What do you mean?"

He backs away from the bed frame like I've burned him with a red-hot iron. "I got you a meeting with Bella Fashion Design Group, and I brought you clothes for it."

"Do you mean that you'll let me out of this prison?" Hope blossoms in my voice.

"Don't get too excited. I'll make an exception for the meeting but you'll have four bodyguards, and Marcel. Also no phone." Dammit, there's going to be zero chance of me running away from five men. "Now strip off that"—his brows furrow as he points at my pajamas—"skimpy lace thing so I can concentrate and give you my advice."

My nipples pucker at his command, something I never thought I'd like. He's dressed in a plain black T-shirt and jeans, sporting numerous tattoos and a silver cross pendant. A combination that's never looked this sexy on anyone I've seen before.

"So you want me to strip for you?" I undo the bow.

"You're killing me, Stella." His voice is low, hoarse.

"Then you should've stayed dead." I whisper in his ear.

His jaw hardens, and he turns away to walk to the couch, throwing a file with documents on the wooden table.

"For fuck's sake, just look in the garment bags."

I gasp when I unzip the first one. It's a black and white suit I made exactly for an occasion like this one. I never used it. "How did you know? And how did you get it? It was in Rosehill."

I can see his smirk in the reflection of the window. "Ivy did it. I was just the messenger."

"Thank you." My chest warms up. "It was very thoughtful of you."

"Don't open the other bag yet. If you get the deal, I have a surprise for you, so wait until then."

"And what might that be?"

He buries his fingers in his dark curls. "Curiosity killed the cat, princess. Did you get dressed?"

"Yes," I laugh out loud.

I don't know what possessed me to say that but he turns around and the look on his face is sure to haunt me for an eternity. I'm completely naked, shameless and bold. Something about this new Lucifer provokes my darkest sides.

"Jesus fucking Christ," he growls.

A chuckle escapes my lips. I can't decide if he wants to kill me or fuck me. Or fuck me until he kills me. "Stop acting like a baby. You've seen me naked before."

He doesn't say anything, just stares at me while I'm taking my time dressing. His thoughts might as well be written on his face. He's trying to fight this. Us.

"I've seen you naked once," he finally manages to say aloud. It sounds more like I've pressed a knife to his balls.

"That's not entirely true. Remember that time when—"

"You're so thin," he says, interrupting my jog down memory lane. Instantly, a hot flash of shame runs over me, and my spine bends a little. He pushes away my fingers as I'm trying to hook my bra, and he does it for me. "I tell you what. You get this deal, I'm cooking you dinner."

I snort out. "If you want me dead, you should just do it fast and painless. Why do you want me to suffer?"

"Ha ha, very funny, Ms. Morelli," he mumbles sarcastically. His fingers slide from the bra hook down along my spine to the end of the curve. Chills break on my skin from his deep voice in my ear. "I learned some tricks while you were gone, princess."

I don't want to think who taught him those tricks.

His thumbs press on the dimples of my back only for a second before he moves away. I slide into my black and white cashmere suit quickly.

"Now we can proceed." His voice is far and when I turn, I have a flashback to when he was nineteen, sitting in my room so similar to this one. He looks so out of place it's hilarious but he manages to pull off the tall, tatted-up, Sicilian scary-guy look even on a white couch with pink fluffy pillows. How is that fair?

"Who am I meeting again?" I can't recall anything after the thin comment. It always sucks when people talk about your weight without being prompted.

"BFD Group."

My thoughts vanish as I stare at him wide-eyed, mouth agape. "Are you kidding me? Their stores are on Fifth Avenue. No way."

"Good, so you know why you should sit your perky little ass down and listen to me."

In the back of my mind, I register his compliment, but all I'm capable of right now is, "How?"

"You underestimate me."

"But seriously, how? I've been trying to get them for years, and they never respond to my emails. Are you in the fashion industry too?"

His laugh is deep and pushes buttons inside of me, tingling the wrong side of my body. "No, I'm afraid not. However, I have a very close friend in fashion."

"A girlfriend?"

"A girl that's a friend, yes."

I fold my arms across my chest. "I don't want any favors. I told you."

"Princess." He stands up and grabs me by the shoulders, shadowing me with his broad figure, and piercing me with his stormy eyes. "This is a one-time opportunity. You can't let your pride get in the way of your dreams."

I drop to the couch and sigh, burying my fingers in my hair. "You know what it was like having someone manage your whole life. I always felt obligated to my father, may he rest in peace. I don't ever want to feel that way again."

"I'd never want that from you. And I'm not coordinating your moves. I'm simply giving you an opportunity, and what you do with it is up to you."

I lean on the backrest and stare at the ceiling. "Okay. Teach me your magic ways."

He grins like a wolf, knowing damn well his prey just jumped straight into his trap, and he grabs the folder from the table. "First thing is…"

CHAPTER TWELVE

STELLA

The meeting takes longer than expected, and on the way to Lou's house, I'm jumping through the roof of the town car from excitement. I don't even wait for Marcel to get out of the front passenger's seat as I take off to the elevator, running on my four-inch Manolos straight to Lucifer's office.

A delicious smell swirls in the air, and when I don't find him there, I burst through the kitchen doors, shouting, "I got it. I got it." But there's no one inside. In the middle of the counter rests a wooden board and a white piece of paper next to it.

The first words I see in big bold handwriting are *Congratulations, princess!*

How did he know? I grin and take the note to read the rest.

I had to attend to some business, I'm sorry. Open the second garment bag, and meet me at eleven in the garage.

P.S. It's no lasagna but it's nutritious. Eat all of it. You'll need it.

My stomach growls, and I look up to the wood board, my

disappointment for him not being here vanishing. There's no way Lucifer arranged this mouthwatering Pinterest-ready meal of juicy grilled steak with marinated broccoli and rice decorated with sesame seeds. If he did, then this new *trick* of his is one I'll enjoy immensely.

I dive right in to it, moaning with every divine bite. Well, well...if that isn't a surprise. Mr. Big Shot can cook like a pro.

The satisfaction of achieving something on my own is clouding my mind. Lucifer might've gotten me the meeting in the first place, but he wasn't joking when he said it's serious business. I met the vice of the BFD Group, and I could tell he was very skeptical at first, but after my presentation and the samples I showed him, that little frown on his wrinkly face curved into a smile. I'm so freaking proud of myself. Raquel almost pierced my eardrum on the call in the car.

I take a long bath and hydrate with the expensive cosmetics Lucifer got for me. He seems to remember what I used years ago. I can't afford those brands anymore seeing as I decided to be independent, something I still regret when I look at the electricity bill. However Ivy and I always found a way to make it work in the discount sections. I miss her so much, I wish I could tell her about my success but I can't pick up the phone to call her. I still haven't figured out what to say, or how much. I'm a little ashamed of how much I let this situation affect me. So many years of hard work to fight the bulimia and insomnia, and yet here we are. I don't want to lie to her.

Lucifer informed me Damien arranged the suit to be delivered. I should be mad at Damien for not breaking the doors down and getting me out of here but I don't know what Lucifer used on him. Maybe he threatened him or someone else. With a baby on the way I can't hold it against Damien. I wouldn't put it past this new Lucifer to use that as leverage, he seems hell bent on keeping me here. I can't think of another reason why Damien wouldn't be looking for me.

With a tinge of excitement I take a peek at the last black garment bag. The zipper hisses as I pull it down to reveal a dress I know by heart. It's my favorite one from my newest collection—a rose silk midi dress. The softest fabric that ever touched my skin, it slides on me like second skin. If you ignore the fact that it's a little too loose around the hips and butt area, it's the perfect siren dress. The neckline falls loose, revealing a hint of my cleavage. Spaghetti straps hold it, crossing behind me and continuing down my bare back in a corset pattern all the way to the end of my waist.

I trip on a Louboutin shoe box on the carpet that I didn't notice before. My heartbeat accelerates. What has Lucifer planned? I open the lid to find Follies Strass four-inch pumps with transparent fishnet and little rhinestones.

Everything is better if it's pink or sparkling.

Underneath the garment bag there's a blue Harry Winston leather box with a handwritten note.

Wear this tonight, princess.

My eyes water, staring at the little piece of paper and the beautiful diamond pendant necklace with a pear-shaped drop of ten carats hanging from the middle of it. A little Harry Winston card says the whole necklace is thirty carats, which by my knowledge means it must be somewhere in the six or seven figures. But it's not this exquisite jewelry that makes the tears roll on my cheeks, ruining the makeup I so carefully applied.

Why is he doing this? What is his game?

This is the Lucifer I dreamt of having. The one I gave my firsts to. He's so conflicting these days. Does he hate me or does he love me? One day he locks me up, the next he throws expensive gifts at me. It's like he's trying not to want me but he's failing. First, the kitchen, then the meeting. He even let me out. A thought blossoms in my heart. What if he's trying to win me back?

He doesn't deserve my forgiveness but God I want to give it to him. He can be quite the asshole but when he's sweet… it's better than my wildest dreams.

My palms are sweating, and I almost drop the necklace as I try to put it on. I press the intercom button. "Nina, could you please come to my room?" The shoes slide like butter on my size-five feet as I wait for her.

She arrives two minutes later with a polite smile on her face. "Oh Stellina, you look meravigliosa."

My eyebrow tics. "Please, don't call me Stellina. Literally, call me anything else, just not *that.*" She nods. "Could you please help me with this?"

"Of course, dear." She pats me, gleaming like the godmother in *Cinderella*. This whole thing feels like a fairy tale. I gave up on wanting to be a princess a long time ago. But I could be *his* princess.

I turn around to face the mirror.

Nina's beaming from behind me, holding me by the shoulders. "Mr. Visconti better realize what he's found before you leave us because, dear, you are a gem."

Visconti? Why does that sound so familiar?

"Grazie, carina." It's so nice to feel the presence of a grandmotherly figure. I never had that in my life, except for Melanie, and if she hears I referred to her as a grandmother I wouldn't hear the end of it.

She turns me around and squeezes my cheeks. "Here. A little blush always brings the boys to their knees. Now you're good to go."

I hug her and thank her again. I take my little sparkling clutch that came with the shoes and navigate my way to the parking lot at exactly eleven. I meet Marcel, whose lips twitch when he sees me, but he doesn't let the smile get to his face.

"Where's Lucifer?"

"He's meeting you there," Marcel says as he takes my hand. One of the bodyguards, dressed in all black attire, opens the door to the garage to reveal a shiny black limousine. As my heels hit the sidewalk, I inhale the dirty air of New York and welcome it like a sea breeze. If that's what freedom beyond these walls feels like, I'll take it.

Another bodyguard opens the door to the limo for me, and Marcel leads me to it. My legs and hands are shaking as I slide onto the black leather seat and inspect the luxurious interior. Marcel slides onto the seat opposite me, and we take off.

"You're not going to try to run away again, are you?" he asks, a smirk on his face. He knows I'm stuck with two armored cars in front and behind us. Even if I wanted to run, which I'll admit I'm not a hundred percent sure of anymore, I have nowhere to go. No phone, no money, no documents.

Besides, I'm interested in seeing what Lucifer's got in store for me.

"Where are we going?" I've never been on a date with Lucifer if you don't count the sneaking around in the manor, kissing in the barn, or stealing a touch in the pool when Father wasn't around. We were inseparable whenever possible, so this is all new to me. The little amount of dates I've been on were mostly terrible and not much more than ice cream at Rosehill Park. Don't get me wrong; I'd bathe in mud with the pigs as a date with Lou. But he wasn't like this. We were simple, enjoying the little things in life. All of this lavishness is Damien's style and reminds me of the ball he took Ivy to.

"I can't tell you. It's a surprise." Marcel opens a bottle of water and offers it to me.

"No, thanks." I can't drink anything right now. My stomach is in knots. "Come on, give me a little hint." Going out twice in one day is unexpected. It's throwing me off balance just when I started having some.

Marcel only smirks, clad in a crisp white shirt, which contrasts his tanned olive skin and gray slacks with a black Louis Vuitton belt and moccasins. We don't speak a word through the twenty-minute drive, and he doesn't seem to notice my squirming on the leather seat. I can see by the way he's looking out the window his head is somewhere far away from here. As I stare at my reflection in the opposite window, wearing my best dress and all these luxurious gifts, I can't help but question what Lucifer's agenda is?

Thankfully, I don't have to wonder much more because the limo stops and security opens my door. I step out, too concentrated on putting one foot in front of the other to notice anything in the dark, and I lift my gaze to see the other guard opening a red metal door to a Chinese restaurant.

"Come on, this place is amazing." Marcel takes my hand once again and leads me through a dark hallway.

"I dressed in this"—I gesture to my outfit—"for a bite of Chinese?" I raise an eyebrow, but before he answers me, a black-haired woman dressed in a black dress with a purple mask on her face comes into view.

"Welcome back, Marcel," she purrs and stares at his eyes a second too long for me to see they're acquainted. "Miss, you look lovely tonight. I think the mask I chose would suit your outfit perfectly." She smiles at me and hands me a black masquerade mask with a delicate design.

"I love it, thank you," I say as I put it on.

Marcel winks at her, and she melts under his gaze as she hands him a silver and black mask. She takes us through the hallway, our security trailing behind us, both of them wearing black masks.

It's all becoming clear now. We're at Masquerade. The big red neon sign on the center of the wall is the first thing I see when the woman pulls a curtain, and we step into the room. This is Damien's second branch of the club that I was supposed to be at when I got kidnapped. The original club is in Rosehill, where Ivy used to dance. Masquerade is housed in a hidden location, with a secret entrance and exclusive membership. Hence, the Chinese restaurant front.

"Welcome, I'm Sarah and I'll be your server for the night." A tall blonde comes from some direction, pulling me out of my thoughts. Marcel smirks at her, and she giggles. I barely contain my laugh, so I turn my back on her and stare at Marcel, who shrugs. "Let me take you to your table," she says behind me and saunters to the farthest, darkest black leather booth. I notice we're the only people on the terrace of the club, which is the VIP area, and there's security on every corner, which is unusual judging by my experience at the Rosehill's club.

I walk to the railing, looking over the first floor. It's bursting at the seams. *Masquerade* requires wearing a mask, and they give you one at the entrance. It was Damien's idea after many years of being in the spotlight, to have a place where you can put a mask on so you can show your real self. And judging by the people dancing, grinding against each other, laughing and having casual fun, it's working. Typically, most of them are celebrities, politicians, important figures, enjoying their freedom before they go out into the world of expectations again.

The club is lit by its signature purple and blue lights, neon red mask signs on the walls. It's a lot bigger than the club in Rosehill. There's a big stage in the center where aerial performances, including air hoops, silks, and pole routines are held by the best dancers in America. I've seen Ivy and the other girls' shows at Rosehill, and they are incredible. I'd like to see how these will top them, knowing Ivy has choreographed them too. Usually, there are themes for the shows, and sometimes they do Burlesque.

As I search the floor, my eyes land on the target. Lucifer is smirking, propped up on the center bar, dressed in all black shirt, slacks, and mask, staring at me. My knees buckle, and I grab the railing before I fall on my butt. His eyes drill into mine as he raises his glass, taking a sip from a brownish liquid. I sashay to the stairs.

This reminds me of when we were little at my father's masked balls. They were straight out of a fairy tale, only the two of us weren't allowed to be at the actual event, because Giovanni was hiding me from his enemies. Which makes zero sense because why would you invite your enemies to your home? Lou used to steal masks and wait for me at the end of the stairs to my wing, so we could dance to the music in the back hallway all night. Later, Aunt Melanie started throwing them every Halloween, and even though she acted unbothered and said they were for investors, I knew she started it for me. But it just wasn't the same without Lou.

And here he is now, in this fucked-up fairy tale, walking over to me just as I reach the last stair, and he bows, offering me his hand. "Princess."

"Lucifer." I place my trembling hand in his as he raises his head, looking every bit like the devil himself. I'd let him lead me to hell and bathe me in the fires of his passion.

CHAPTER THIRTEEN

LUCIFER

"May I have this dance?" I clear my throat. I'm a goddamn man for fuck's sake, not a giddy teenager.

"Just this once." She curtsies.

I lead her out onto the dance floor and place my hand on her back, hers going on my shoulder. We sway to the rhythm of the slow song, lost in our own little universe, much like the dozens of masked people around us.

I whip her around and whisper in her ear as her bare back presses against my heaving chest, "You look marvelous, princess." Her scent is everywhere around me, dousing me like a drug. She smells like strawberries and heaven. I smell like sin and everything wrong. A deadly combination.

She shivers as I brush my nose against her neck. "I thought I wasn't allowed to go out." Her voice is a soft velvet, head tilted sideways granting me access to her pulsing neck.

When I was younger I used to hate Damien Black with a passion. The pretty billionaire prince of Florida—a perfect match for the Sicilian mafia princess. Who do you think

Giovanni would've chosen for her? Not the errand boy, rejected by his own family. In my fantasy I was the one who kidnapped her on the day of their wedding.

Judging by the gossip rags (why, yes, I stooped to the level of a teenybopper stalking the columns for eight years to make sure my girl's face wasn't printed next to Damien's) it's suffice to say he's been thoroughly pussy-whipped. Can't be grateful enough for this Ivy girl. She's sure as hell getting a gift from me the day she puts a wedding ring on his finger.

"Damien promised you're safe here." I smirk against her skin. "Plus I've taken some extra precautions." The building is swarming with soldiers. No one would dare cross the threshold armed. "It's your treat. You've been a good girl after all."

"So you know that I got the deal." She turns around and buries her head in my shoulder.

"I was talking about wearing the necklace." I whisper in her ear. "It's your gift for a job well done."

The DJ changes the song to a slow ballad. He's been paid off to accompany my agenda. I pull my head back, and Stella smiles timidly, her eyes shining brighter than all the diamonds I could gift her. This is the time to use all the arsenal I've gathered in the manor. Stepping away, I hold her hand and make her twirl, the silk of her sexy dress swaying in the air as she makes a full spin. I pull her to my chest, my heart pounding as her nipples graze my shirt. Fuck, she didn't wear a bra.

It feels like floating as she follows my lead blindly, never once bothering to look around. The heat between our bodies grows more powerful with every beat of the melody. Every breath we take is in sync with our moves.

My hardened cock brushes her stomach. I press my lips to her neck, feeling her throbbing pulse. Damn, I really need to focus on this dance before I put a hasty end to the lives of these innocent people just so I can fuck her right here, right now on the dance floor. Not that I'm shy but they shouldn't have the privilege of seeing her divine body naked.

We savor the rest of our movements as we let go. Of our past, our pain. Living in this moment where we can have the perfect illusion of everything the singer is singing about. A bright future, a family. Our hearts beating as one like it was meant to be.

Stella slants her gaze sideways, looking around the hall. Her eyes widen when they land on the big screen reading *The night of the lucky star*. She turns to me, "The theme of the night…"

Her waist bends as I dip her back, hovering an inch short of her lips and finish her sentence. "Is you."

She gasps as I pull her up and make her twirl around me once more before she lands straight into my embrace with the end of the song. The lights go out, and I can't help but steal a small kiss from her cherry-tasting lips.

Enzo was right about one thing, though. I don't deserve her. She's too perfect, and I'm too many shades of fucked up.

"Ladies and gentlemen." A man is on the stage as the lights come on again, and I pull Stella up against my chest. "May I introduce to you the ladies of the night?" Dramatic sounds play while he hypes the crowd.

"The show is starting. We should go up," Stella whispers against my neck. I guide her through the gathering throng to the VIP floor. She leans on the balcony's railing, her ass pressing against the silk, and I almost trip over Marcel. Damn, she can be a little vixen when she wants to.

"Never thought I'd see the day when Lucifer Visconti is pussy-whipped." Marcel laughs in my face.

"Watch your mouth where your family's concerned, play*boy*." Emphasis on *boy*.

My security guy laughs behind him.

"Fuck you, you're not my family," he mocks while pouring me a glass of whiskey.

I slap him behind the neck. "I almost became your brother-in-law"—he makes a gagging sound—"so I don't think this arrangement would work. But I'm sure there's a nice lad out there for you, though."

He flips me off.

The lights go out once again, and I take it as my cue to slide behind Stella and away from these shitheads. She squeals as my dick presses against her ass, then relaxes when I grip around her waist and huddle her body into mine. The music starts, and a red light illuminates the stage as the curtains open to reveal four masked dancers on their knees.

"They're wearing my costumes!" Stella gasps at the transparent mesh bodysuits with rhinestones covering the right places. The dancers' hands are tied by silk fabric hanging from the ceiling as they squirm on the ground.

Damn, my mind immediately goes to a half-naked Stella all tied and ready for me, and my dick twitches. I'll take a wild guess and say her mind is in the same place because her ass presses against me harder as the silks ascend and take the dancers into the air, hanging by their tied hands. They entangle their feet around the fabric and fall face down, letting their bodies hang loosely in the air. Stella digs her nails into my skin every time they make a sudden move, the pain arousing me. The dancers swing and twist around the fabric in perfect sync with the music, making the show just provocative enough that it can't be called trashy. Stella's hand slips behind her back, gliding on my thigh. I like the confidence this club is giving her. "Aren't they gorgeous?" She bends her head back and purrs in my ear, sliding her teeth over the soft part.

Fuck if I know how any of them look.

I slide my hands under her hip bones. "You tell me. I've failed to notice any other woman."

She moans, "Lou" and her hand glides on my dick. I close my eyes, holding my breath.

Someone taps my shoulder. "What?" I growl, turning to face them.

"We should get going, boss." Fucking Marcel ruins the moment.

Fuck am I thinking?

There shouldn't be a moment. What I'm doing here is wrong. So, so wrong.

"Come on, princess. Our time is up."

She nods, her eyes an aqua pool of lust. Her thoughts are written on her face, in her ragged breath and puckered nipples behind the thin silk fabric. If anything, I hate me even more for giving her hope of something we could never be. For letting myself wander in the forbidden possibilities.

Security escorts us through the dark hallways to the limousine waiting at the back. The one I shouldn't have gotten in the first place. Same for the million dollars hanging from her neck. I couldn't help it. Call it a complex or whatever, but I wanted her to know I have the means to give her everything I couldn't when I was young. Bathe her in gifts until there isn't a thing in this world she wouldn't have. What an idiot. Of course she'd want the only one I can't give her. My heart. I'm not willing to pay with her life.

Stella slips onto the seat and makes room for me as Marcel and our security divide between two cars in front and behind the limo. "Are we going home?"

The one thing she can't have slams against my rib cage at

the word *home* with the weight of a fucking stone. God, I am pussy-whipped indeed. I need to get my head in the game immediately.

I nod and take a bottle of water as the limo takes off. All of a sudden, she throws one leg over my lap, yanking the bottle out of my hand and straddles me. Her lips press against mine softly, timidly. I growl as I do the hardest thing known to man and push her back. "What are you doing?"

"You know you want this too." She buries her head in my shoulder, kissing my neck, but I know she's hiding her flushed cheeks.

"We can't do this." I restrain her, holding her arms. Her cheeks redden even more, and I don't think it's embarrassment I see. "We can't."

"Why?" She actually whimpers. I relax my hold on her as I realize I'm squeezing her, and she uses the moment to sneak her little hand to my cock. "I like it when you're rough. Please, Lou." Her dress has ridden up to her ass. She's grinding on my thigh. "I can't take it anymore. Plea…"

She doesn't get to finish her plea as I put a finger to her lips. "I can't give you what you want."

"What I want is for you to take my body." She sucks on my finger. I growl, barely holding on to the last of my sanity. She moans as her panties are wetting my slacks, rubbing and throbbing. "I want you to do dirty things to me."

"Yeah, princess? Like what?" *Shit. Fuck.* Her voice is blurring my mind.

"You know…" she mutters and bites at the sensitive skin on my neck. I grab her ass and squeeze.

"You're going to have to be more specific. There are a lot of filthy things I want to do to you." She pushes her hips farther so my fingers glaze the wet lace of her panties.

"Then do them all. That's all I want from you and nothing else." Her doe eyes beg me, and then she fucking pouts.

I bite her lower lip between my teeth, and my cock pulses in approval. It's threatening to burst at the seams of my pants as she squeezes it between her little fingers through the fabric. My hands move to her damp panties and slide over the lace. "You're making me do bad things."

She smiles against my face. "Vanilla was never our style." A low chuckle rumbles out of my chest. "There are so many things we never got to do." She bites her reddened lip between her teeth.

She doesn't need to remind me. I fucking hate myself for it. It might sound like I was a loser (which I was) but I didn't have sex until I was twenty; I wanted to wait for her, until she was ready. Until she turned sixteen, cornered me in the stables, and asked me to take her virginity on her birthday. And I did because I could never deny her anything. We were so juvenile, I didn't even know where to touch her. How to pleasure her. But God did we have chemistry. I knew I'd give her all my firsts long before she wanted them.

Life had other plans.

It turned me heartless, mercilessly fucking every woman on my way to forget her. But I never did. And these women, they changed me. Nameless, faceless, they took everything that was supposed to be hers, molding me into something darker. A monster, holding their pain in his hands to try to dull his own.

"I'm going to hurt you, princess."

"I can take it. I want it."

I'm not talking about physical pain and she knows it. Her eyes spark when I give her orders, when I squeeze a little harder. She needs to feel the pain too.

"I fear if I give in now, you won't bear the pain I'll leave behind when I leave you. And make no mistake, I will leave you, princess."

Her throat bobs, but her face is confident when she retorts, "I'm a grown woman. I can take care of myself. But watch your heart, 'cause I might break it on my way out."

I smile at her, knowing goddamn well I left said heart in the manor eight years ago right next to her sleeping body when I kissed her goodbye and disappeared through the window, knowing I was giving up my life to save hers and set her free.

"Only one night."

CHAPTER FOURTEEN

STELLA

"Yeah, just this once," I repeat, staring at his darkening eyes. The limo comes to a halt, and Lucifer grabs me by the hips and moves me off him.

"No one can know. It's too dangerous." He stares me down as I fix my dress. Who am I going to tell? The babysitter he's got following me around?

Security opens the door and Lou climbs out, giving me a hand. Marcel joins us on the sidewalk, giving us a knowing look before he opens the door to the garage. Shoot, is my hair messed up or are we just that obvious?

The ride in the elevator is silently awkward with me huddled in the back, Lucifer standing way too close to me, and Marcel and the guard staring at the metal doors, unmoving. I take a deep breath when the doors open, my lungs choking on the air like I was suffocating before. Or maybe it's because my heart is beating so loud everyone in the elevator can probably hear it. It feels as if it's bruising my chest, anticipating what I've dreamed of for more than a decade. I have a feeling it will be much more than my brain fantasized about.

"Marcel, I won't be needing anyone on this floor tonight," Lucifer commands, coming to a stop before his bedroom door, making me almost bump into him. Marcel gives him a hard stare, saying something with his eyes I can't decode, but Lucifer's scowl is final.

I still don't get their relationship and exactly what Marcel's part in Lucifer's life is. Sometimes he seems like the best friend, other times like an errand boy. It's also weird that Lou has so much security. I know he's rich and all that, but I don't think the construction business is that dangerous, is it? And why would the Russian mob deliver me to him? They obviously have an insider from the manor, which means someone actually survived the massacre to tell. But why not kill me instead? Do they want a piece of his business? Are they punishing him for something? Maybe he owes them money. I know little to nothing about the way the mafia operates, ironically.

Marcel says nothing as he whirls around and stalks to the elevator, followed by the guard. I'm about to open my mouth to ask Lou my questions when he pushes the door open and grabs me by the hand, dragging me inside.

The door clicks behind me as he presses me against it and kisses me stupid until I've forgotten my name.

"You like to see me taking control." It's not a question; it's a statement. His hand wraps around my jaw and squeezes. His teeth dig into my puckered lips, until I taste the copper blood on my tongue. I press my body onto his but he backs away. "Nah, princess. You'll only get what I give you." He drops my jaw and moves his hands to my hips, turning me around and pressing my cheek against the cold wooden door. I hear the hiss of removing a belt. His breath is hot on my bare back as he traces his tongue from my neck to the end of my spine where the dress ends. "Remember the boy who took your innocence, princess?" he says against my skin.

I moan, arching my ass back, searching for some kind of contact. To feel him, to know this moment is real. Not another dream I'll wake up from.

But then the familiar hiss of the belt slashes the air as it connects with my butt cheek, leaving a sting behind. "Answer me with words, Stella," Lucifer grunts in my ear, one of his hands soothing the pain.

"Yes."

"Good." I feel his devilish grin against my neck. "Because I'll make you forget him and anyone else who touched what's mine in the time I was gone."

The pain in his voice gives me strength. Making me feel like a dangerous woman, a vixen. "See, that's where you're wrong, Lucifer. I'll never be yours, and you're the one who applied this rule. So take everything from me. But do it knowing you'll never have what you really want."

He kneels behind me, licking his way up from my calf, pushing my silk dress with the top of his head. I shudder as he sucks on my inner thigh and bites, dragging his lips to my pussy. "I'm used to being dealt the wrong cards, princess. But I bet you all of mine that no one has or ever will touch you the way I'm going to." He flicks his tongue over the wet lace of my thong. I'm trembling with need I never knew could be this strong.

I tease, "I'm not sure. See Max…" I never get to finish as he flips me around, banging my body against the door. Hot red fury takes over his eyes as he grips the side of my silk dress with both hands and rips it apart like a wild animal. The tearing sound makes me clench my thighs as the dress falls around my ankles, exposing my bare body to him.

"I can promise you, you won't fucking remember his name when I'm done," he growls, ripping the lace of my panties, them joining the pile of fabric on the ground. He grabs me by the hips and lifts me up, my legs entangling around him. He's still wearing all of his clothes, making me wish I had the strength to tear them like he did. But I don't, so I start unbuttoning his shirt as he carries me to the king-size bed, the only thing I managed to see before he took all my attention.

"No, no, princess. We play my game here. My rules." He slaps me over the hands and throws me, my back hitting the bed sheets with a soft thump. "Spread your legs for me."

I do as he commands and he hovers over me, tracing a finger over my bare pussy. "I'm going to ease you into it. Do you like that?" He pushes a finger inside me. I throw my head back, a hot wave passing through my body as I moan a little *yes*. He pulls it out. "Good girl. Give me your hands." He takes both my wrists in one palm, holding the belt in his other hand.

"Do you trust me, Stella?" he asks with his no-bullshit look.

I nod before I even think about it. Being kidnapped *twice* gives you some reservations about having someone tie you. But I trust him with my life.

"Turn on all fours."

I roll over and rest on my knees and palms. I can't make myself feel any shame about exposing every inch of skin to him. Usually, I'm self-conscious when it comes to being naked.

A tortured sound comes out of his chest. He hovers over me, taking my wrists in his hands, making me arch my back as he traces his tongue over the length of my spine, eliciting a shiver from me. I curl my ass, searching for more.

"My greedy girl." It sounds like the sweetest compliment I've ever heard. His right hand drops, and he slides it over the crack of my ass, making me clench my hole. "Relax. I'm not rushing, but sometime in the near future this ass will be mine too. Remember that." I don't know when one night became more nights, but I like the way it sounds.

He slides his fingers down to my pussy, pressing his thumb against my entrance. "You're dripping with need for me." His gruff voice is full of lust.

"Yes," I moan out and press against him, making him slip his finger into me.

"Bad girl," he hisses. Cold leather connects with my pussy, and it sends a hot sting of pain through my body.

"Oh," I call out but it only makes me more aroused. "Please."

"What are you begging for?" *Slap*. Another pang of pain shoots to my ass. I feel a wave of moisture dripping on his fingers.

"Fuck me. Please."

He growls, "Shit." I hear the sound of his slacks hitting the floor, the tearing of a foil package, and the next thing I know he enters me without any warning.

"Oh God!" The pain of his thick cock expanding me is too raw. Too sweet.

"He won't help you, princess. You sold yourself to the devil." He ties the belt around my wrists behind my back, making me dig my head into the sheet so I can have some support while my ass is perched in the air.

He pulls out to the tip and then slams back into me. Again. And again. Until my moans echo off the walls of his dark room. As I expand to accommodate all of him, he grabs me by the shoulders and pulls my head back, arching my spine.

"Princess, make no mistake, I'm not your savior. I will destroy you."

A strangled moan escapes my lips. "I don't need your confessions. I need you inside me."

"I'm warning you. I fuck dirty, There will be no lovemaking."

"Good. I don't have any love to give you."

I nod and he bangs into me, throwing me off balance as I slam forward and fall face down on the sheets. He grabs my hips in a bruising grip and does exactly as he promised.

CHAPTER FIFTEEN

STELLA

I wake up in my bed at sunrise, alone and sore. Just like the last time I fell asleep in Lucifer's arms, he carried me to my room.

I can't believe he didn't let me sleep next to him. Old Lou would never miss a chance to sleep together. He really has changed.

I slide off the side of the bed and as soon as my feet hit the floor, my legs buckle. I fall onto my knees on the white fluffy carpet and burst into laughter. At least one side of him changed for the better. Or, the best, if I have to be precise. Every muscle, even some I didn't know existed, burns like it's been set to cook on slow fire. Torturing but with a sweet heat.

When I get up, my legs somehow manage to work with me. I get to the dresser to grab the phone Nina leaves me in the morning and head for the bathroom.

Okay now, not only sitting is a bitch but peeing is my newest enemy. Dio, I'm so pathetic. I should do some exercises or at least have sex once in a while. This can't happen every time I get some action. Although, as much as I don't want to admit it, it's never happened with Max or my ex-fiancé. Last night was something completely different.

What I can have of Lucifer will never be enough. I still feel him in my blood like venom, poisoning me and ruining me for every other man. It's different this time. What scares me is I don't know if there's a way back because I'm pretty sure there isn't one forward.

The screen on my phone lights up from the sink where I put it.

It's Ivy.

I stare at it, contemplating answering. I want to, so badly. But I don't know what to say. Every time I pick up the phone to call her, I can't. I can't even check how many calls she's made, but my guess is at least a hundred.

I reassure myself it's okay as long as I can keep myself from going back to old patterns of unhealthy behavior all on my own. I imagine what Ivy would've told me, and I force it on myself. I haven't puked in a while, and I've slept a few hours every night, sometimes not even dreaming at all, which is a great improvement to returning on the path I was before all of this happened. I know Ivy would always be there for me but soon she'll have a baby, a lot more responsibilities, and she has Damien. I have…no one.

The screen lights up again with a text message from her. I barely refrain from reaching out to read it. I shouldn't have brought it with me. Stupid habit. Lucifer said only emergency calls. Another message beeps through the silence and then another. Heck, what if it's an emergency?

I grab it just when Ivy's name comes across the screen again.

"Hi."

"Stella." Ivy's voice makes my chest blossom with warmth. "Is this you?"

"Yes, who else would it be?" My nervous chuckle is too high. She'll smell my bullshit all the way from Florida.

"Oh, God, I can't believe it. Are you okay? Who is this old friend you're staying with? Damien's told me next to nothing. How are the meetings going?"

Lucifer let me talk to Damien once because he wanted to make sure I was alive and well. He made me tell Damien that I'm staying here for business meetings and my flight was delayed, I got robbed and stayed with a friend. I don't know how much he bought it but he didn't protest.

"Yes, yes. I'm fine but I have tons of work. Sorry I haven't called. I lost my phone and…"

"Spare me the bullshit. I know you and I don't believe a word you say. But I know you have your reasons. You'll tell me later, as long as you're all right."

I hear someone calling her in the background, and Ivy yells back she'll be there in a minute.

"Listen, I don't have much time. I'm going into labor, but I had to call you."

"Wait, what?"

What date is it? It's not supposed to be for another… month. It's been a whole month?! What's in the air in this house? It feels as though it's been two weeks.

"I'm scared, Stells." Her voice trembles, and that's how I know it's serious because she's usually really strong. "I don't have my mom, and my nonna couldn't make it in time. I need you. Can you come? Please," she whimpers.

My heart shatters to pieces on the marble floor. All I want is to be by my best friend's side for the welcoming of my niece. Blood or not, chosen is still family.

"What about Damien?" Tears well, threatening to fall down if I say no.

"He's been my rock through all of this, but he's a guy.

You know him. I need a woman to understand my stress, take it and stress along with me. If I have to listen to his calm voice telling me to breathe one more time, I'm going to make my daughter a half-orphan."

Damn hormones.

"Okay, babe. When are you giving birth?"

"We're heading to the hospital. Damien's waiting by the car. He doesn't know I've called you. Don't tell him. He thinks he's the man of the hour, which he kinda is, but I need you. No one else. Please."

"I'll be there as soon as I can. I promise."

She hangs up when I hear Damien calling for her again, and the phone slips from my hand to the floor.

What is the fastest way to Florida? *Shoot. Shit. Double shit.*

I have to find Lucifer.

I throw on the first clothes I see, which are some ripped jeans and a Beatles T-shirt, and I run straight to his office on the second floor, swallowing down the pain shooting from my sore muscles. I find him there, bowed head under a desk lamp, eyes focused on some papers.

"Yes?" He doesn't even lift his gaze from the documents.

I walk to him, placing my palms on the desk. "I need to get to Rosehill."

He raises an eyebrow. "Since when do I take orders from you?"

Hearing Ivy's voice and the memory of what we did last night gave me a shot of confidence. I stare him down. "Ivy's in labor. I have to be there for her."

He shrugs. "Sorry. No can do. She'll be fine."

"You don't understand. She's my family." I hate the way my voice sounds. Weak, begging. I want it to be strong like I feel in this moment.

"That means very little to me." He avoids my eyes, returning his gaze to the documents as if I'm a stranger begging for spare change on the street.

"You don't understand. I. Have. To. Go." My voice is quavering, hands shaking. How can he act like last night didn't happen? Like I don't mean anything to him?

"There will be no lovemaking."

He doesn't have to love me to respect me.

"There's no way for that to happen. Sorry. Bye now." He waves me off like I'm a hovering fly.

I turn around and pad to my bedroom, anger radiating in waves from my clenched fists. *No way for that to happen.* Bullshit. Lucifer is about to see how real friends always find a way.

I grab my purse with credit cards and passport, that magically appeared before my meeting the other day. Lucifer should know better. He's the one who taught me how to escape unnoticed when I was ten. *Observe the little details. Your way out is through them.* It's his steps I followed when I learned how to move silently. He might've forgotten all about me, but I haven't. I remember everything.

Placing the towels to look like a human on the bed and tucking them in, as I'd done a million times in the manor, I realize I might've not changed as much as I thought I did. I certainly care about the people I love the same. And I'd do anything for them. *My greatest weakness*, as stepmother dearest loved to say. I always took it as my greatest strength.

I sneak into the hallway, knowing the staff won't be coming on this floor until 7:30 a.m., as per Lucifer's orders from last night and I have fifteen more minutes. I can take the stairs and reach the garage if I go unnoticed. There are hidden cameras everywhere, but Lucifer must be too busy staring at the bunch of papers to notice I'm gone since he hasn't caught my sneaky ass yet. Or he doesn't care. Anyway, I'm thankful as I slip through the hidden back door in the wall of the garage, no one should know about it. But of course, I snuck in here a few times after the failed attempt at running away. I looked around, touched everything and let my imagination play out the scene of my kidnapping over and over again until I realized from where the Russians got into the house.

As my feet hit the sidewalk, I place my huge sunglasses on and a baseball cap I don't even know why I own. Oh, right…Ivy and Damien had paparazzi following them when we had to meet for the opening of Masquerade, and I didn't want my picture taken. I flash a grin. Well, I guess life has its ways of putting everything to use.

I realize it's either dumb luck that let me sneak out or I just haven't been trying hard enough. Who am I lying? I saw the man I loved was alive, was I really going to try too hard to run away without getting the answers to my questions? No.

I sneak to the other side of the street and run as fast and as far away as I can until my muscles start to give up. Which isn't much to be honest. I hop in the first cab that stops.

"To the airport, please. And fast."

The taxi driver nods and takes off. I check the flights to Rosehill and there's only one today. I'll be able to catch it if fate and traffic are on my side. I smile so wide my cheeks hurt. *I escaped my prison.* It takes all of me to calm down and refrain from dancing my victory dance in the backseat.

I did it. On my own. I'm stronger than I thought.

I send a prayer out to the universe. Hang on, Ivy. I'm coming.

CHAPTER SIXTEEN

LUCIFER

"*D*o you need anything from me, sir?" Meghan, a red-haired flight attendant with a body more suitable for a Playboy cover, leans over me like I'm a toddler. Her tits are spilling from the tight blue uniform, and she makes a point of stuffing them in my face. Uncle certainly chose someone *qualified*.

"No." I get back to pretending to read the newspaper, flipping one ankle over my knee. "Off you go now." She frowns in my peripheral vision, and sashays her way to the end of the aisle, swinging her tight ass in a uniform that makes me question whether she even went through the course for being a flight attendant, chancing a glance over her shoulder at me.

Not gonna happen, baby. Keep walking.

She finally disappears, and I plaster the newspaper to the small wooden table before me, grunting. Maybe I should fuck her; I mean, that's why my uncle and cousins hired her. She expects to get a tip out of it. That'll teach my little fleeing hellion a lesson. But it's not the kind of man I am. I've already tried everything; Stella is engraved in my memory forever. I'd much rather flip her ass over my knee and spank the disobedience out of her. And that's exactly what I plan to do as soon as this jet lands in Rosehill.

She thinks she's so clever, escaping past me while I was engrossed in doing the calculations on my freedom. I didn't need to check her credit card statements to know where she's heading.

Though, she really did screw me over by forcing me to take the family's jet on such short notice because she landed the only flight for today. If any Visconti is sober enough to notice it, they'll know something is up.

"Mr. Visconti, prepare for landing," the captain's voice booms through the speakers.

Fucking finally.

I don't even take the time to say goodbye to the captain as I run straight to the car waiting for me on the tarmac. It's bad enough it took me six hours to do all the paperwork and pull my head out of my ass to actually notice she was gone. And then another two for the jet to prepare. She could be dead without security by now if someone else found her first. And that motherfucker Black isn't picking up his fucking phone.

The car stops at the curb in front of Rosehill hospital.

"Wait for me here," I bark at my security driving in the car behind me.

The smell of sanitizer and bleach assaults my nostrils as I push through the glass doors of the "Black Industry" wing. Where else would that billionaire heir have his offspring than his own wing? Fucking rich people.

I have to remember I'm one of them now as I clench my fists and the door behind me closes with a thud.

"Can I help you, sir?" A petite woman in her forties, eyes me and flashes what I can only presume is her most charming smile.

Yeah, they all like what they see when I'm dressed in a

crisp Armani suit. Stella's the only one who sees the dirty little boy underneath it. It drives me nuts.

"Yes, ma'am." I lean an elbow at the counter, and she flutters her long fake eyelashes. "I'm looking for Damien Black. His fiancée, Ivy Thanos, was admitted here."

"Are you family?" She twirls a lock of hair on her finger.

"Not exactly but it's an emergency." I smirk at her and her cheeks flush. One of the first tricks I learned. Works every time.

"I'm sorry, sir, I can't give you any information." She pouts like that's supposed to somehow soothe me.

"Visconti," a taut voice comes from behind and heads turn from all corners of the room.

There he is in a cloud of arrogance and God complex. Damien fucking Black. He's the king in this city. The clear annoyance in his clenched fists doesn't reach his green eyes, though. It's like he's…happy? He nods his head toward a small corridor, and I follow.

"I was wondering when you'd show up." He crosses his arms in front of his extremely wrinkled white shirt. Was he wrestling bears behind that door? "You were protecting her, huh? Seems like you couldn't carry out your part." He throws my words in my face, smugness dripping from every syllable.

A door clicks behind him. "Lucifer?" Stella's sweet voice searches for me.

I side-step Damien, growling, "You're in so much trouble." But when I face her, it's one of those moments where a choir of angels sing above my head, illuminating her and the little baby she's cradling tucked in a pink blanket.

Both Damien and Stella shush me and she whispers, "I'm not going back to New York. I'm staying here with my beautiful niece." Her eyes are big aqua hearts looking down at the tiny human calmly swallowing and blinking at her.

There are very few occasions I've been left speechless. For the life of me, I can't force a single word out. All the dreams I buried hit me in the balls with an iron fist. All the times Stella and I planned for a perfect little family of ours. The reality of what an empty dark life I've been living is suffocating.

Damien snorts from my side, bringing me back to reality. "You couldn't keep her safe even in that fortress. It's my turn again, *bro*." He shoulders past a stunned me and takes his daughter from a puzzled Stella. His whole face lights up like he's doped or something. "Where's my little girl?" He cocoons the baby. *Another thing I'll never have.*

"Wait," Stella finally speaks, looking like she, too, just got out of a trance. "What do you mean again?"

Damien, the shithead, basking in a bliss of endorphins, answers her without thinking. "He had his shot with you. It's more than he deserved after he brought the trouble to your door because of his uncanny inability to stay on the other side of the country away from you."

All of the joy on her face evaporates into a furrowed forehead and glistening eyes.

Her voice is wobbly when she speaks to Damien. "So, you're telling me all this time you knew Lucifer was alive?" She turns to me, glaring like she's already organizing my funeral. "You knew I was alive? And you both lied to me?"

Her hands shoot up, burrowing her fingers in her golden hair. She stares at the ceiling wide-eyed, barely balancing the tears on her lower lids. "And both of you let me torture myself for eight years?" Her voice rises, almost shrieking, "Eight! Freaking! Years!"

The little bundle in Damien's arms cries out, raising her tiny hand above the blanket as if she's reaching out to find Stella.

"Calm yourself. Ivy's asleep," Damien scolds her.

I reach out to take Stella's hand, but she backs away from the three of us, shaking her head. "I can't believe it. You knew what it did to me. How much I suffered."

"Stella…" Both Damien and I say at the same time. He nods at me, barely noticeable, and I continue. "Come with me. I'll explain everything."

She raises her hands in defense and cries out, "No!" She starts walking backward. "I'm done with taking orders from you. From Damien. Everyone. I'm done." She turns around and disappears through the door, running.

"Baby? Is everything all right?" a woman calls out behind the door.

We exchange glances.

"I'll take care of it."

He nods and enters the room to attend to his family. I'm left chasing the vision of mine that seems to have disappeared from the world.

CHAPTER SEVENTEEN

LUCIFER

"Open the fucking door, princess. You don't want me to break it down."

There's shuffling on the other side. I can't believe I spent two hours searching the city only to find her hiding in plain sight.

Watching for years from the sidelines, I never had the courage to come this close to the place Ivy and Stella live. I feared I might accidentally break inside and throw her over my shoulder like a caveman. Now I know I should've.

I can't believe I let her live in this hideous house. The only good thing about it is the little neat garden of fire bushes and shooting star flowers in the middle of the backyard's brown lawn. This neighborhood isn't so bad; why the fuck does this house looks like that?

I stop my gaze at the peephole. "Princess?" No sound comes from the other side. "Now, remember, you asked for it. Back off if you're still here." I count to ten and drive the heel of my foot against the door. The soft, hollow wood splinters, and the door flies open. This was way easier than it should've been.

The first thing I see is her, staring with bloodshot eyes at me from the kitchen space.

"Why don't you just leave me alone?" Her voice is weak, broken.

The second thing I see hurts even more than the first. A suitcase and a duffel bag thrown on one side of what is a surprisingly good-looking vintage living room. "You're running away from me?"

She shrugs, looking down at the laminated flooring.

I take a step toward her, but she takes a step back. "You don't think you can really escape me, do you? I'll find you if I have to search the world."

"I don't want you to find me. I just want to live free," she mumbles, avoiding eye contact.

It cuts deeper, but I don't have the luxury of having feelings. Not when her safety is the price. "My jet is waiting. We have to get back to New York." I walk over and take her bags from the floor.

When I turn around, she's behind me, arms defiantly crossed, eyes stabbing me with a thousand knives. "I'm. Staying. Here."

"Not when you can get killed. This isn't a discussion."

She takes me by surprise when she lunges forward, raining her little fists on my chest, screaming, "I'd rather be dead than live my life by yours or anyone else's demands anymore. I hate you. Leave me. Go. I'm not your puppet. You can't control me."

The tears welling in her eyes tell me otherwise.

The bags drop to the floor with a thud. I wrap my arms around her, squeezing her close to my body. She squeaks, both of us surprised, when I dive in for a hungry kiss. She meets me midway, desperate for whatever I'm willing to give her, and I realize I haven't been breathing until our tongues meet.

It takes her a few beats to let me go and stare into my eyes, surprising me by lifting off her shirt and throwing it in my feet, followed by her jeans.

I grab the back of her neck, having the urge to drink from her lips. She's ablaze, burning me, hurting me with her every touch. For bossing her around. For hiding the truth. For the fire I thought I extinguished the night I left her. I sure as hell won't be the one to put it out this time.

I grab her hips and lift her up, and her legs wrap around me like a vine. "Where's the…"

"On the right," she shoots out before I finish.

I kick the door open and throw her on the bed. She doesn't open her eyes, just lies there, waiting for me, trusting me even though she screamed she hated me just minutes ago. She can hate me all she wants if it'll keep her safe and close to me. And in this matchbox of a bedroom, there's nowhere to escape.

I know exactly what she needs. "Kneel. Eyes closed."

She does as she's told, clasping her hands behind her back.

"Such a good girl." My suit jacket is the first to fall, followed by my gold cuff links. The vision of her trembling as each cuff link hits the floor with a clink will haunt me in my dreams. I cup her chin, and she flutters her eyes open.

"Closed," I bark out. She quickly obeys, wetting her puffy lips, begging me to lick, kiss, and bite them. So I do. I squeeze her neck and dig my teeth into her lip until she cries out.

"Shh," I place my finger on it, unbuttoning my shirt with the other hand. "You know what you need, princess?"

"I..." she starts. "I need you."

"No." I caress her blushing cheek. "You need to learn your lesson." I sit on the bed. "On my knee."

She stares at me. "What are you... Ah!" She gasps when I pull her over my knees.

Whack! The sound of the slap of my palm on her bare ass cheek bounces off the walls.

"Don't." I land another one on the same reddening spot. "Fucking." She squirms under my caressing palm, arching her bottom up. "Run." A smack on the other cheek follows. "From." She moans as I hit the last one, striking harder than the others. "Me."

My fingers hover over her wet cotton panties and press against her center.

I bend down and whisper in her ear. "I bet you're dripping for me, princess, aren't you?" She nods, and I bite the soft part of her ear. "Let me put my mouth to work."

I slide my arms under her body and flip her over so she's lying on her back now. Her wide eyes stare at me as she squirms, trying to sit up. "What?"

I slide my arms under her knees and lift her against my bare chest. "I've been dying to eat you out."

TELLA

Oh, Dio mio. My whole body shudders in his arms.
"I... I've never..."

Lucifer's mouth curves on one side, and he raises an

eyebrow. "What? You look perplexed for a woman in this position."

"I've never had anyone…eat…lick…you know," I stutter. His smirk is now a full-blown grin.

"That's unbelievable. What kind of morons have you dated?" he mumbles as he pushes me back to relax.

"I… My fiancé hated it…and Max never mentioned it, so I just… I haven't done it," I blurt out, staring at the fascinating ceiling, terrified my cheeks are melting from embarrassment.

"Remind me to send them a thank you note for leaving me another one of your firsts." He shakes his head, still grinning. The way he looks at me through his hooded gray eyes with so much heat and carnal need…

"I've had this fantasy…" I blurt aloud. There's just something in his wolfish gaze that gives me confidence. "Ever since the kitchen incident."

"Oh?" he says oh so innocently.

I open my mouth to explain, but I realize it'll be easier to just show him. I shoot out of bed and run straight to the kitchen, grabbing what I need from the fridge. Checking the expiration date, I turn around and see him leaning on the doorframe.

Sweet heaven, I almost choke on my breath. Six feet and two inches of pure godly perfection. I take a second to appreciate it, following an invisible line from his tousled curls down his defined abs and almost drop the can at the bulge in his pants below the mouthwatering V-line.

There's a knowing look in his eyes when he sees what I'm holding. I count my steps on the way to him, trying to tranquilize the butterflies.

A small smirk rises on his face. Oh, he knows. He's the

only one who ever saw the playful vixen beneath the fragile flower.

"You never disappoint me." He wraps his arms around my thighs and spins me in the air, carrying me into my shoebox of a bedroom. "My good girl."

A hot flash of pain when my ass hits the bed serves as my reminder I was just spanked by this gorgeous specimen. Giving up control when I was on the verge of breaking felt oddly freeing and satisfying. Call me crazy but I feel stronger.

"Spread your legs," Lucifer commands as he pulls down his pants. I close my eyes when he hovers over me, leaving a tingling trail of kisses on my lips, my neck, and that dimple on my shoulder that makes me go wild.

A dark angel, seducing his way out of heaven.

The hissing sound of the whipped cream can makes me clench my eyes. A cold wet feeling grazes my nipple, making my pussy clench around nothing. Lucifer flicks his tongue over it. I arch my head back, moaning. He growls against my puckered nipple and swivels his tongue around it, sucking off the cream.

"You've got a little…" I notice when I open my eyes and show him a place on his scruff where a little dot of white cream has escaped.

He wipes it on his middle finger and smears it on my lips. I part them for him, and he pushes in. "Suck on it, baby." The sweet taste makes my mouth water when I wrap my lips around his finger.

"Fuck. If that's how you suck, I can't imagine what you'll do to my cock." I tense a little under his touch, but he kisses me stupid, whispering, "Not just yet."

He slides his tongue along my throat, tits, all the way to

the lowest point of my belly, and he kneels on the floor before me, as if I'm equal to a goddess. My gaze is glued to him as he positions my center right in front of his face, glances at me under thick lashes, and flicks his tongue over my clit without warning.

"Lucifer," I moan when he grips my knees and pushes them down to my stomach, spreading me wide open.

"You've got no idea"—he sprays a path of whipped cream over my pussy and licks it clean—"how happy it makes me knowing I'm the only man who'll taste this pussy. You'll only ever be mine, princess." The wet fluffiness sticks to my clit as he spritzes the last of the bottle. I grip the cushions on the verge of having an orgasm just from seeing him staring at my pussy like it's the most delicious cake and he hasn't eaten in a week. "I'll feast to that."

He dives in, tongue chasing my clit and sucking off the cream, making my eyes roll in their sockets and eliciting shivers down my spine. My moans turn into screaming as the sensations build into my center and erupt like fireworks on the fourth of July. It's like nothing I've felt before. My hands find his wild mane and pull at his curls.

"Harder," I growl.

A deep chuckle rings on my sex, tingling me from the inside. Gripping my thighs, he sucks harder, deeper. All over my pussy, diving his tongue in and out of my hole, circling my clit, and devouring me until I writhe against his face, screaming profanities as I come harder than I ever have before.

"What did you do to me?" I ask, fighting to catch my next breath.

He's all smiles when he stands up, giving me a hand. "Come on, let's get a shower."

"I can't." I shake my head, beaming. "My legs are... Whoa!" I yelp as he lifts me off the bed.

"Just show me the way." He winks at me.

We take a long, hot shower with an even hotter image in the mirror of him fucking me against the wall until I come a thousand times. He has to carry me back to the bedroom because I can no longer feel any part of my body. I finally fall asleep, with my hair still wet, curled up in his arms and hidden away from all the nightmares.

Or so I think...

Until I wake up in the middle of the night, screaming and panting.

"Hey, hey. I'm here." Lucifer kisses my temple, trying to calm me down. I huddle into him until he's wrapped around me like a glove.

"I can't go back, Lou. I've been losing my mind and my health in New York. I've already lost so much. Please, don't make me go back. Please." I weep, his hot chest burning my wet cheeks. "Stay with me," I whisper, too scared to hear the answer.

His heart rate accelerates. "I'll see what I can do, princess, but I'm not making any promises. Either way you're bound to me."

I lie there, listening to my favorite sound as his pulse calms down again for what seems like hours in perfect sync with mine. He doesn't get a second more of sleep either. I know he's up every night because I hear him coming from his office in the early mornings when I'm usually working. But tonight it feels different. Like we're teenagers again, savoring every moment we can steal, trusting each other unreservedly to protect one another from our demons as we fight through another cruel night.

When the sun starts rising, I dare to look up, and I see a

glimpse of that boy. That's when it's time to get my answers. One thing I know is Lucifer will always crave to be mine.

"Something isn't adding up, and I promise to support you whatever it is, but you have to tell me. I need more, Lou. Otherwise, I don't know if I can be with you."

CHAPTER EIGHTEEN

STELLA

The storm in Lucifer's eyes is long gone, and in its place are the nostalgic ashes of our memories.

"You wouldn't be with me if I tell you either." He sits up in the bed and leans against the headboard, sighing. "You can't be with me at all. This is just a temporary situation."

I push closer into him, afraid he's getting ready to retreat into himself, but he opens his arms for me to nestle on his chest. Right above the proof I need to never trust a word out of his mouth.

"Is that why you have a permanent reminder?"

Without even asking me to specify he looks down at the tattoo on his rib cage. It's a gray wolf howling under a shooting star.

"You've always been a lone wolf." I run my finger over the ink.

He shrugs, playing it off nonchalantly.

I stop my finger on the star tattooed under his peck. On his heart. "Why?"

He takes my hand and kisses my fingers one by one, saying nothing.

"Lou." I look up at him. He's watching my hand intently, avoiding eye contact.

"I wanted to keep a part of you to guide me through this world."

"You knew I was alive. Why didn't you come to me if you wanted to keep me?"

"It's complicated, Stella. Dangerous."

"I am already in danger, Lucifer. And keeping me in the dark might hurt me more if I don't know what I'm hiding from. Or who."

"I never wanted you to get involved in this world. I'm so sorry."

"Your world. I want to be in every part of it. Damn the consequences."

"You don't know what you're asking. You'll hate me forever."

"Try me," I counter.

His chest rises more rapidly. "All of this, everything that's happened to you, is because of me. I'm the one poisoning your life."

I take his face in my hands. "Look at me, Lucifer. You're not the villain in my story. Do you hear me? Don't make me figure this out on my own, 'cause you know I will."

He shifts, his hands balling into fists. "I should've told you long ago, but I'm a selfish bastard. I wanted to keep the perfect illusion of the boy in your head because it's the only good thing left of me in this world."

"I could *never* hate you," I say to his back and he laughs. A freaking sincere laugh deep from his chest.

"God, this is going to hurt," he mutters, running his hand over his wild curls. He turns around. "You deserve to know the truth. At least we had tonight, right?"

I have the sudden urge to chew on my lip. How bad could it be?

He traces his hand over my thigh and slides down to lie on the bed again. I follow, fitting every curve of mine into his until we're perfectly aligned without a gap, like two pieces of the same puzzle.

"You know what Giovanni's business was, right?"

The butterflies in my stomach turn into knots at the mention of my father. I nod. Then the realization sinks in. My eyes bulge out. "You work in Morelli's organization?"

"Not anymore." He looks down and squeezes my hand. "I lead my family's."

"I don't understand."

"For the last ten years, every one of the Five Families, the five biggest criminal organizations in New York, has been trying to scramble to the surface because the pressure by the authorities doubled after the massacre of your family."

I don't blink an eye at the mention, too enthralled by the revelation.

"I'm still on the mission of pulling my family out of the dark by legitimizing our businesses. We own one of the biggest construction companies in New York and some other smaller businesses that are being used as umbrellas. Unlike my family, Giovanni had morals. He didn't kill for fun, he didn't do human trafficking or prostitution, and he didn't sell drugs to kids. I consider that as close to sainthood as one could get by the mob's standards."

Although I wished my sixth sense wouldn't be right, it seems like once again I've guessed it right. One thing doesn't sit right with me though. "I thought you didn't know your family?"

He sighs. "I wish I didn't. But it's more complicated than that."

"Stop saying that as if I'm too dumb to understand. What does your family have to do with all of this?"

"Morelli and Visconti were the two most powerful mob families in Sicily. Well, yours was the leading and mine…"

"Visconti," I repeat, cutting him off. "That name…" I scour my brain, trying to figure out why it sounds so familiar when a distant memory swims to the surface. "My mother." A little whisper falls out of my lips. Time freezes along with my heartbeat as I turn to look at Lucifer's face. "You have the same eyes as him." The gray eyes of the man who shot my mother. How did I miss that?

His features grimace an apology, but all I wish is to make the memory play out faster than the thousand times I've seen it in my dreams. A man's rough hand around my mouth. The roar of a desperate mother. A hole in the wall of an abandoned building. A little blonde girl in a blue dress running toward the sunlight. My knees hit the gravel road beneath at the sound of the shrilling scream behind me. *Visconti.* That was my mother's last word before the shotgun echoed off the walls of the building I just escaped.

I still remember the sound of the gunshot and her little gasp like it was yesterday.

I ran as fast as my feet would allow me, crying and hurting in a way I shouldn't have known at the age of five. Or ever.

My therapist said it's normal to vividly remember a traumatic experience at such a young age, but how could I forget this little detail when the memory haunts me every time I close my eyes? Why remember it now? So many questions are swirling in my head as a tear slips down my cheek and Lucifer catches it on his thumb, chasing away the intense picture.

"I'm so sorry, Stella. You have every right to hate me."

I can't move or say anything, staring at him blankly. I can't feel my heart beating. Has it stopped? Is it too fast? It's like the small room has doubled in size, and I'm still that little girl trying to run away.

"Punch me, slap me, scream at me. Please, princess, just say something." His eyes are begging me, both of his hands squeezing mine. "Please. Anything."

"Why?" It comes out so small, like the way I feel now. I clear my throat. "Why did your father kill my mother?"

"Our families were feuding. Angelo came after Giovanni by kidnapping you, but your mother found you before your father did and became a casualty."

"But we grew up together. You lived in my home. My mother's home!" My tone rises with every sentence. I need to close my eyes and breathe. *Deep breath in, deep breath out. You can do this, Stella.* I open them and try again, but my voice is broken. "You came mere days after my mother's funeral. Why?"

"Giovanni wanted to avenge your mother and since mine was already dead, he took the only son of Angelo. Your father was no saint, but he wasn't a monster. He couldn't kill me, so he made me his servant."

"And your father just let him? The man who went to incredible lengths to destroy my family just gave away his own?"

"He named me after the devil, did you think he loved me?" He shakes his head, chuckling softly, and against all logic I burst out laughing. Laughing. Laughing. Until the tears of shock turn into sorrow. I feel like a lunatic. I have so many feelings swirling inside I don't even know what's appropriate.

I wipe my eyes with the back of my hand, producing something between a sob and a laugh. "You got it all wrong. Lucifer is an angel who didn't get a second chance."

"You're doing it again. Stop justifying what I am. My fucking family tried to kill you. They are responsible for what happened eight years ago. They massacred your entire family and your friends. How could you not hate me?" he growls.

The police never found evidence, and they didn't say names. It's all coming together now. "So that's how you got out alive?" The thought of him betraying us seems so unrealistic to me.

"I warned Giovanni, but he wouldn't listen. I had to do something. You were supposed to have a happy weekend with the Blacks while your father and I won the battle that left you homeless." I pull down his hands before he plucks his hair out. He raises his head to look me in the eyes. "Sometimes I wish Angelo would've left me to die. At least I would've been a man worthy of your love." He looks down at his hands. "Instead, look at me now. A murderer. A liar. A fucking traitor."

"I…" I don't know what to say. This is too much to digest. His family is the reason I don't have one. He opened the wound I thought I healed but oddly enough it doesn't hurt as much as I thought it would. There's this feeling I can't put a name on. Almost like…closure. I should probably report him or at the very least throw him out. But all I can think about is how fucked-up our lives are and yet being with Lucifer still feels so simple.

He's looking at me intently, and as much as I try I can't see a glimpse of his father in his eyes. Maybe that's why I never noticed. All there's ever been is pain. It makes me uncomfortable, and I look down at the sheets. Lucifer suffered as much as I did, if not more. My father was many things but at least he loved me. All he ever did was for me, even if it was wrong. I can't imagine what it's like knowing your only parent hated you enough to give you up.

The pain in his eyes isn't from his family, though. He's beating himself over things that had nothing to do with his decisions.

"Lou…" I slide my palm over his cheek, but he draws his face away and rises to pace the small space.

"Stella. I could kill you in a blink. Finish what my family started. Run. Hide. I swear I won't look for you. You'll be free like you wanted. I'm the monster keeping you imprisoned. Think of yourself first for once in your goddamn life."

"I am thinking of myself. But without you, there's no me."

"How could you be so good and forgiving? Why?" He grabs me by the shoulders, shaking me. "Hate me for fuck's sake. I need you to despise me so deeply that even the thought of me repulses you." He grows angrier by the second. He finally lets me go, and I fall back on the bed. He roars above me "Hate. Me."

I grab a hold of his face and plant a kiss on his mouth. A long kiss that says more than words could ever.

His voice is broken when he whispers against my lips. "Why?"

Fingers buried in his hair, I keep a strong hold of him, eyes leveled with mine.

"I could never hate you."

He crouches down, letting his head fall into my lap. "You can't love me either. I'm the boss of the Visconti famiglia, and you're my enemy's daughter. It's forbidden, princess."

"Let's run away like we planned to. Let your father lead his own mafia organization. I'll kill him myself if he comes after us." The fury in my blood could boil a thousand Angelos if he ever so much as stepped close to his son.

"Princess, you don't have a bad bone in your body." He chuckles, shaking his head in my lap. He looks up and squeezes my cheeks between his palms. "You don't need to worry about him."

"Why can't we be together then?" I try to say, but his squeezing is causing me to sound like a whining little kid.

He releases me and sweeps his palm over his face, sighing. "Do you understand why I keep you locked up? If someone from the other families finds you now that your father's not here to protect you... My guess is they'll either want you dead, too, or married to one of their spawns."

"No way," I shoot out but then another idea comes to mind. "Can't I just marry you?"

He almost chokes on his own breath. I'm pretty sure he stopped breathing for a second there before he quickly masks it. "No, it's complicated."

I can't say his quick rejection doesn't leave a brand-new wound on my already crumbling body. A bigger one than finding out his parents killed mine. Does that make me a bad person?

There's a lump in my throat pressing so hard I want to vomit.

"You're not made to be a mob moll, Stella. This life almost killed you once. I won't let it get to you a second time."

"But I'm already involved, Lucifer. What are you going to do, keep me locked for eternity? Only so you can deny being with me some more?"

"I'm searching for a way out of this situation, and I'll find it. This isn't a discussion." There's not a hint of doubt in his tone. The most serious face I've ever seen. "Once I know you're safe our path splits, and you'll never see me again. I told you at the club. I will leave you."

My heart is shattering all over again when I thought the pieces he left eight years ago were so small they couldn't possibly be broken anymore. He seems hell-bent on jumping over them, crushing them to dust. And there's nothing I can do. He already proved he's able to live without me. I almost died thinking we could be together on the other side. I can't imagine what this round will do to me. I'm getting more nauseous by the second. I jump out of the bed and run to the bathroom. I can't stop it. I barely open the toilet lid before I vomit the burger and fries I got when I ran away from the hospital. The memory of stuffing it whole in my mouth, thinking about binge eating another five to relieve some of the stress triggers a second round of vomit.

There's a knock on the door.

"May I?" Lucifer asks.

"No!" I shout through another gag.

"That was just courtesy. I'm coming in."

I don't have the energy to give a single fuck, so I just sit on the tiles, resting my head against the wall and wiping my mouth with my hand. Classy.

"Stop fucking lying to me. This isn't okay, Stella." He points at the disgusting toilet and flushes it. I shrug.

"I'm fighting it." I'm not lying. Technically, I fought it today when I wanted more food. I could've gotten a bag with everything on the menu but I didn't, and I'm proud of myself. I just wish I managed to suppress my gag reflex before I let this slip.

"Fuck that. I'm taking you to a doctor."

I shrug again, looking at the blue tiles. Does it matter what he does now when he's going to leave me someday? I'll have to fight everything alone again, and I'm so tired of being alone.

"Hold me," I murmur.

"What was that?"

"Just hold me. That's the only thing that will help." Ivy would bitch slap me if she knew I'm leaving my health in someone else's hands again. Someone who could leave me any day now. As pathetic as it is, I'm not beyond taking advantage of his pity to spend whatever time we have left together.

He helps me brush my teeth and wash my face and carries me to the bedroom, where the sun is shining through the transparent curtains. I huddle against his hot skin, closing my eyes instantly.

"Promise me you won't leave until you have to. And no more giving me the cold shoulder." It's a dick move to take advantage when he'd do anything right now to make me feel better, but I can't feel an ounce of remorse. This new him provokes the new me. Bolder, unapologetic, manipulative. I want every second I can get of him. I'll think about the consequences of his disappearing later.

"I'll see what I can do, princess." He kisses my forehead, and I fall into a dreamless sleep for the first time in months.

CHAPTER NINETEEN

STELLA

"Thank God, you're still in Rosehill!" Ivy exclaims when she opens the door to welcome me. Six, Damien's huge black Doberman, pushes by her to stand protectively between us.

"I've missed you, buddy!" I crouch down and squeeze him in a suffocating hug until he yelps and rushes inside the house again. Ivy's little postpartum belly is showing under her red velvet tracksuit, and even with eye bags the size of Texas, she still looks as gorgeous as ever, her long brown hair up in a messy bun. "Why is Six acting weird? He couldn't have forgotten me in a month."

"Don't pay him attention. Ever since the baby came home, he doesn't leave my ass for a second. He's so overprotective of her that Damien had to lock him in the kitchen 'cause he wouldn't let Melanie through the door." She rolls her eyes and gives me a kiss on the cheek.

"Now I see why you're so happy." I giggle. Ivy and her mother-in-law are…something else.

"Melanie's actually been oddly warm these days. The ice

kingdom must be affected by the global warming or something." She takes the baby gift basket out of my hands and walks inside the house. I stay rooted at the threshold, holding back happy tears. She notices I haven't followed her after a few steps. "Are you waiting for a written invitation? Come on."

I step inside Damien's beautiful mansion and follow her.

"I don't know how I survived without you, babe."

"Aww." She hugs me, and I can feel her relaxing in my hands. "You're stronger than you think. Me, on the other hand"—she lets me go and points at a yellow stain on her blouse—"not so much. Thank goodness, I have Damien because Lord knows I'm on the verge of losing my mind." She puts a hand on the side of her mouth and whispers to me, wide-eyed, "And it's only been a week."

I chuckle, taking the basket back from her hands. "What can I help with?" We reach the lavish living room where a pile of baby presents is taking up half the room. "Maybe I should've gotten something bigger?"

She huffs, shaking her head. "We keep receiving packages from people I don't even know, but Damien says they're friends. How many friends could a person possibly have?" A lot apparently by the looks of it. "I was thinking of giving them away 'cause we don't need them, since Damien bought the whole store when I told him I was pregnant."

"That's a very Damien thing to do." I roll my eyes, a habit I got from her. "So did you choose a name?"

A cry comes from a nearby room.

"Yes." Her whole face lights up, and she pulls me by the hand, dragging me through the hallway. "We turned the guest room into a nursery for now," she explains as we walk into the cutest baby room I've seen. Six is lying on the ground in front of a white baby crib. "Miss Devora Black." Ivy takes the little bundle in her arms, beaming and glowing like I've never seen her, and the baby's cry slowly subsides.

Baby Devora smiles at me, melting my heart, and it's one of these enlightening moments where you realize nothing else really matters. Money, fame, nothing can compare to this little human, dressed in mint-colored pajamas, staring at me with her big green eyes.

"She's got her father's eyes." I snivel, unable to stop the tears. She's a perfect mixture of both of them, brown hair and fluffy lips.

Ivy removes one of the straps of her top to breastfeed her. Her eyes water, and she nods, sniveling as well. "His temperament too. She's already the most spoiled daddy's girl ever."

We take a moment in silence to admire the beauty that two of the most stubborn people I know made.

"May I?" I extend my arm inches from Devora's ivory skin when she tears away from her mommy's boob. Ivy nods, giving me permission to caress her rosy cheek. She opens her little hand and squeezes my finger. "Oh my, I'm gonna cry so bad." I fan myself. I'm a sucker for sweet moments, and Ivy knows it. I've cried at every romantic comedy we've ever watched.

"Do you want to hold her?"

I nod and Ivy places the little munchkin in my arms. Something brushes off my foot, and I look down to see Six sitting protectively at my feet. The baby fits so right in my hands. "Hello again, baby D. I'm going to be the best auntie, I promise. I'll cover for you if you want to go to parties, and I'll give you a sip of my beer when your mother isn't watching."

Ivy snickers beside me. "Good luck with that. Damien's

already masterminding how to keep her as far away from those as possible. Boys too." She laughs. "It's gonna be one hell of a show to watch these two growing up."

"I can't wait." My heart is going to burst from happiness and love. Ivy directs me to return to the living room. "Where should I put her?"

"Wanna see a trick?" Ivy smirks at me. She whistles, and Six immediately goes to her. Once I lay the baby on a plush blanket on the couch, he climbs and lies between her and the edge, wrapping his big body around hers. Devora places her tiny hand on his paw and a few seconds later, she's dozed off.

"Wow," I whisper.

Ivy's smile is up to her ears, eyes shining. "I know. Best nanny ever. No one can make her fall asleep faster than Six. He won't move until she wakes up. You'll see. I swear this dog is smarter than most humans I know." She yawns, sitting next to the baby and placing a hand over her so she's completely safe.

"I can't imagine how tiring this is."

"It is, but it's so worth it. She introduced me to a love I never knew possible."

Seeing Ivy gleaming when the nurse placed the baby in her hands for the first time was worth all the trouble I went through coming here. Well, that and the smuggest man I know—Damien—not knowing what to do with himself as Ivy cursed him in every language she knows while pushing and cracking all the bones in my hand. It wasn't the easiest natural birth.

Ivy leans her head on my shoulder and continues speaking softly. "Enough about me. What is the deal with New York and the man I heard at the hospital? I don't have the energy, so cut to the truth."

I sigh. "Remember when I told you the story of my childhood? The boy I used to love?"

"Holy cow!" She raises her head, looking at me with a gaping mouth and wide eyes. "I thought he was dead," she whisper-yells.

"Apparently not anymore."

"So that's why you lost all this weight." She pinches the skin on my belly because there's no fat left there. "Have you been eating at all? Sleeping?"

"Yeah, a bit."

Her lips press in a line, and she shakes her head. "I know when you're lying. You're staying with us."

"I'd love nothing more but I can't." Her face is a whole question mark. "I don't know how much more time I have with him."

"Oh, dear." She wraps her arms around me, squeezing me in a hug. I knew she'd get it without many words. She's been through the wringer with Damien herself. "I'm sorry. Is there anything I can help with?"

We go back into our previous position, only this time I'm the one relaxing my head on her shoulder. "No. It's a matter of time before he leaves me."

"Then he's not worth it, baby. Any man would die fighting for you."

"He almost did," I whisper. It hurts too much to talk about it right now. I've been overthinking it this whole week we've been here. Every time he goes out to do whatever he's doing and won't tell me. Every night when I fall asleep in his arms.

I've got a limited amount of time in Rosehill, so I'd rather try to think of something else for a change. Something that makes me happy. Like my best friends. "How's the wedding planning going?"

"You won't believe it. I found this amazing woman who knows exactly what we want. She's supernatural, I'm telling you. Damien and I are clueless. I thought he'd want a big flashy event, like a thousand guests on a floating platform and Beyoncé and Jay-Z performing, but he actually surprised me with wanting to keep it intimate. Just the closest family and friends, which is fine by me. All I want is to get some damn sleep before the thing."

"Where is he, by the way?" I'm still mad at him though from what I've heard over the phone, he hasn't left her side for a minute. I swear my best friend who hosted a party every week has turned into the biggest homemaker I know. It's so cute and heartwarming. We were all wrong about him.

"He had to step out to some emergency meeting at the hotel. He's been neglecting his job recently. I feel bad." She yawns again.

I tap her thigh. "Come on, switch places. Six and I will be on baby duty, and you'll sleep."

"Really?" She snickers, rubbing her palms like a little devil. "You're the best."

"Yeah, yeah. I know." We switch places, and I put one hand on the sleeping baby and use the other to caress Ivy's head in my lap. "Do you have a date?"

"Not yet. I can start doing light exercises soon. I have a dance routine in my head that I want to do for Damien at our wedding. It'll be spectacular, so I have to be in shape by then."

I'm glad to hear her first love—dancing—hasn't been pushed out of the picture.

"Let me know if you need any help."

"Yes, actually. I want you to dance with me," she says drowsily.

"What?!" I whisper-yell, but she's already asleep in my lap. Uh-oh, more embarrassment is awaiting me.

Yet, somehow I can't help but wonder if Lucifer is going to be there to see it. You know what they say—dreams are free.

CHAPTER TWENTY

LUCIFER

"Princess, I'm home," I shout from the new door of Stella's little house.

"Do you want something to eat?" she asks from the couch while I untie my running shoes in the entryway.

It suddenly hits me. The domesticity of it all.

I've always wanted to know how that feels. Normal life. Away from all our problems, like we've been transported to a world where the dreams I once had have become a reality. This fucking city is messing with my head.

What am I doing playing family with her when this could kill us both?

Fuck me.

Fuck fate.

Good Lord. Fuck her.

Stella's lying on her stomach on the green couch, her ass showing underneath her teeny-tiny pink shorts. It's a thousand degrees in the summer, but holy motherfucking shit I want to unwrap her like an early Christmas present.

"Lou?" She turns to me. What? Ah, she asked me a question.

"Yeah, I have to restore these muscles." I flex my chest and biceps under the white sweaty T-shirt, and she chuckles.

"Be careful there or you might steal Superman's shine." She stands from the couch and saunters to me, then plants a brief kiss on my lips. "I'll get you a plate of spaghetti Bolognese. Go shower. You stink."

She scrunches her nose in that adorable way and shrieks a second later when I can't help but pull her to me, rubbing sweat all over her clothes and bare belly.

I chuckle, winking at her, "That fucker ain't got nothing on me, baby."

I take a quick shower and don't bother dressing up in anything else other than my Tom Ford black boxers. Stella's eyes almost bulge out the second I walk back into the living room. *That's right, princess. Two can play this game.*

"It smells delicious." I inhale the steam of the plate waiting for me at the coffee table because the dining space is taken up by her sewing machines. Basil, tomatoes, and perfection. "Where's yours?"

Stella shrugs and looks the other way toward the TV screen.

"Come on, now, baby girl. Don't tell me you already ate without me?" I pout, fluttering my eyelashes the way she does when she wants something from me. She always gets it, my weak spot.

She will be your downfall—Giovanni's reprimanding voice echoes in my head. He knew I was lost to his daughter; everyone in the manor knew. I was running after her ass like a puppy and protected her from everyone else like a wolf. He didn't like it, but he respected that I took my punishments for it without a word. The punishments became harder, but not because of something I did. He wanted to test if I was good enough to survive in his world. Take the throne with his princess by my side because Lord knew I wouldn't have let her go. In my head there was never a plan for us to live this life. I was waiting for Stella to turn eighteen so we could escape.

Look at us now. Giovanni got his way even after he died. The motherfucker must've had some deal with his beloved God or something.

Stella stirs beside me on the couch, actively avoiding my gaze. "I'm not hungry."

"Bullshit." I purse my lips, looking at her body. A couple weeks ago there was meat where her ribs are visible now. What the hell happened? I thought she was getting better, not losing ten pounds a week.

She wraps her hands around her middle, hiding the view from me. "I'm not. Can we just watch TV now?"

"Nah." I unwrap her hands and squeeze her wrists. Not too hard but enough for her to know I'm serious. "You're doing as you're told."

She sighs and rests her head on the headrest. "Fine. But only a little. It's like eight-hundred calories per serving, and I…"

"Stella?" I raise an eyebrow. "Run your ass to the kitchen, I want to see you with a plate of food in hand."

Stella shakes her head, unable to hide her smile as her lips curve and she bites the lower one. "You sound like a misogynistic prick."

"Blah, blah, blah," I mock her, standing up to get her a plate of spaghetti. "Don't want to hear it. You're fucking perfect the way you are."

She takes the plate from my hands when I park my ass back on the couch.

I smile and voice out my thoughts. "I'll always be here when you need me, princess."

Shit. What a fucking a lie.

Well, not really because I've been here all along. She just doesn't know it. And I'll still be here after I have to part ways with her. Lurking in the shadows, stealing little glimpses. Basking in the bliss of seeing her happy and successful. Then going back to the dark, lonely life of a deceased man.

"Can you promise me?" Her eyes light up, glowing like two big stars in a crystal-clear sky. What did I get myself into? Stupid fucking mouth. Giovanni was right all along. I have to be tougher, or I won't fucking survive to see her happy.

"No. I can't…"

Her soft lips press against mine, swallowing my denial. She pulls away and leans her head against my shoulder. "Don't. We have tonight and that's all that matters."

I stab the fork into my plate and carry it to her lips. "You're absolutely right, princess. Now get your sweet ass on my lap so I can feed it." I pat my thighs, and her laugh breaks through the thick summer air as she takes a mouthful of pasta Bolognese.

Blonde hair brushes over my face as she settles on me, leaving a trace of strawberry scent behind. "Baby, if you keep wiggling your ass on my dick, I'll be the one doing all the eating."

Her cheeks turn a sweet shade of pink, and her lips part. Before she says something that'll make us both skip dinner and go straight to the dessert, I push another fork of spaghetti inside her gaping mouth. "Now swallow it down, princess."

I watch as her throat bobs, and she turns a deeper shade of pink. Damn, this color calls straight to my dick. She can feel it, too, because she's slowly, barely noticeably grinding over it. Stella turns half her back to me, trying to keep the illusion that we'll watch TV as if we both don't know where this is heading. The news is on, something about a dog shelter getting a big donation. I stab the fork on the plate again, rolling until there's a solid bite on it. Stella looks down and shakes her head. I grin.

"Come on, you can do more." I take it to her mouth and watch as she greedily sucks the last drop of sauce from it. In my head this conversation is playing in a whole different atmosphere. But it's good to know she can take a big chunk in her mouth. She'll need it soon. Very, very…

"*Dio mio!*" Stella exclaims, spitting the spaghetti all over the floor. She jumps from my lap, her fingers burrowing into her scalp like she's trying to pull her hair off. What in the actual hell?

"Barry!" she roars, pointing at the TV.

Shit. The face of her ex-fiancé is staring at us from the screen.

A woman in a suit is standing next to a frightened girl at a lake, reporting: *"The body was found floating in the waters of Lake Myakka. This young girl was taking a walk when she stumbled upon the gruesome view in the early hours of this morning. According to the police, the victim's cause of death is not drowning. As of now this is a murder investigation…"*

Blah, blah, blah. A victim. Ha. Give this reporter the joke of the year reward. This con was no…

"Oh God! Oh God! Oh God! Barry!" Stella stands frozen in place, spitting out cry after cry like a prayer. I wish I could see her face. She sounds like she's pouring her eyes out. From where I'm still sitting on the couch, I see she's covering her open mouth with her right hand and massaging the left one over her heart. *Her fucking heart.* This five-foot-five blond piece of horse shit didn't deserve her heart. Not then and certainly not now.

"What do you care? The man was a scumbag." I scratch

my stubble, trying to look as unbothered as possible but inside I'm dying.

"He was my... He should've been my..." *Come on, princess. Don't say it. Don't make me lose my mind.* She spins to face me and surprises me. There's not a single tear in her eyes. Unlike in her voice. "Wait. How do you know that?"

I shrug it off, staring at her aqua pools, still trying to see tears. A lazy grin I can't help, spreads through my face. *That's right, you dumb fucker. I'm the only man she cried her eyes out for.* I realize how wrong that sounds, but I also don't give a shit. I want her to cry only for me. I want her to smile only for me. I want everything of hers only for me. I'm a selfish motherfucker, but I'm her motherfucker.

I can see the rusty wheels in her brain slowly turning, and I know it's a matter of seconds before she comes to the right conclusion. My princess is no fool. If anything she's fucking brilliant. She should know to stay the fuck away from a monster yet she keeps wandering back into his lair.

"Lucifer, tell me you didn't do this?"

"I don't know what you're talking about." I stab the fork into the pasta and finally take the first bite of her divine recipe. *God...the mozzarella...and the...*

Stella's high-pitched voice takes me out of my bliss. "Tell me you didn't kill Barry, Lucifer."

Nothing to spoil your appetite like your girl's dead ex-fiancé. Why do her exes keep fucking returning? Didn't they get the memo? Hello, she's fucking mine. M-I-N-E. They just can't leave her alone. Like that fucking Mike dude or whatever his name was. He'll follow in Barry's steps if he keeps "keeping tabs on her." Yeah right, I read her fucking texts. And I sure know I wanted to bang her brains out when I was *just keeping tabs.*

"You know I can't tell you stuff like that, princess." I feed myself another forkful before I sing like a canary because this girl can milk anything from me. She stands, still frozen in place but her hands are no longer on her heart and mouth. She's picking her nails, trying to stare me down in a silent conversation.

What did you do, Lou?
Yeah, fucking right I killed him.

He was trying to contact every one of the Five Families for weeks after he found out who she was. What for, you ask? To get the best deal on her head.

And then he fucking hit her. On their fucking wedding day.

Smacked. Her. Precious. Little. Face.

As far as I know Barry was a deceased man the second he laid his eyes on Stella. Surprisingly, with my life path it was just my second murder. The first one changed me forever. But, oh, how good this second one felt. Having the face of the man who slept next to *my* woman, fucked *my* woman, and disappointed her fragile golden heart over and over again, crushed under my boot and begging for mercy like the fucking peasant he was. He didn't deserve the time of day from a goddess like Stella Morelli. But she gave it to him anyway so I backed off. Gave her the freedom to be happy without me.

I can't say it didn't feel good knowing he'll never touch her again.

I can read every emotion on her face. Shock. Realization. Disappointment hurts the most. But I'm not giving up over something like this. If she decides to throw me out, I'll haul her ass over my shoulder and take her with me. I don't care if she protests. I did every single thing in my life for her. The good and the bad. Especially the bad.

"Well, now that the cat's out of the bag, we should probably pack your stuff and get the hell out of Rosehill," I say nonchalantly, successfully covering my desperation. There's no way I'm letting her run away from me again. She can hate me all she wants as long as she's safe. And she should. I fucking hate myself for everything I've done. If she knew everything, she'd be running, screaming, in the opposite direction.

Out of the blue, she leaps forward and jumps on me, straddling my lap and burying her face in my collar. "Thank you. Thank you, Lou."

What the fuck?

"What are you thanking me for, princess?" I don't understand. I was expecting her to tell me to leave, but instead...

She raises her head and glues her lips to mine. Her tongue is desperately searching for mine. Hot tears coming down her cheeks and sliding over to mine. I dig my fingers into her back and slide them down to her ass. She moans and settles over my dick, biting my lip hard. Like she wants to punish me. And then licks it because she can't stand to cause me pain. Even though I deserve it. I'll take it. Hell, I'll take everything I can from her, even if it's her hatred. I just don't know how I'll take losing her again. Never again.

She pulls her lips away from mine and slides them over my neck. I know she doesn't want me to hear her quiet, little sobs. And I know she isn't crying because of fucking Barry. He deserved what he got, and she knows it. Deep down on some level, she knew what he wanted from her all along.

She's crying because of everything we are. Everything we were. And everything we were supposed to be.

Stella's quick to remind me when she digs her teeth into my pulsating flesh. Hard. Punishing. This time she doesn't lick it. She jumps out of my lap, a new look on her face. I can't decipher it. She just stands there, silent, looking between me and the front door.

"Do you want me to go?" I ask, too afraid to hear the answer.

"Please." She's staring at the front door, her broken voice smashing the rusty piece of metal in my chest to a million pieces. Fuck. This is a goodbye kiss.

I stand on my feet. She whips her head back to me. Her hands wrap around my neck, squeezing, leveling me to her height, her reddened eyes staring at mine, breath coating my lips. "Please, never stop protecting me. Even when I don't know it. Please." She looks down to my dick, which is still up and ready to go despite everything, and closes her eyes, exhaling hard before opening them again. It's not the same frightened little girl looking back. It's a vixen, knowing damn well she's holding my heart to stab it or heal it like a freaking voodoo doll in her hands. "Take me to the bedroom and never ever fucking leave me."

Maybe we're not so different after all.

I grin and bite her lower lip back. "I thought you'd never ask."

CHAPTER TWENTY-ONE

STELLA

As much as it hurt, I had to say goodbye to Ivy and Damien again. Lucifer was adamant we had to flee before the police came knocking on my door since I was one of the last people to see Barry before his untimely demise. This morning on the news they announced that according to the autopsy, he died shortly after our split. Damien was left dealing with the explanations of where I am, and since he has the whole city in his back pocket, I'm pretty sure I won't be hearing from Rosehill's PD in New York.

Three days later it's still hard for me to accept it. On some subconscious level, I knew that when Barry suddenly stopped showing up at Melanie's looking for me, he wasn't alive anymore. Everyone says I'm "too good," if that's even a thing, but deep down I wanted that. It all makes sense now that Lou told me the whole story. The late-night text messages, the closet phone calls mentioning my name. I foolishly convinced myself it was probably some big surprise for our wedding day. Oh what a surprise it was when he raised his fist in the backroom of the church to punch the hell out of me and spewed out my real surname. I knew it right then and there. I wanted him dead.

Maybe I'm not so different from my blood after all.

The minute Marcel picked us up from the airport, the energy between Lou and me shifted. My home in Rosehill might be my safe place, but Lucifer's Manhattan castle is his ruin. He's been actively avoiding me, ghosting around the house. Just when I thought we took a step forward, he sprinted backward all the way to the starting line. For three nights I've heard him lock his bedroom door the second he steps inside. For three nights I've pressed the handle anyway, shamelessly and silently begging him to let me in so I wouldn't have to face another sleepless night lying in my cold bed, missing the heat of his body, afraid of what's on the other side of my dreams. I know he can't get any rest either, and he sees the handle dipping, yet he lets me suffer in the confinement of my room.

Tonight my head is hanging over the sewing machine as I relentlessly make my sketches come to life. A new idea was born the night I saw Barry's face on TV, and later after Lucifer took my body and soul to a whole new level of delight, I drew my new collection. It's so different from everything I've done so far. Bold. Fierce. Defiant.

Ugh, the sound of pacing in front of my door has been distracting me for the last minute. "Lucifer, I can hear you."

The handle dips, and the butterflies in my stomach awaken. Until I see the face that protrudes from the door. "Marcel?"

"Hi." He waves and steps inside. "Just wanted to check on you. How's it going?" He's dressed casually in washed-out jeans and a black T-shirt. Such a stark contrast from all the suits and the seriousness he wears all the time. I've been wondering what he's doing in a mob house, how he got himself in the middle of all this? He's older than me by a couple of years; he should be out of college, making a name at some company.

"Not bad. I've done quite a lot of work for the fashion show."

During my time in Rosehill, my new partner sent me the documents I signed with Lucifer's help. I am now officially a BFD Group brand, and my first introduction will be in an upcoming fashion show for all their brands. My clothes are going to be presented in front of the biggest names in the fashion industry. I was going to offer the pieces I did over the past month but when inspiration strikes, you don't push it back. I have to be absolutely perfect for my big break.

Marcel, however, looks less than the perfection he masters. His brows are creased, and his eye bags are bigger than his blue eyes. Doesn't anyone in this damn house sleep? Like a spell, my body reacts and I yawn. Looks like my mind is finally giving up, and I'll be comatose for the next few hours soon.

"Is something on your mind?" I ask when Marcel doesn't speak for a long minute, staring at the floor.

"I have something I want to talk to you about." He continues avoiding my gaze. My gut is telling me I won't like what I'm about to hear. I'm too worn out for another big thing right now. I haven't slept since the Barry news, and I need to recharge before I tackle the next.

"Is it urgent? Can we do it another time because I'm really tired?"

"Sure." He scratches the back of his head and turns to face the door. He stops before opening it and looks at me for the first time. "Stells...don't tell Lucifer I came here. This is between you and me."

Okay, weird. I'm not a snitch, though.

"Of course. I'll find you in the morning." If I don't sleep through it.

After a much-needed shower, I slip into my baby blue silk shorts and tank top and give my cold bed the stink eye like it's at fault somehow. Lucifer freaking promised me he wouldn't leave me while we still had time. How dare he after everything we went through. I won't take this anymore!

I waltz out of my room, barefooted, and head down the hallway. I stop in front of his bedroom. I swear if he doesn't open this time, I'm going to yell. So loud, the whole staff will hear me. I knock once, but there's no answer. Just when I'm about to take out my anger on the poor door, his piercing scream stops me with my fist in the air.

"Stop!"

"Lou?" I call out. This can't be right. Too many years have passed.

He screams again, louder. "Stop. Padre, no."

Shit. Just what I thought.

I push the handle and yelp when I almost fall inside the room. He must've forgotten to lock it.

"It wasn't my fault. I swear," Lucifer shouts again and my heart skips a beat. Déjà vu.

The first night he skipped sneaking into my bedroom at the manor, I went to the servants' house. The window to his room was always open, so I climbed through it only to find an empty white space safe for a worn-out desk he kept his study books on and a dirty mattress on the floor. There he was curled around a quilt, shaking and crying. He was rambling something I couldn't understand. I lay down and spooned him when he started screaming for help. It took him a couple minutes before his body went soft in my hands and the nightmare finally stopped.

That night I realized we had another thing in common,

but he never spoke of it. Most nights he came to protect me, suffering both my nightmares and his. So the few nights he didn't show up, I did the same for him until the sun started to rise and it was time to go. I never learned what his nightmares were about. The scars he came with when Giovanni brought him probably had something to do with it. I just hoped comforting him was enough.

Here we are now. A lot more scars on his bare body, but it's the ones in our minds that are frightening.

I saunter to his bed and crawl under the flat sheet. Lucifer is shaking, breathing ragged, lips parted. He looks so vulnerable. Like that nine-year-old boy who stood in my front yard.

Not the boss of a mob. Not a killer.

An angel.

"I didn't want to. You made me," he screams, snapping his teeth. "No." He almost slaps me with his big hand as he tosses in the sheets.

"Lou?" I caress his damp head. He jerks awake, slithering up the headboard to sit.

"Stella." My name sounds like a prayer on his lips. He blinks, looking around the dark room. "Did he hurt you?" His voice is torn, pained.

"Who?" I sit up. He winces when I put my hand on his biceps. He's searching my face.

"Tell me he didn't hurt you," he demands but the pain is still there. In his gray eyes, in his shaking fingers. In that high note. Before I can answer he looks down. "Of course he didn't hurt you. I killed him."

"Barry?" I ask, confused. If Barry's the one haunting my Lou, I'll resurrect and kill him myself.

"Angelo."

"What?" Even though it's dark as hell in here, I can see

his face perfectly. The crooked grimace, the apology in his eyes. *What?* He couldn't. No. *What?*

He takes my hand. "I'm not a good man, princess. I killed my father."

"I... You..." My words are lost, and my jaw is resting on the floor. I try to collect myself before he decides to shut me off again. "Why?"

"It doesn't matter why. I did it. I cornered him and I pushed him off that roof." He takes my hand to his lips and closes his eyes, placing a long kiss on it.

It all flashes back to me. One morning I was sitting at home in Rosehill, laughing with Ivy when they said it on the news. *"Angelo Visconti, the rumored head of the Visconti family committed suicide last night in..."* I didn't listen to it very intently, as Ivy was telling me a story about the Masquerade club, even though I knew the name Visconti stayed in my mind for a while. I couldn't remember where I knew it from. Just like I couldn't when I first heard it in Lucifer's home.

Lucifer looks lost in thought when I brush a strand of fallen hair off his brow. He sighs and rests back.

"My father hated me since I took my first breath. His beloved wife gave away her life so I could be born. It wasn't hard, even at the age of nine, to understand that Giovanni taking me as blood tax was my way out of being beaten and starved until I followed my mother's fate."

"Blood tax?"

"It's a practice from the Ottoman empire to forcefully collect young boys from the Christian families, convert them and raise them to serve in the military. Later, they sent them to kill their own people. Ask your friend Ivy, she's Bulgarian, it's her history. That's where Giovanni got his inspiration from."

I hold my breath, too scared to move.

"Angelo sought me out before the massacre. He warned me, thought I'd change sides. He needed an heir to his throne but he never had any more children. I warned your father, begged him to get you out of that manor but he dismissed it." He's staring at the darkness, the wrinkle between his eyes warning me he's lost somewhere in the war. "That day I fought as a Morelli. I would've died as one if Angelo hadn't found me in the ruins and taken me to New York. He got what he wanted. His place in the mafia secured, his heir back in his home, his enemy defeated. I lost everything."

"You had me." I place my hand in his lap.

Lucifer squeezes my palm before he leaves it on the bed.

"I never was and never will be good enough for you, Stella." He only uses my name when he's dead serious. He caresses my cheek. "I'll understand if you're scared to stay with me. I can have the jet send you back to Damien's first thing in the morning. Lay low for a while. I'll take care of everything, you'll have my security and you'll be made aware when you can return back to your normal life. You can forget about me." He takes my cheek in his palm. "Do you understand me? Let me go and know that I've kept my promise to you. You'll never have to look over your shoulder ever again."

He pushes the flat sheet off him, dropping his feet to the side of the bed. As he places his palms on the mattress, getting ready to stand up, it hits me. It hits me and it fucking knocks me down. He's trying to save me from himself.

"Do you think you're getting rid of me that easy? Mark my words. Never. Fucking. Ever." I climb on top of his lap, knocking his body down to lay on the bed. His eyes widen. "I don't care what you did. How many people you've killed. Dammit, I don't care if you pour the poison down my throat yourself. But remember this, Lucifer. I'll come for you, and I'll stab that knife through your chest so we could burn in hell together. We'll be Romeo and fucking Juliet for all I care."

A ghost of a smile sneaks up his face. "You're crazy."

"I sure am. I've already been through hell and back, and I'm not letting you go. Not now, not when all of this is over and certainly not in death. I swear I'll take you with me even then."

The flexing of his six-pack as he perks up on both elbows distracts me enough for him to take advantage and spin me around, pinning my wrists to the bed. With a devilish smirk, he lowers his mouth to my ear, whispering "I was hoping you would say that, Miss Morelli." The thickness of his voice crawls on the insides of my thighs. A whimper tears out of me. "I'll do anything to keep you. You know every dark thing about me. I'm yours if you want me."

When he bites my ear, I take the advantage to wrap my legs around his waist and flip him under me again. My hands moving fast, I tear off my tank top. His eyes roam over my bare upper body, lust and carnal hunger taking the wheel inside his brain. He reaches to touch me, but I slap his hands off.

"My game, my rules. Now, let me take care of my man." I slide my hand over his briefs and pull them down. His lips press against mine, hot tongue invading my mouth in a whirlpool of sweet saliva and fight for power. I draw away, but he pulls me back up and sucks a nipple into his mouth.

This man just can't let anyone do anything for him.

His hands creep on my ass, taking off my shorts and my panties in one go. I use the opportunity to pull away and slither down his body, leaving a trail of kisses.

Wow. You've got no idea how big a dick is until it hits you in the face.

That thing is a monster, threatening to poke my eye out. How the hell did it fit inside me?

"Having second thoughts, princess?" he teases. I look up to see his devilish gaze. I bet he's dying to have my mouth wrapped around his cock. I know I am.

I pretend like I'm thinking about it. He laughs, deep and low, and his dick pulsates in my hand. Fuck it. I wet my lips and take it into my mouth, closing my eyes and having no idea what's going on. As I failed to tell him a couple of times, this is my first time giving a blow job. I move up and down, licking the tip and however much of the shaft I can, trying not to bite him. I curl my fist around the bottom because that's what I've seen porn actresses do and pump it. Fake it 'til you make it, baby.

His roar has me opening my eyes, afraid I somehow hurt him but when I look up, there's only adoration and lust written on his face. He lets me play a little more before he grabs me by the biceps and pulls me up.

"Let me teach you how it's done, my little princess." He stands up on the bed, grabbing the canopy frame. "On your knees."

I kneel on the bed at the altar of this Roman god, staring into his eyes in awe.

He slides his finger over my mouth. "Open up." My lips part and little by little I take him in. He fists my hair into a ponytail, pushing farther in until I choke. "You can do it, princess. When you feel it at the back of your throat, swallow me down."

Bobbing my head up and down, I suck him off until I gag and then repeat, taking him a little farther inside. My confidence grows with every swallow, every moan of his.

When I feel adventurous enough, I flick my tongue around the crown, and his legs start shaking. He roars, pulling my head back and falls down onto his knees. I don't even have time to close my mouth before he kisses the hell out of me.

He lays me down and returns the favor, licking on my pussy until I'm riding his face into oblivion. Just when I'm about to come, he slips his finger from my pussy to my ass. "Come for me, baby. I want to taste your cum."

I give up the fight and crash into little pieces in his hands. When I come down from the high, I realize there's something cold touching my asshole, creating a thin line between mild discomfort and arousal.

"What?" I don't have the strength to ask the whole sentence.

Lucifer's mischievous eyes twinkle, and he kisses me stupid. "It's a small butt plug. You like it, don't you?"

I bury my face in his chest as if he could see the heat rising on my cheeks in this darkness. "Yes, I do."

I can feel him grinning against me, his breath burning my sensitive skin. "Don't be ashamed, princess, 'cause you won't be able to look me in the eyes after what we're about to do."

He flips me on all fours as easy as he could playing with a doll. He could do whatever he wants to do to me, and that actually thrills me.

I don't want to be the fragile princess or the good girl. I want to be bad. Really, really naughty for him. I want his punishments and his rewards, and I want to be black and blue in the morning, when I can't walk just so he could bring me breakfast in bed and caress and massage my bruises all day.

Lucifer squeezes something behind me and cold liquid drips down my pussy. It slowly starts warming as he massages it back and forth.

"Lou," I moan when he slips two fingers into my throbbing pussy, and he grips my hair, pulling back my head.

"Say it again," he orders gruffly in my ear. His thumb slips to my ass as he pumps me. The butt plug inside me stirs, causing my back to arch from the delicate pain. "Shh." His fingers leave me as he uses his hand to caress my butt cheek. Whack! A slap comes out of nowhere, making me clench my asshole and to my surprise the pain has almost faded, and in its place is a hot feeling, making my pussy drip. He places his cock at my entrance, and a shiver runs through my body as I wait impatiently. "Say it again." He grips my throat.

"Lou," I moan his name, and he plunges inside me, wrecking my nerves and shooting me straight to the top. The unfamiliar feeling of having both my holes filled makes me go wild, moaning and thrashing in his arms as he bangs inside me until I'm screaming from pleasure. "Oh, Lou. Promise me you'll never leave," I beg as I collapse, and he wraps his hands around my body, holding me so I don't fall.

"Stella." He squeezes my cheeks, twisting my head around to face him. "Never!" he roars as his cum spills inside me, dripping down my thighs, and I pass out in his embrace.

CHAPTER TWENTY-TWO

LUCIFER

There's a loud knock on the door of my office, where I'm burying myself in documents all day, trying to figure out why my calculations don't work out. We should've been in the clear long ago, but there's always something that comes up, and I can't cover it up financially.

Another knock.

"Come in."

The door opens slowly, and Marcel steps in. Fucking finally. I've been waiting on news forever.

"So? What did Enzo tell you?"

He gives me a sign to zip my mouth as a sweet female voice comes from behind him.

"Marcel, dear, would you be a darling and move the fuck away?" Tiana Carter pushes him out of the doorway to step into the room.

"Hey, T." The first genuine smile for today rises on my face.

Tiana looks as stunning as ever, strutting in her five-inch heels and a dress that looks like she wrapped herself in a washed-up rag but probably costs a small fortune. *Couture*. I'll never get it.

Surpassing my desk, she throws herself on my lap and suffocates me in a big hug.

"My handsome devil, I've missed you so much." I get a hint of a French accent in her speech, which means she's been in France until recently. She has a tendency of adopting the accent of whatever country she's escaped to.

"You're the one who got lost, Miss Carter. I haven't seen your eyes in…" I pretend to think about it when I know for a fact Tiana has been gone from New York for more than four months. It's the longest I haven't seen her, and I've missed her. Especially now that everything's going to hell, and I'm barely holding the pieces together. Myself too.

I'm too far gone for Stella at this point. I need a distraction. Tiana's the perfect remedy; she always knows how to get me out of my head and on the right track. In short, she's my only best friend other than Marcel.

Marcel raises an eyebrow from the doorway, and I give him a sign to fuck off. He exits with a sigh and a shake of his head.

"You eating well? 'Cause you weigh a ton more," I tease her.

She slaps my chest, standing up and straightening her posture. "Ha-ha. Very funny. If you must know, I've lost a couple of pounds." She swivels around showing off her perfect five-foot-nine supermodel body and killer legs. The raven hair (a wig, I presume, since she's always been a platinum blonde kind of girl) does wonders for her pale skin and dazzling smile.

"But I see you've gained some." She crosses her arms, wiggling her eyebrows.

"You could say I got a new cook?" I scratch my nape.

"Oh, Luci. My poor, poor, devil. You're so screwed up." She shakes her head with a shit-eating grin. "That Stella girl is messing with your head, isn't she?"

"I don't know what you're talking about." The second I finish this lie, I know I shouldn't have said it because one, she always sees through me, and two, her face is now as serious as a fucking heart attack.

"I sure as hell know and so does everybody else in the Five Families, Lucifer. Why are you being so careless, flying her around and sending her off to business meetings? Meetings I fucking arranged you with." She waves her hands in the air, exasperated. "You're going to screw us both over."

"What do they know?" I saunter to the drinking cabinet to get us both a drink because we'll sure need it for this talk.

Tiana throws herself dramatically in one of my leather chairs. "They know who she is, and they know you're protecting her." She salutes me with the glass of bourbon I provided her and gulps it down in one go.

"Wow, slow it down, T. Are they angry?" I have to take a measured sip of mine because if I let go of the illusion of control, I might just go nuts and finish them all in their sleep.

"The Russians are surprisingly calm. They haven't spoken about it." And by "they" she means her boyfriend Sebastian Fucking Federoff. The golden offspring of the Russian mafia. "The other two families are mostly curious. They didn't know Morelli had a daughter, but they don't feel threatened." She pauses, giving me the glass so I can refill it.

"But..." I prompt her, tensing under my clothes, waiting for the other shoe to drop.

She throws her head back and stares at the ceiling. "But Daddy is furious."

Shit. I had a feeling about the old Carter—Tiana's father Thomas Carter—when he didn't call the previous two weeks.

He favors me as his own. Or at least, he pretends so he can get what he wants, which I've been postponing for a while now.

"What did he tell you?"

Tiana rubs the platinum ring with the big sapphire on her finger. "You know he keeps me in the dark. I overheard him telling our consigliere to prepare for war if you don't deliver what you promised soon. Mother's been pressuring me over the phone, too, sending new designers. She booked a fucking planner." Her voice wavers, and she gulps down half the new drink I brought her.

"Hey, hey." I take her face in my hands, and there are tears welling up in her eyes. Tiana never cries. "If anyone's gonna throw a pity party, it's gonna be me. I promise you I'll fix it."

"How?" She pouts, rolling her eyes. "How are you going to fix this? We have to make it official soon."

I drink a larger sip of the bourbon, feeling the glass slipping away from my hand. I grip it harder, my knuckles turning white. "I know. I'll keep my promise to you, but buy me some time to figure it out."

Tiana leans in, and I wrap my free arm around her shoulders. "Do you think she'll forgive you?"

"She has to." I let out a sigh, trying not to break the glass. "Otherwise, it would mean the end of me. You might as well take the gun and put it to my head 'cause living without her again would make me regret not dying eight years ago."

Tiana is the one person, save for Marcel, who knows everything about me, including the reason I killed my own father. Our fathers introduced us before I went off to college, and they had made plans for us by the time I returned to take over my family's business.

I was rude to her, pissed off at the world, but she clawed

her way to my heart one night when we accidentally ran into each other at a casino in Monte Carlo. We got so wasted at the bar that she unloaded everything from her broken heart into my angry hands. I bought us a third bottle and by the end of it, I spilled the beans on everything from my early childhood to my embarrassing first time with Stella. The third time I've opened up in my life to anyone, and I fucking cried like a baby. We agreed to never speak of that night again, though, and she might just stab me with her heel if I ever remind her how she cried the whole night, first about herself and then along with me. We didn't have it the easiest to say the least. It's not joy that creates the strongest bonds; it's trauma. When you know someone's hurting like you do.

"You really do love her," she says with pain in her voice and empty eyes looking at nothing in particular.

"Do you love Sebastian?" I snort out.

"I got it." She sighs and finishes her drink.

I stand up to pour her another one but stop when I hear Federoff's voice echoing in the hallway. "T, what's taking so fucking long?"

That motherfucker. He's so jealous he won't leave Tiana for twenty minutes alone with me. I finally got Stella to see a psychologist and if that Russian bastard disturbs her…

Tiana should know better than to bring him to my property. The last time he barged in here like he owned the place, we got into a fight, and she was mad at me for a month. She stormed off to some unknown island, leaving Sebastian to run after her ass like the lost golden retriever puppy he is.

And there he is, storming through the door in…what the fuck is he's wearing? He'd blend perfectly with the Versailles palace interior. Fucking little shit.

"Baby?" Tiana calls out like she just saw the leader of her cult and jumps to her feet just in time for him to grab a possessive hold of her and make a show of kissing her by lifting her in the air. It's a scene straight out of a teen movie, triggering my gag reflex.

I refuse to acknowledge the green feeling it stirs in me. I miss Stella so fucking much, and she's just upstairs, battling her own demons. I miss her even when she's in my hands because I know it might be the last time. The mere thought of it compels me to open my desk drawer and run a hand over my gun.

Her words from the night before stuck with me all day.

Romeo and fucking Juliet. Shakespeare didn't sugarcoat the world with all that happily-ever-after nonsense. He brought the real, and the raw, and the pain. The question is, will I bring the courage if by any chance all my efforts don't work out?

Tiana's moan inside of Federoff's mouth comes just in time to pull me out of my darkest thoughts. It doesn't take a genius to figure out she used me as a cover-up to meet with him.

"I hate to ruin the free porn, but I've got work to get back to, kids." I open the door of the office and gesture with my hand when Sebastian lets her go and turns to me. There's something in those sly pale eyes of his. His smile changes from a head-over-heels to a I-fucked-you-up in seconds.

Dammit, how didn't I figure it out earlier?!

Tiana exits through the door, looking for something in her purse. I grip Federoff's arm on his way out. "It was you who tipped off your father, wasn't it?" I knew I hated him for a reason deeper than just the fact he's an ungrateful arrogant waste of air. He knew if I got back with Stella, I wouldn't be able to let her go. Or that Tiana's father would've killed me before I manage to find a way to escape with Stella. Turns out he's dumber than me; he probably thought it would be a win-win for him.

He gives me that shit-eating grin he's popular for and shrugs. "I just gave fate a little push."

"You motherfucker," I growl in his face and push him against the door. "You fucking risked my woman's life for what? To keep me away from Tiana?"

"It brought you and little miss mob princess together, didn't it?" He pushes me back and brushes off his tacky jacket. "You can thank me later."

"You aimed for me, but you shot yourself in the foot, moron. Now the old Carter is—"

"You can measure your dicks later, boys. I've got shit to do." Tiana cuts me off, sliding between us. She must've figured it out already because she wouldn't have allowed it if she knew his plan. That's probably why she hasn't shown her face in so long. I can't really fault her for protecting the one she loves, but I can sure as hell beat his face in.

Tiana silently begs me with her eyes to let it go. Just like the first time I met Sebastian in Monte Carlo. He literally bulldozed through my hotel room's door, looking for Tiana, who had stormed out of New York after she saw him talking to another model at the show she was in. We tore down the room, fighting because I thought she didn't want to be found. Turned out that was exactly what she aimed for: running away from him. These two have the weirdest, most toxic dynamic I've ever seen, but they'd kill for each other. I broke his nose just when Tiana slid between us and almost crushed my balls with her knee. I was just trying to protect her from the son of her family's sworn enemy. Spoiler alert: she doesn't need protection; she's a whole other level of crazy. She has the heir to the biggest Russian mafia wrapped around her pinky.

Trying to avoid a repetition of history, I instinctively protect my junk with my hands. Tiana smirks and turns around. Sebastian finally gives up the silent stare-off when she faces him, and he wraps his arm around her waist. He whispers something in her ear and she giggles, whispering something back. They kiss and finally let go of each other so she can hug me goodbye.

That's when Stella shows up around the corner of the hallway.

CHAPTER TWENTY-THREE

STELLA

The nice woman with honey-colored hair gives me another one of her comforting smiles. Patricia Harbor—the best shrink in eating disorders, as Lucifer drilled into my brain. She graduated from Columbia University Medical Center, as she already mentioned twice, and is a professor of psychiatry there.

"There's a major difference between having a lapse and a relapse, Stella," Patricia explains. I give her a weak smile.

I insisted on having our little talk on the fluffy carpet with our legs crossed where I usually sit when sketching. I've had some of my most creative ideas in this spot, so I thought it might be easier to endure this session.

Hmmm, maybe I should add a slit to the gown I sewed yesterday? That would give it...

Shrink Harbor cuts off my line of thought, continuing. "A lapse is a temporary slip. You show signs of returning to your previous behavior, but you're trying to control it. Whereas, a relapse represents a full-blown return to the pattern of behavior."

Ugh. I don't even want to be here, staring at this carpet

while someone's telling me everything that's wrong with me. I shouldn't have agreed to Lucifer's demands. I've been to a thousand psychiatrists and help centers; it never helped me. I want Ivy and Damien, and Rosalie, and little baby Devora. I miss Six licking my face. I want my small house and my yellow-grass backyard, and midnight drives for new fabrics with Raquel. I want my life back. But I want it with Lucifer lying on my green couch while I make us our favorite pasta.

"Are you listening to me, Stella?"

"Uh, yeah. Relapse, I got it." I raise my gaze from the carpet back to Patricia. She looks like she doesn't believe a thing I tell her.

She'll never get it. If I told my shrink everything I've been through, she'd run out of here in horror. I only told her what I could've without risking her calling the cops on us.

"Please, this is for your own good. If you don't listen to anything else I say, at least try to listen to this. You're not having a relapse. Yet. You're trying to fight it. The last step that takes you from lapse to relapse is giving up. You haven't given up because you're strong, Stella."

I roll my eyes and huff. "If I was so strong, wouldn't I have avoided this whole process altogether?"

"More than ninety-five percent of the people that have eating disorders experience lapses. It's natural, you're fighting the battle of your life against your biggest opponent. Yourself. Think of it like you're writing a story. In every story there is the good and the bad, and the writer decides which is stronger. You define whether it controls you or you control it."

I sigh and look at the ceiling, murmuring, "I'm tired of fairy tales. In my story the bad always wins and takes everything away from me."

"Really? Then why did you succeed in fighting this

disorder the first time? And why do you continue to do so now? You said you've managed to keep the urge of throwing up or binging for the last two weeks. You know what that means?"

I shake my head, still staring at the ceiling, tears prickling in the corners of my eyes.

"It means the good has already won. The last time you did it with the help of all your friends." I finally meet her eyes. The corner of her mouth quirks up. "This time you didn't even know you had a lapse. You thought it was a relapse, which means you fought a bigger monster without even realizing it. You did it all by yourself without the help of anyone else."

Well…that kind of makes sense. I didn't call Ivy when I needed her. I didn't have my usual surroundings that calm me. I found a way to beat it without having anyone or anything to comfort me. "Then why do I have this feeling in my throat every time I feel unease? Sometimes I look in the mirror and all I see is a bag of bones. Then I eat a pan of food and when I look again, I feel disgusted."

"Because the monster is still alive. It lives inside you, and it's looking for power, pulling strings in your brain. You have to kill it. The same way you killed his brother when you first completed all the steps of the circle of recovery. And you will. I can see it in your eyes. You're a fighter. Remember my words when you need them. Repeat them. Look in the mirror and tell them to yourself. If you have to, fake it till you make it."

This earns her my first genuine smile and a chuckle. This is exactly the same thing I've been telling myself.

"Lucifer insists on feeding me because he thinks I'm way too skinny, so I won't have a problem at that front."

"Sometimes your closest people are too worried, and they

don't think about the consequences of their advice. Urging someone to eat or drawing attention to someone's body weight and shape is unlikely to be helpful. I told him the same thing. You should be eating, but it shouldn't be forced on you. You're the only one who knows the best way to a healthy body and a healthy mind."

"I don't know… I've just done so well with hiding from my monsters so far. I blame myself for leaving the door open so they could trickle back in and seat themselves at the couch like time hasn't passed at all."

"If you want my advice, and I can tell you don't." She smiles when I bite my lip. Is it that obvious? "Sorry, I'm being unprofessional here, but I can clearly see you're being forced into this meeting by a man who loves you and worries about you. From what I've heard from you both, you've been to enough shrinks to recite me everything they taught us in med school, you don't need me explaining it all over again. You can get away from toxic situations that trigger you, but that'll be putting a Band-Aid on a gunshot wound. Most of the time eating disorders are not about self-love but about unresolved feelings we hide deep down in ourselves. Grief, anger, disappointment. Toxic relationships breed toxic environment for your mind. My advice is take some time to self-reflect. Maybe there are people in your life you haven't forgiven. Maybe there are good feelings you never got to express, so they've turned rotten after being kept for too long. Find a way to overcome everything you've been afraid of but won't admit to yourself, and you'll be free. Your friends, your love partner have been a good support system so far but at the end of the tunnel, we're all alone. You need to be enough and you are. You just have to heal to believe it."

"Thank you." I look at the clock on my wall, glad to see this session is over.

The second I walk her out, I waltz back in to the second floor to let Lou know I've done my part of the deal. His part was promising me we'll be sleeping in one bed from now on. What I didn't expect is shrink Harbor's words to keep repeating in my head on the way there.

After all, I'm not in control of other people's actions, but I'm in control of my reaction to them. If I could just continue fighting without overthinking every single thing, maybe I could finally get everything I want—the business deal, my strength back, coexisting peacefully with Lou.

As I speak of the devil...there he is in the hallway with two more people. A tall and attractive blond man with pale skin. I can smell the Russian blood in his veins all the way from the corner. I can tell Lucifer doesn't like him by the way he glares daggers at his direction, but he seems quite familiar with the raven-haired, well-dressed woman in his arms. A pang of jealousy shoots arrows into my heart as I'm staring at Lucifer whispering something in her ear.

Is the Russian her bodyguard or something? He isn't built like a bull, but he looks strong. He could know martial arts or some shit like that. Wait a second, isn't that...

"A vintage Versace?" The end of my question slips out, left in the thick air as the three of them whip around to see where it came from.

Holy freaking shit! Tiana Carter. The highest-paid model of the year is in Lucifer's hallway, giving him hugs.

"Why, yes it is. Thank you for noticing," the blond guy says, confirming my suspicions with his Russian accent, but I can barely see him now behind the shine of Tiana. "You must be the infamous Stella Morelli."

Now that gets my attention. How does he know my last name?

Lucifer sidesteps them to come and wrap his arm around my shoulder and give me a reassuring forehead kiss.

Tiana freaking Carter beams at me, brushing off thick strands of black hair from her shoulder. How is it possible she looks even more gorgeous in person than on a *Vogue* cover? There's grace in every move of her body, in every breath she inhales.

The Russian man slips his hand into hers, and that's when I notice the huge sapphire engagement ring she's wearing. I didn't know she was engaged, and she's been in every fashion magazine I've read. I know so much about her daily eating habits, her workouts. What her mansions in Paris, Los Angeles, and New York look like. But I've never once seen her with this guy. Who is he?

They stop before us and Tiana extends her hand. "It's so nice to finally meet you. Luci has told me so much about you." My jaw drops as I stare wide-eyed at her, unable to move any part of my body or produce a single thought.

This woman is like a myth in the fashion industry. She's perfection in a human form. She does all the biggest shows on fashion week, and she's personal friends with the biggest designers. Once she went live on Instagram when she had the biggest designers gathered for brunch in her Paris mansion.

She knows who I am.

And she calls my man Luci.

I stagger backward a little bit, but Lou's got my back. He gestures to her hand, still hanging in the air. "This is Tiana Carter, a very good friend of mine."

"Hi, I'm Stella." I squeak out and extend my hand, expecting her to shake it, but she's quick to pull me out of Lou's hands and wrap me in a hug. She gives tight and warm hugs, something I never would've suspected. Raquel and I have talked about how she looks like a very reserved person under this socialite façade. Damn, Raquel won't believe this...

"And I'm..." the Russian man starts when Tiana releases me, but Lucifer cuts him off.

"Leaving. Tiana and he were just leaving, so let me walk them out and I'll come get you."

The Russian man's Cheshire-cat grin makes me uneasy. "It was nice meeting you, Stella."

Lucifer leads them down the hall, but Tiana stops short and turns around. "Congratulations on the BFD Group deal. They're the best you could've gone with." Her smile implies there's more meaning behind her words.

"Thank you." My mind is finally ready to produce some thoughts, and I grab the once-in-a-lifetime opportunity to voice the most ludicrous of them all. "Would you consider coming to my fashion show? I would be so honored."

She beams that perfect set of teeth at me and chuckles. Even her chuckling is gracious and cute at the same time. "I'd love to. In fact, let me check my calendar..." She fishes her phone out of the designer clutch and taps a few times on it. "Great, I have the whole evening free. You know what? Send me the photographs of the collection. I might even model a piece if I like it."

"Like show up at the after party in a dress of mine?" I chirp like a fourteen-year-old at a One Direction concert. I didn't prepare my mind for this turbulence. This is more than everything I've ever wanted in my career path. I never thought I'd get to meet Tiana Carter, much less have her wearing something of mine.

The men are already down the hall, waiting for her by the elevator. "No, silly. Maybe close the show or something? We'll see." She fishes a business card from her clutch. "Here, call my agent. He'll go over details with you." She starts walking backward down the hall. "By the way, I'm dying for that pink one-shoulder dress you showed at the Black Rose Hotel. Oh, and give Damien Black my best. I haven't seen him in ages. I heard he's got a daughter now." She's already by the elevator, and the three of them disappear inside.

What the freaking hell just happened?!

Ladies and gentleman, I address the brain cells popping like bubblegum balloons in my head, *please fasten your seat belts, we're experiencing some unexpected turbulence.*

Did I just get Tiana freaking Carter to walk in my fashion show?

Again, what?! This is too surreal. My brand's status will skyrocket. Am I ready for something like this?

The hell, I am. I've worked relentlessly, days and nights, to get where I am. I deserve everything.

Why am I not surprised that she knows Damien. Everybody who's anybody knows Damien Black. Especially the models.

CHAPTER TWENTY-FOUR

STELLA

I peek behind the curtains of the stage. My goodness, there are so many people who came to watch my fashion show. Critics and celebrities in the first two rows. Oh, there's my godmother, Melanie Black, right next to a fashion magazine's editor. And...she brought a camera crew with her.

I wish Ivy and Damien were here, but they had to tend to Devora.

"Okay, people, the show is starting in ten. Tim, line up the models. Stella, I need you with me!" I hear Raquel's orders in my headset.

There's Tiana's Russian boyfriend or fiancé or whatever standing at the back. I take one last look around the crowd for more familiar faces and take a deep breath.

You can do this, Stella. This is your big break.

"Is this your first?" A female voice startles me.

I turn around to see the opening model and the others lining up behind her, chatting with the makeup and hair people doing last checks. It seems like everyone knows everyone here.

I offer her a tight smile. "No, my second. But it's my first major one. I didn't know so many people were coming."

The stunning blonde, whose name I forgot because of the anxiety eating at me, could blind me with her pearly white smile. She rubs my shoulder reassuringly. "Don't worry. Your work is amazing. I'm definitely buying the piece my sister is wearing." She looks back where her twin is laughing with one of the makeup artists.

These are the super-famous Instagram model twins. Raquel said they are, quote, "*the* thing" in social media. If you combine their individual and joint accounts, they have over a hundred million followers.

"Five minutes, people. Stella, I'm waiting!" Raquel squeaks out.

"Last minute selfie!" the blond model calls out, and the other women whoop. A girl dressed in jeans and a T-shirt shows up out of nowhere and gives her an iPhone with a light ring attached to it. "Come on, Stella. You've gotta be in the front." The model pushes my small body between her and another equally tall and toned woman. "Say vegan, gluten-free cheese," she calls out, and everybody cracks up. "Sweet! I was thinking of posting on my story but this is feed-worthy."

The girl in the jeans takes the phone and says, "I'll upload it" before she disappears in the back again. The twin model starts saying a prayer, and I move away to give her space.

"One minute. Stella!" Raquel roars in the headset, and I start speed-walking before she shows up here and whoops my ass. Tim, who handles everything in regards to the models, from the castings to the lineup, takes the lead and gives last-minute instructions.

The backstage is full and buzzing like a beehive.

Suddenly, I freeze when I hear applause, followed by a

male voice. "Ladies and gentlemen, BFD Group is proud to present Femme Fatale limited collection by our newest designer Stella Morelli."

Mixed emotions of pride and fear invade my body when I hear my real name presented to the world. Yesterday, Lucifer came to the rehearsal to give me a present. My own logo design that BFD's marketing team made for me printed on a box of cookies. It read Stella Morelli instead of my fake name Stella Jacobs.

I looked at his unreadable face and stuttered confused. "W-what?"

He grabbed my hand and declared with undeniable sexiness, "You're a Morelli, and you should present yourself with a name that once instilled fear and respect in everyone who crossed it."

"Yeah," I retorted. "A name of an underground Sicilian king."

"But a king nevertheless. Know your worth, princess, and you've already conquered the world." My heart melted on the floor right then and there in this same hall. "Damn, I know I'm proud to be sleeping in the same bed as the brilliant daughter of the most powerful Sicilian family."

I wanted to climb him like a tree and stake a claim in front of all the models who ate him up with hungry eyes like he was a fresh lemon cake for dessert. I love him so much, and I've never even told him. I'd be rectifying the situation after today's show when he strips the dress off me.

"What about the other mob families?"

He fixed a strand of hair behind my ear. "All of them already know, princess. Let them come. You're the kind of woman wars are fought for. They'll have to run through Marcel and me before I ever let them get to you."

That was it. I decided on the spot I wasn't holding up my

promise of letting Lucifer go when all of this is over. Now that people know my real name, it might never be over. I just hope we all make it out alive and in one piece.

He made a secret deal behind my back with BFD Group for my rebranding. Stella Jacobs was never bigger than some customers in Florida, so it shouldn't have been a problem. BFD likes to erase the history of their smallest designers if possible when signing them so no one can form a wrong opinion from old collections. They are very particular in the image they decide to create for your brand, which I have to admit was a little unsettling at the beginning, but after we talked it through and they respected my opinions, it made the whole business part easier. Like a good parent, they let your imagination roam free but direct you when you get too out of line. This whole show is their planning and they've done brilliantly. The music we chose for the runway starts just as I find Raquel dressed in one of my designs that didn't make the cut for the limited-edition collection but will be presented in the ready-to-wear collection. Her black hair is up in a messy high-bun with some strands falling down on her face as always.

"Oh my God!" she squeaks and slaps a handful of all her "special crystal" rings on her mouth. "Are you crazy? Why aren't you dressed? We're starting."

"I didn't want to ruin my dress when I got makeup and hair." I shrug. The hairdresser took some special time adding hair extensions to my real hair to make it fall down like a rich waterfall of blonde curls. And the golden makeup I went for... Dio! I've never looked so good in my life.

"Bring her dress. Fast." She barks the order to Bobby, her newly-appointed assistant, who's taken so much yelling I couldn't possibly endure. I watch the blonde twin model strut down the runway on the TV-screen on the wall. "I can't believe this is happening," I mutter to myself, but Raquel hears me and pulls me into a hug, the oriental notes of her perfume suffocating me. "I know." She squeaks in my ear. "I'm so proud of us."

Bobby brings my dress, and Raquel's jaw drops to the ground when she sees it. "Stella, you little minx! You've kept this beauty all to yourself."

"I know. I wanted it to be a surprise." I stare at it, contemplating walking down the runway. I'm the type of girl who loves to watch everybody turn their heads when looking at my designs from the safety of the backstage, where I can help and talk with the models. The people who actually can and should walk this runway.

Raquel and her assistant help me put the dress on, and when I look in the mirror, Raquel is behind me, clasping her hands as she bites her lower lip, and a tear rolls down her cheek.

"My girl." Her voice catches an even higher note I didn't know the human ear could hear. "This is the definition of divine."

A smile rises on my face as I marvel at the first design I sewed for this collection on me. It's a deliciously decadent red, one-shoulder, floor-length dress. A slit reaching my thigh, the silk A-line silhouette, and the cape drape detail hanging over my shoulder are the declaration of the message my collection sends. Regal beauty.

Lucifer's revival was the final nail in the coffin of my old, innocent, gullible self. I've discovered a whole new side of myself the past month or so. The goddess. Every time he pulled her out of the cage, she left little pieces of her in my mind, my heart, my body until she chose a moment to settle for good that day the shrink made me realize how much I've achieved on my own.

The goddess is not only for Lucifer now. It's for me. It's for the world.

The whole limited-edition collection is composed of golds and reds. Silks, velvets, and laces. It's very different from everything I've done before, not that I'll ever give up the pinks and the shiny, God forbid, but I feel like I've outgrown that phase, and I'm ready to create a new one. A collection for women who know their worth. Who aren't afraid of their inner seductress.

"Here, shoes." Raquel hands me a pair of golden heels with red soles. The perfect finish to my bold look.

We watch the rest of the show on the screen until it's time for the last model to walk out. Tiana Freaking Carter. She's wearing a golden tea-length corset dress, and she's rocking it. It's my second favorite from this collection.

"Come on, it's your turn." Bobby waves us over by the curtains, where all of the models who were previously on stage are lined up again so they can make the final collective walk.

I peek at the screen while waiting, looking for Lucifer, and as usual I spot him right away sitting in the back so he won't draw attention. I get mesmerized by his wild curls spilling everywhere, a burgundy suit I sewed for him, and a huge smile I've only seen a couple of times since we were kids. I totally zone out, failing to see Tiana is already gone off the stage. A hand creeps on my back and I jump, startled only to see Tiana's tall figure towering over me.

"Sorry." She chuckles. Damn. Her looks make me cringe a little inside. We have to get out on stage together. I feel mighty powerful in my dress, but there's no heels high enough to hide the fact that Tiana looks and moves like a siren, and I'm just a cute, petite girl. I'm not made for the catwalk, but I sure as hell want to impress Lucifer.

Which is going to be harder than I thought standing next to her—the scared girl, who apparently isn't buried as deep as I thought, chirps in my head.

Shut up, bitch. Confidence, remember? You're going to walk out like a goddess, and you better make it fucking sparkling! The new me makes the old one crawl back into her corner.

The models walk out, making two lines on either side of the runway for Tiana and me.

"Are you ready?" she asks. Gosh. I could fall in love with her smile only, and that's not even the best part of her.

I'm going to fuck Lucifer's brains out tonight for introducing me to her.

Focus, Stella. Catwalk now. Fucking later.

I feel like throwing up.

The man's voice booms through the speakers. "Ladies and gentlemen, Stella Morelli."

CHAPTER TWENTY-FIVE

STELLA

I somehow strut to the curtains and disappear behind them, overwhelmed with emotion and energy from the still-booming applauses. Thank God (and Raquel, which sometimes is the same thing) for making me walk down the runway with my head held high alongside Tiana because alone I would've stumbled, blinded by the camera flashes. My head feels dizzy for a moment as my vision clears and I stagger sideways, grabbing onto something. Or rather someone. Someone who makes my eyes bulge out the second the black dots disappear.

"Uncle Thomas?"

Another ghost of my past grabs my hands in his. "Stellina!" My eyebrow tics. His voice is as thick and hoarse from all the cigarettes as I remember it. He was a good friend of my father who lived in the US and came to visit at the manor often. One of the very few people who knows me as Giovanni's daughter and who knew my real mother before she got shot.

What in the ghostly reunion's name is going on? I couldn't have blacked out; I ate a whole plate of healthy food earlier, and I managed to sleep six hours after Lou exhausted me.

I can practically feel the blood draining from my face and my fingers getting colder in his hands. "What are you doing here? I haven't seen you in ages."

His big frame is taking a lot of space, and his presence is demanding respect. I've forgotten how that feels. It's like I'm standing in front of my father again.

"I came to watch my daughter and who do I see instead? My little Stellina is a big star now. How have you been, kiddo?" He rubs his rough palm on my head and messes my hairstyle just like he always did when I was a kid. *Dammit.* Why does my past keep haunting me?

I stutter. "I… I'm good. G-great, actually." Until it hits me. "Wait, what? I didn't know you had a daughter." He never brought any kids, not even his wife. Only him and his security.

"I do. A very beautiful one for that matter. There she is…" He looks behind me. I turn around and see Tiana Carter walking our way. Dio! Tiana Carter is this Carter? Uncle Thomas Carter?

"Daddy." Tiana gives him a hug and a peck on the cheek. "What are you doing here?"

"I came to see my little girl. You haven't returned my calls the last two weeks." He scolds her with his eyes, never with his tone. I know that look all-too-well. Although neither uncle Thomas, nor Aunt Melanie could measure up to father's scrutinizing gaze. Both Tiana's and my shoulders slump a little. She looks down at the ground. "I've been busy with the fashion show."

Never in a million years did I expect to see Tiana, the most confident woman, bow her head and look uncomfortable.

"I understand. Still, I came to let you know tonight is the night." He grabs two glasses of champagne from the passing tray and hands them to us. Then, he takes one for himself. "We're announcing your engagement at the after-party. I hope Stellina won't mind." He directs that look to me, and all I can do is nod silently. "She could use all the publicity, right Tiana?" He doesn't even glance at her.

I can feel discomfort radiating out of her. Instantly, it makes me question what would have become of me if my father were still alive?

"My daughter is quite well-known. You've got half of the press already here, and her announcement will cover the other half. Everyone will be talking about my two princesses." He chirps the last sentence, like it makes him the happiest person in the world.

Thomas Carter isn't a bad person from what I've seen. He's always been super careful and thoughtful with me, considering I saw him mostly around my mother's death. He doesn't look like a villain, either, with his bulging belly under his brown suit. Why does his energy make chills crawl up my spine then?

"Congratulations." I turn to Tiana and clink the glass against hers just to do something with my hands, but she's white as a sheet, staring at her father, speechless. I try to lighten the mood and nudge her in the ribs with my elbow. "Where's the lucky man?" I saw that Russian guy somewhere in the audience, he's probably making his way here.

"There he is." Thomas Carter points with his glass behind us. I turn around but there's only Lucifer coming this way.

"Uncle Thomas, your sight has gotten progressively worse." I giggle, secretly admiring Lucifer's confident stride. "That's my man, remember? You used to tease Giovanni that I was going to marry the pool boy. He grew up, didn't he?" I say a little too dreamily. "Russian Ken was here earl…"

"Hahaha." Tiana cuts me off with a vicious glare that comes out of nowhere and an ugly chuckle I'd expect from a wicked witch. "Don't mind her. Lucifer should be here any moment now."

"What?" It suddenly feels like the world has collapsed on my unstable shoulders. I have a feeling something is colossally wrong.

"Carter, what are you doing here?" Lucifer growls at him.

No. This isn't right. My heartbeat accelerates through the roof.

A server passes by us with a tray full of food as if to test me, but I don't let my gaze linger on it. I repeat what that shrink told me.

"I should've known you were a wretch like your father, Visconti. Fooling this poor girl while my daughter waits for you to marry her." Uncle Thomas's eyes flicker with mischief.

"Tell me it's a joke, Lou." I desperately search for the truth in his eyes as my voice begs him.

Regret is written all over his face when he finally looks at me. "Princess, I can explain."

"What's there to explain? Don't make me cut off your pretty head and send it to your uncle for unfulfilling your duties, boy. As a matter of fact, he might even thank me."

I can't listen to anything more. This isn't real. This isn't happening. Carter was a good man who always brought me dolls, not this vicious mobster who threatens my Lou.

It suddenly sinks in.

Lou… He isn't *my* Lou. He's been engaged to another woman the whole time. That's why he said he'd leave me. It was never a selfless thing to keep me alive. He caged me in his Manhattan castle and let me lose my mind and my health progress while making love to my body and my mind with his lies.

I'd rather know he's dead than know he broke me on purpose and he's another woman's husband.

Listen to yourself, Stella. This isn't you—the little Stella whispers from her corner, scared of her own thoughts.

But as a matter of fact, it is. Lucifer was right about one thing. I am a Morelli; this is my blood. There's darkness inside of me, and I can feel it rising to the surface.

I hear Uncle Carter's laugh behind me as a background noise, silenced by the humming in my head. My heart is trying to tear apart from my chest and run away to die somewhere alone.

That's what I do.

I push through Tiana, knocking her on the ground and dodge every person on my path as I run away, escaping all the eyes glued to us. Lucifer is behind me, calling my name, so I kick away my heels and run out the back before he could reach me. The people on the sidewalk turn and gape at me, when I, dressed in a ten grand designer dress, step onto the pavement, barefoot, and yell for the nearest cab.

What the hell was I thinking loving a dead person? I should've expected it all along. You can't play with the devil, moaning his name like a prayer and expect to land in heaven.

It hurts so much.

We're fucked up beyond repair. Shakespeare made it pretty tragic and yet he had the decency to let them love each other in their deaths. Our story ends with my heart ripped out of my chest and fed to the wolves. To the one lone wolf sitting under the hollow gap on Lucifer's chest howling at the stars.

I bounce in the back seat all the way to his house, praying

he isn't there already. I only need enough time to get my documents so I can run away for good. I don't want anything to do with that man.

When I step inside my room, I freeze on the spot. There's a man inside with his back to me. It's not Lucifer nor Marcel. He twists around, and so do my guts. My heart stops for a second, the sound of the sudden silence in my head deafening.

"Daddy?"

The man. The ghost. The most feared mobster. My father. Giovanni Morelli smiles and raises his hand to caress my cheek. His fingers are cold, like those of a dead man. "We're going home, Stellina."

I grip the door for support, but it's too late. My stomach spasms, and I can feel all the food I ate before the show coming up my throat. The last thing I remember is puking my guts out on his Italian loafers before I hit the ground.

CHAPTER TWENTY-SIX

STELLA

Sicily, Italy

I wake up in a moving car. My head is fuzzy, resting on someone's thigh. Afraid I might have been kidnapped again, I evaluate my surroundings, doing my best not to move. Beige leather interior. Uniformed driver. Italian loafers. Wait a second.

"Buongiorno, my little star." I catch the voice I never thought I'd hear again and look up. "Did you hit your head?"

Oh, so I'm lucid dreaming. That would explain why my very dead father is caressing my head.

"No, I don't think so," I mutter.

The car comes to a halt. I rise up on my elbows and look out the tinted window. A private airport.

"Wait, what? Where are we going?" I whisper to myself. I've been through this labyrinth before. We get in the airplane, and the bad guys kill us numerous times before we even get to the exotic destination I've thought about most recently.

Ugh, I'm too tired to go through this labyrinth lucid.

"We're going home, Stellina. I told you right before you ruined my new loafers." My dad scoffs.

It won't matter if I scream; this is just a dream, and as long as I can keep it from turning into a nightmare, it's a win. Giovanni would never hear me anyway. *Not even if he was alive.*

We step out of the car. The wind grazes my shoulders. I look down to see I'm wearing the red dress. My fingers glide through the silk. It feels so soft, so real. The wind blows my hair, and goose bumps rise on my arms.

Dio mio, this is all too real. Am I hallucinating?

"Daddy?" I try to call after him while he's walking toward a black jet, but my voice is gone. I try again but it comes out as a whisper. I try again and this time I yell out of my lungs, "Giovanni!"

He stops short. "I'm sorry, Stellina. Where are my manners? I should've helped you. You must be exhausted." He takes his time walking to me. Never running. Giovanni Morelli runs for no one.

It's loud here, but the silence between us is the only sound I hear as we make our way to the jet and settle in. He's the first to open his mouth.

"I've missed you."

Okay now, this is most definitely a dream. My father would never show affection; he considers it weakness, not even for his children. I just smile and excuse myself while I go lie down a little. I've fallen asleep in my dreams a few times, and it seems like this is the cheat code to breaking out of the nightmare. I'll just fall into a black hole of nothingness for the remainder of my sleep and manage to rest…

When I open my eyes again, my father's face is in front of me. "Ciao, bellissima. We're here."

The reality of his breath on my face hits me like a kick to the gut. There can't be a second person resurrected in my life, right? I raise my hand to touch Giovanni's stubble as I did when I was little.

"Is this real?"

His faded blue eyes stare at me. I notice there are new wrinkles on his face. "It's very much real, Stellina. I'm sorry I didn't come for you sooner."

I'm so confused.

I want to scream. I want to slap him across the face for letting me believe I lost my father. For making me feel like I'm losing my mind.

But I also want to hug him and never let him go again. Tell him I love him.

And cry. Oh, how much I want to cry.

I hear the voice of a man in the background. "Sir, the car is ready for you."

I pace the golden-lined hallway in front of my father's office, too afraid to knock and face another one of the demons of my past. I can't take all the memories of this haunted mansion drowning me. Father explained the firemen put down the fire in the mansion first because they thought there might be someone to save in there. He has been living here for the past eight years in the shadows. It's been preserved safe for a couple of burn marks and the smell of charred wood sealed in the walls. The rest of the manor property, including my animals, has been completely destroyed.

How and who he paid off so that he could keep living here is beyond me. The man had more connections in the government than the president.

"Are you all right, Stellina?" he asked.

"No!" I wanted to scream, but I couldn't because a second wave of nausea rose to my throat.

Of course, I'm not all right, seeing the father I mourned give me his custom Italian-made handkerchief. I haven't been all right since I was five and being eaten away by guilt. Guilt that I killed my mother. Guilt that you hated me for it. Guilt that I kept having these nightmares where I couldn't save her over and over again. Guilt that I weighed just a tad bit more than a girl my age should. Guilt that your wife planted inside of my brain. Guilt that you saw and you let overwhelm me.

Guilt I let once again get to me as I watch the stain getting scrubbed off the rug.

In my defense, I couldn't have prepared for this.

For me standing in the childhood home I thought I buried under ruins and my relatives' skeletons.

Little Stella is staring at me from the corner of the hallway. In her blue eyes there's so much pain she doesn't even realize she holds. It's my duty to free her of it. To make all that she's been through worth it.

I push the doors open, and waltz inside, not bothering to wait for an invitation. His office reeks of power. Golden desk, golden painting frames, thick curtains and massive chairs. If this room was touched by the fire, there's no sign of it.

I sit in one of them and stare at my father, who didn't even lift his head when I walked in.

"Your brother will attend to your needs. Please, let him

know if you need anything," he says matter-of-factly.

My eyebrows rise. "Marco? Matteo? They're still alive?" I crack my knuckles. "Is…" I can't say her name out loud. I still hate her guts. "*She* alive too?"

Giovanni's face twists into a scowl. "No, Regina and your stepbrothers are dead. I'm talking about your other brother. You know him."

Just in time Marcel walks in.

My jaw falls slack to the floor right next to my blown brains. "Stellina, are you all right? You look a little pale."

All right? All-fucking-right? This family is dropping bomb after bomb on my head. How the hell am I ever going to be all right again?

"Hey, I wanted to explain to you." Marcel raises his palms, taking a calculated step toward me, but father's ahead of him.

"What is there to explain, boy? Sure, everybody knew I had mistresses all over the world. I was bound to have a bastard or two along the road. And did I give you permission to step inside? Out!" Giovanni scolds him, and Marcel quickly scoots back to the door and closes it on the other side.

I'm starting to question my sanity. Maybe I've finally gone mad and I'm locked in some mental institution where they feed me the periodic table of pills. You know, like that Leo DiCaprio movie.

"By the look on your face I get that he didn't do what he was supposed to and ease you into this whole situation." I can only nod, staring at a little golden soldier on his desk. "Great." He scoffs. "Stellina?" He waves his palm in front of my face, and I snap back into reality. Or illusion. What is reality anymore? I'm so confused. I haven't slept in ages. I haven't eaten in a day. I've puked my guts out. And every time he calls me Stellina, I cringe inside. I just want to sleep, to forget. To remember the better times. But most of all…I want Lou.

I shouldn't. But I do. This mansion…it brings back memories of a better time. When we were young and in love, and I, stupid and reckless. But innocent. Oh so innocent and trusting.

I should hate them. My father, who betrayed me not once or twice. Lucifer, who took a page from his book. Even Marcel, whom I thought was my friend, who knew about all of this. Somehow they didn't manage to kill the good in me, but it wasn't for a lack of trying.

"I understand this is a lot with my return and everything." Giovanni tries to ease me with his famous negotiation tone. I once heard Aunt Melanie say the man could convince the devil to wear all white at Sunday mass. "You have to get on track fast. There's a war coming, and I can't afford any more casualties. That boy will get what he deserves for dragging you back into the mafioso life."

Goose bumps rise underneath my clothes, and I pull my sleeves to my knuckles. "What do you mean war? Is *he* going to get hurt?" The lump in my throat is threatening to suffocate me. I have to get out of here.

"This isn't your concern, Stellina. I'll make sure you get his head when Carter is done with him."

That lump drops into my chest. *No. Just no*. I can't handle another death. Not my Lou of all people. There's a strong voice in my head that snaps back at me. *He betrayed you, and he's marrying another woman.* The voice of the woman in the red gown. I choose to direct her fury to the person grinning at me from across the desk. He wasn't a bad father really; he just always thought of himself first.

Just like now, when he's smiling probably thinking he got what he wanted.

But I didn't.

My fairy tale isn't quite over, even if there's no one to stand beside me. Not a charming prince, not a fairy godmother. Not even a mouse or a bird. This princess is prepared to go to battle alone, and she refuses to wait on anyone to save her. My heart has been forged and sharpened like a sword.

"Stellina? I'm talking to you. Did you drift away again?" My father scolds me from his throne. He'll never see it coming.

I plant my fists on his golden desk and stand up, feeling a foot taller. My smile stretches. I take a moment to memorize the little squirm he does when he realizes he screwed up majorly. I've only ever seen it once when he found me hiding in the bush, and I told him what happened to my mother. That face haunted me for years after, like I did something to break the king of the mafia, when it should have given me strength.

I thought I did good on my own avoiding my issues, but it isn't until this moment when I look at my father's dilated pupils, his old, rusty heart probably skipping a beat, making him lose a breath every now and then, and the vein on his neck pulsating fiercely, that I realize we are all responsible for our choices regardless of our feelings. I choose to face my demons, dirty armor and all, starting with the ghost in front of me.

He might be the scary monster to everyone else, but he is still my father. He isn't going to harm me with his hands—he did it best with his words. I chuckle and shake my head, looking down at his gold-plated desk. The power-game he played fooled me, too, but I learned a trick or two trapped in his golden cage. One of them is nothing and no one makes Giovanni Morelli nervous.

My chuckle fades as I can feel his foot tapping under the

desk. "Stop calling me Stellina. I'm not your little star. You left me for dead, but it wasn't eight years ago. No. The first time you left me was when you let those Visconti bastards kill my mother."

Giovanni shoots to his feet, slapping his palm on the desk. "I'm not responsible for your mother's death!"

I continue, well aware that his fingers are trembling on the desk, sending vibrations toward me. The woman in the red dress feeds off his anger and turns it into poise. "Whatever lets you sleep at night, Father. 'Cause I haven't. I haven't slept in a long time, and I'm tired of it. You left me again when you stopped reading bedtime stories to me and pretended you didn't hear me pacing the hallways at night. Because I know you did and it kept you up, too, but you chose to ignore it. Just like you chose to ignore the clothes that started hanging loose when your second wife gave me laxatives because I was a little bit chubby."

His eyes widen and he clears his throat. "I didn't know."

I chuckle darkly and push off the desk, crossing my arms under my chest. "Sure you did. Isn't that why you turned your head the other way every time she took my plate at dinner and gave half of it to my stepbrothers?" I round the desk, feeling like he's suddenly shrunk and I'm a giant. "For years I thought I was sick, but no. All of you were." I get in his face. "You sure tried hard, but you couldn't break me. I'm a giant star now, Giovanni, and I'm going to shine so bright I'll leave burn marks on your skin. Just like all of you left your marks on me."

It's the first time I see my father, the king of the Morelli mafia and the scariest person I know to date, fall to his knees, tears streaming down his cheeks.

See? I told you he isn't a bad father. He's just a selfish one.

CHAPTER TWENTY-SEVEN

STELLA

I get a long dreamless sleep after I return back to my room. I guess it comes with the territory of being an unapologetic bitch, and I could get used to it. Slapping my father with the truth felt way better than slapping Lucifer would've. I was tempted but I wasn't capable of it. My loss will hurt him more.

In spite of everything, the old me and the new me both still miss Lucifer. Even when I want to wrap my hands around his neck and squeeze until his last breath. Especially when I want to meet his lips and breathe new life into his lungs. I wish he could feel what it's like dying a thousand times every time I'm away from him.

As I'm lying in my childhood bed, all of our memories flood me in a pool of pain.

I was seven when Lucifer sneaked into my room for the first time. He climbed up the ivy surrounding the mansion's façade. I was at the balcony, awake from yet another nightmare, when he jumped over the stone railing. He was eleven. A scrawny boy with wild dark curls and jaded gray eyes. He looked like he hadn't slept in ages. Back then I didn't know he had his demons too. He'd heard me scream and climbed up to check on me. We were just becoming friends, spending every free second hiding around the manor because he was the servant boy, and I was the mafioso principessa. Forbidden friendship turned into forbidden love.

Of course back then I thought boys were "*eww.*" Like that boy, Damien, who came to visit with Aunt Melanie. He pulled on my braids and chased after the servants' daughters. His sister, Rosalie, was glued to him, always whining.

But not this boy. Lucifer carried a different energy I always found myself gravitating toward. Even at eleven he had expressive eyes. There was pain in there I could relate to. So I let him in my room, and we talked for hours before we fell asleep. He lived in the servants' houses, my bed was much more comfortable.

My nanny found us in the morning, curled against each other. She was all smiles while she scolded me and made me promise that would never happen again. Years later, when she found us again, she told me she didn't tell on me because she knew Lucifer was my knight, and he'd fight my demons until his last breath.

That first night became the start of something bigger than us. Lucifer came the night after too. And for another five years he kept on climbing up my balcony at midnight, fighting my demons all night and disappearing at sunrise. Until my father stormed into my room one night.

Lou and I stole my stepbrothers' new wooden horse because they were being mean to me. It was my idea. Lou told me to go to Giovanni and tell him they'd been bullying me, but I knew father had known about this, and he didn't do anything to protect me. I once heard him tell my nanny "Boys will be boys. Stellina will get through it."

I was twelve and he was sixteen, I pretended to sleep so I

could stare at Lou when he fell asleep. He was so beautiful it hurt my eyes. I didn't understand why my heart did somersaults in my chest whenever he took a deep breath through his plump lips. Or every time he brushed his long hair off his beautiful face. He grew up a lot the last year, towering over me. His body wasn't that scrawny anymore; he had muscles on his arms that flexed when they reached out to find me and wrap around me. He was always wearing a T-shirt, and I wondered if he had belly muscles like those actors in the Italian dramas Regina was watching. His cute face was turning into a strong, cut jawline. I was having unfamiliar feelings.

Giovanni opened my door with a bang. I jumped up in bed. I usually locked it, but that night I was too distracted by Lucifer's story about him harnessing Giovanni's new stallion. He paid for my mistake.

My father dragged him out by his hair. I cried and begged on my knees. He didn't listen to me for a second while he was dragging him to the barn. I curled in the corner of my balcony and listened to the sounds of the whip on Lucifer's skin echoing in the silent night. He didn't make a sound. The whole house was awakened by my cries, and no one came to our rescue.

For a year we barely saw each other, stealing a minute or two hiding where no one would see us talking. Father had guards in front of my balcony and had my nanny check on me three times a night. Without Lucifer I had nightmares and eventually, I decided to stop sleeping at night. I had a catnap or two in the daytime, and that kept me going. I filled my days with sewing and cooking. The first became an obsession that kept my mind off things. The second was a hobby that eased my anxiety. I was a bit chubby from the start, but when

I started eating everything, I learned to cook from our chefs, and I gained a few more pounds.

For Regina it was an apocalypse. She was the thinnest woman I've seen to date. Tall, with two sticks for legs, and a stomach glued to her back. Her sons were chubbier than me but she never made them exercise or diet, like she made me. When I didn't follow her routines, she slipped me laxatives as sleeping pills. Later she took me to the bathroom after a lengthy speech about how I should feel guilty for eating, and she showed me how to provoke my gag reflex with my toothbrush. She used the *boys don't like fat girls* card, and she bought me new clothes that fit me better along with underwear for young women as she called it when I got my first period. I was only thirteen. I bought it, thinking Lucifer would stop avoiding me. I didn't know Father made him one of his soldiers and sent him on lengthy trips to keep us apart.

I didn't last long without him.

One night I finally broke down and managed to escape through the hidden exits in the mansion. That's when I found him shaking and screaming on his tiny mattress in his empty room in the servants' house. That's when I made the promise to myself we were going to be together forever, despite everything, because I was going to do everything to fight his demons, and he was never going to give up on destroying mine.

My nanny saw everything that happened to me, but she wasn't in a position to say anything. The next day when she hadn't told anybody that I wasn't in my room through the night, I realized she gave me permission to be with Lucifer. Father removed the guards after I played my part of the dutiful daughter for a while.

A sudden urge makes my feet lift off the bed and walk over to the dresser. The white wood is faded by the years just like everything else in this room, but it hasn't lost its memories. I run my fingers over a dark red stain soaked into the wood.

I was fifteen when I had my first kiss right here in this spot.

Through the years father made up his mind that I wasn't going to let Lucifer go. At some point I think he actually entertained the idea because secretly he liked Lou. He was tougher than his sons, disciplined and loyal. Everything my father stood for. But Giovanni Morelli wasn't going to let his daughter go without a fight. He never managed to catch us sleeping together again, although I'm pretty sure everyone knew we couldn't stay away from each other. It made him angry so every now and then, he took Lucifer to the barn and whipped him just in case. I listened every time he did it. It was like the world stopped moving, the birds stopped singing, and the people stopped talking. It taught me how to cry silently. The only sound slicing the air was the whip tearing his skin. Lucifer never said a word. He took his punishments for being with me, bathed himself from the blood, changed into a new shirt and came back to me. I saw his bloody shirts every now and then when I went to the servants' laundry room.

But that night Lucifer came to me all sweaty and bloody. He was on the verge of passing out, when he stumbled into my room from the balcony. He crumpled onto my floor, and I held him for hours, cleaning up his wounds while he was sleeping and wincing every now and then. When he woke up, he didn't remember coming to me. He was devastated that he let me see him like this. That he let me see what my own father had done to the man I loved. He was only nineteen. More gorgeous than ever, even with the blood and all the cuts. That's also the first night I saw his body. He had scars everywhere. Proof of his love for me. He was still an angel underneath the coat of scars, but he had become a man. He had abdominal muscles I've never seen on a man, and he was hard and hot everywhere. Even places I didn't expect.

I knew I wanted him to take my virginity that night. I had the talk about the birds and the bees with my nanny and Regina already. I was ready in theory.

I got up from the floor and slipped one of the strings to my cream nightgown down.

"Princess, what are you doing?" Lucifer growled and got to his feet. His body moved in a sexy, unfamiliar way, his muscles flexing with every step he took toward me.

I took a few steps back, taunting him. "What I wanted to do for a long time now." My back hit the dresser, and I bit my lip. I slipped the other string down, but Lucifer caught my gown before it slipped down my body and brought it back up.

"You're not ready," he whispered in my ear. Every nerve in my body screamed *I'm ready* back at him but my mind wasn't. Still, I rubbed against him. The feeling of his hardness against my bare thigh made me squeal. Lucifer chuckled dark and low and cupped my face. "See? Not ready yet."

I wanted to feel his lips against mine desperately. I caught myself wondering what he would taste like much too often. Sometimes, when he couldn't make it to my room to hold me, I slipped my hand into my panties and touched myself, imagining what it would be like for his callused hands to touch me.

I pressed my body harder against his, and he slapped his palm on the dresser. I turned my head and saw blood from his fresh wounds bleeding into the white wood.

"You're going to be the death of me, princess. You know that?"

I hated when my father called me Stellina. It meant little

star. I didn't want to feel little. Lucifer's princess always made me feel stronger, taller.

He always told me I was his curse and his blessing. The one who gave him life, and the one he was going to die for.

In that moment I wanted him to die for me. Just like I was dying to touch him. To kiss him. To taste his lips. I wondered if his tanned body tasted like the sun.

I swiveled my head and licked his collarbone. It tasted salty and coppery. What I'd found out to be my favorite taste of all.

"Have you done it already?" I asked him the question that was bugging me for a few months now. Since I saw him talking and laughing with Samantha, one of our cook's daughters. She was pretty and almost eighteen. Lucifer could easily be with her without suffering any punishments.

His lips twisted to a lopsided grin, and he raised an eyebrow. A curl fell down on his face. Dio, he was gorgeous. No wonder every girl on the property wanted him. Some even tried to pursue him, despite knowing I had set my claim on him long ago. Somehow their favorite purses and clothes always ended up burnt. A mystery, unresolved.

"Done what?" He was mocking me now. I slapped his chest, but it only made my hand hurt. He hovered over me like a dark cloud. He wasn't always the angel who saved me. Sometimes he was a dark enigma, the devil's fire burning in his stormy eyes. I wanted to get burned, marked by him. Just like he was marked *because* of me.

"Don't fool me. I see you talking to other girls sometimes. It's okay, you know…" I trailed. It was really hard, almost impossible to get the next words out of my mouth. But it was necessary. Lou wasn't my property as much as I wanted to pee all over him. In the figurative sense of course.

"I can't keep you from doing *it* with other girls. It's only fair…"

He crashed his lips against mine, shutting me up and pinning my head to the wood board. There was a part of me freaking out. This was my first kiss. Of course, I've had a few childish pecks on the lips with the other kids and with Lucifer, but this was the real deal. The passionate one. I wanted it with every cell in my body, but I didn't know what to do. Much to my surprise, Lou wasn't very experienced either. We just stood there, lips pressed against each other in a light, playful way. It wasn't until my hand moved up his torso that he opened his mouth and grazed my lips with his tongue. He still had a fresh minty taste from the chewing gum I had given him earlier. I opened mine and let him slide his tongue into my mouth. I followed his lead, and we made out for a few minutes right there, sloppy and inexperienced. I had a feeling this was his first kiss, too, and it made me beyond grateful that he waited nineteen years just so he could share it with me. I was already stupid in love with him by that point.

We ended up making out all year in my bed, in the vineyard, in the stables. Literally everywhere we could without getting caught. I couldn't imagine what my father would have done to Lou if he found out we were becoming a lot more than friends. He'd probably kill him once and for all.

I find myself touching that spot on the wardrobe as stupid as it sounds. It makes me feel closer to the younger Stella and Lucifer. The ones that weren't this complicated. Things between us were easy, natural. It was the world that complicated it. Now…I don't know anymore.

I go sit on the fluffy carpet and wonder if he placed the exact same one in his house to be a reminder of us reaching second base. My thighs tremble at the memory of his fingers inside me.

"Please, Lou, please." I moaned. He shushed me with the same finger he used to rub my clit with, and then he licked it clean. I growled and let my head fall to the ground. "When are you going to let me return the favor?" I was desperate again. That was how he always left me, wanting more. And not because he didn't finish me. But because he never let me touch him. You know, give him a hand job or whatever.

He grinned and pushed his finger back into me so he could finish his job. "Soon."

I sighed and mumbled to myself that he always said that, but he never did let me. This time he meant it, though. Soon after that I gave him my first hand-job behind a rock at the beach where we were hiding from the guards of the manor. Because the Morelli family had its own private beach of course.

Almost a year later, I finally cornered him and told him my wish for my sixteenth birthday. I'll never forget all the color draining from his face. I was finally feeling ready. I was also a bit afraid that since he was twenty by this point, he was going to do it with someone else soon if he hadn't already. But we had this unspoken thing between us. We gave only each other our firsts. Deep down I knew he was waiting for me. I was never more eager about anything in my life than having my body connect with his in a deeper union.

When it happened in the dirtiest place of all, in the barn, it was like millions of fireworks exploding in my blood. The most magical experience of my life. Two souls connecting with each other. Two bodies merging into one. Two people finding the purest love in the most messed-up situation.

Unfortunately, we all know how it went on from the next day. Total massacre, broken heart and all.

Never in my eight years since I left the manor have I

thought about coming back. Never could have I predicted that my magical but wicked fairy tale would have come to this.

My father shed a tear because of me. My love is marrying another woman. And the naïve girl inside me is finally dead, replaced by a stronger woman.

I should be happy. I am. I withstood the storm.

Then why is it every time I look at the balcony, I hear the sound of the whip in my ears and feel the burning marks of it on my skin?

I contemplate going down and seeing how my father is doing after I left him in his office crying on his knees, but I decide h*e'll get through it,* as he once said.

I stretch, drink some water, and slip under the silk sheets. I wonder if I'll be able to sleep dreamless again. But I can't seem to remove my eyes from the balcony. Remembering old times. Longing for a repeat. Maybe I'll dream of this instead of the nightmares.

When I finally close my eyes an hour later, I'm just about to drift off when a screeching noise makes me jump in my bed. Immediately, my eyes drift to the balcony, an old reflex. I convince myself I'm probably imagining it when two hands grip the balcony, and a male figure jumps over it before landing on his feet.

Well, I'll be damned.

CHAPTER TWENTY-EIGHT

STELLA

The man on my balcony is hidden in the dark, and I can't make out anything of him except his form. I immediately jump from my bed and slip into my slippers, putting a robe over my nightgown. My head is telling me to be smart and call for help, but my heart is somersaulting.

Could this be him? Did he come for me?

Butterflies are doing an insane dance in my belly.

Am I going to run away with him? Am I going to forgive him?

The shadow of the man makes a move toward the closed doors of my bedroom. A throwback of the last time Lucifer climbed to my balcony flashes in front of my eyes.

We had just made love for the first time a couple of hours earlier. I had gone back to my room to clean myself, my thighs still trembling with a new and exciting feeling. There was blood on my pink dress we used as a sheet over the hay, and I had just washed it and put it on the balcony to dry out when Lucifer's hands gripped the railing, and he flung himself over it. I let out a little squeak as I wasn't expecting him. He gripped my face with his callused hands and leaned down to kiss my forehead. His long hair smelled like soap. I made a mental note to remember that smell as if I was subconsciously aware this would be the last time I was going to see him.

He was wearing the white linen V-neck shirt I sewed him for his birthday. He was starting to look like an Italian soap opera actor, all tanned, lean, and gorgeous.

But his eyes were two stormy clouds. Something was worrying him.

"Princess, I need you to promise me something," he told me as he pressed me against the wall.

I nodded, and he caged me with his arms. "Promise me that whatever happens in our lives, you'll always shine the brightest."

"Why do you say that?"

"No reason. Just…promise me you'll never let this cruel world put out the spark in you, my lucky star." He kissed me softly. "I need your light to guide me. Can you do that?"

I promised him and he rewarded me with a deep kiss. A thousand feelings, a million unsaid words caught in a dance between two pairs of lips. A promise to be forever mine, forever his.

The kiss of the death I named it the next day when I saw my home, my heart, in flames on the TV news.

A soft knock comes from the balcony's doors, and I snap out of it. I realize my fingers are touching my lips as if I can still feel Lucifer's kiss on them.

I take a step toward the balcony, my feet and hands shaking, but I stop short when I see the face on the other side.

Marcel. My brother.

I remember him more vividly now when we're in the manor. The last time I saw him I wasn't older than fourteen. He used to come around a few summers for a week only, always alone. He was closer with Lucifer than me. I never paid him much attention because Lou was always around the two of us, shadowing Marcel out of my vision. He was just another gross boy in my book.

I open the doors but block the doorway with my hand. "What are you doing here? I don't want to talk to you."

Marcel raises his hands. "I come in peace. Please, just hear me out."

Squinting my eyes, I hiss at him through a gritted jaw. "Why would I do that? You've been lying to me for months. You probably knew Lucifer was engaged all along." The word stabs through my lungs. *Engaged.*

We used to be engaged at the manor. Lou gave me a paper ring after I beat the shit out of one of the capo's daughters when she said she wanted to play the bride in our next game of wedding.

The woman in the red dress has been living inside of me all this time; I just kept her on a leash, afraid to let her out to play because she might hurt somebody. Just like they've been hurting me all my life.

"I did and I'm sorry. I didn't want you to get hurt, but it wasn't my secret to tell." His blue eyes, so much like my father's, beg me to believe him. Liars. All of them.

"Is that what a nice *brother* would do?" I spit the word in his face, and the shock in his expression is almost audible. This tone doesn't suit *nice* Stella, but she's tired of discovering what newest alive relative has been manipulating her. At this rate I wouldn't be surprised if Mussolini showed up at the doorstep and claimed to be my long-lost cousin.

"Come on, Stells." My eyebrow tics at the nickname my friends call me, and I want to punch him for ruining it for me. He doesn't get the right to call me that. "You haven't heard my side of the story. I promise you I won't waste your time."

"You already are." I start closing the door in his face, but he stops it with his hand.

"I'll get you out of here if you hear me out."

That makes me raise an eyebrow and laugh. "To where? The kitchen? My father's office? No, thank you." I turn around and continue pushing the door with all my strength, but dammit, Marcel is too strong. I can't even move it.

"I'll help you get to Rosehill."

I turn around and plaster my hands on my waist. "Why do you want to help me? And why the hell are you here in the first place? Aren't you Lucifer's soldier toy or something? Seems like backstabbing runs in the genes."

He looks behind him. There's some movement in the yard. I can read the anxiety on his face. "Giovanni…um, Father, placed security in front of your door and the backyard. He'll have my head for what I'm doing right now, but fuck him. You're the only person who's innocent and suffering from this situation and yes, a nice brother would want to help his sister. So, if you let me inside, I might be able to save both our asses."

I sigh, feigning exasperation but internally I'm shaking. Security? My father's treating me like I'm thirteen all over again.

"Fine." I move from the door and let him inside. Because I want out of here. Not because I still secretly like Marcel, and I've always dreamed of a brother like him. "How did you get in h—" I start to ask, but Marcel plasters his hand on my mouth and makes a sign to hush with his finger.

"We have to be quiet," he whispers. "I know the guards routine. We have five minutes to talk, and then we'll have our window to escape."

"Then talk," I whisper back and cross my hands over my chest so he'll know he isn't welcome here. I just don't want to have his death on my conscience, and I wouldn't put it past Giovanni to kill him for helping me escape.

"Remember when I wanted to talk to you at Lucifer's?" he asks and I nod, goose bumps rising on my skin. What I remember from that night is Lucifer's confession that he killed his father and then the way he took me. The way he stole my soul from my body so he could toy with it and make it purr his name in the darkness.

He broke my heart for the millionth time, and I still can't see him as the devil. In my head he's still my fallen angel. It makes my blood boil. He isn't even mine, but my heart doesn't seem to have gotten the memo.

"Your point?" I snap at Marcel, and he shushes me.

"Just a reminder I actually tried to tell you that you're my sister. In case that earns me bonus points."

My jaw relaxes a little. "Did Lucifer know?"

He presses his lips together, and I roll my eyes.

But of course he knew. The lies just keep piling up, and I can feel someone's going to snap soon from all the pressure. I pray for others' sake it's not me. "How long?"

"He's very perceptive. He got it even before I realized Giovanni was my father and not my uncle as my mother used to tell me."

"When was that? When you started visiting your oblivious sister?"

"Actually it was on my seventeenth birthday."

I remember that day. The last time I saw Marcel. We were celebrating his birthday. He's three years older than me so that means my father and my mother were married at the time he was conceived.

"Giovanni saw us kiss, and he thought I was committing incest." I raise an eyebrow but the memory comes to the surface.

We were playing the Suck and Blow game where you had to pass around a card with your lips. Most of the kids in the manor were older than me, but I insisted on joining them in the game just because I didn't want Lucifer to kiss someone else accidentally. Marcel was sitting on the other side of me, and the card fell from my lips so I had to give him a peck. It felt so gross. I immediately turned around and wiped my mouth in Lucifer's shirt. He found it funny that I couldn't give someone else even a childish kiss.

"Of course, I didn't know you were my sister back then. I grew up with my Italian mother in New York. I didn't know Giovanni until I was eight when she introduced him as my uncle and sent me to his "farm." You can imagine my surprise when I saw this luxurious estate. I grew up in a one-bedroom apartment in Brooklyn when it wasn't popular. We barely had money for food and bills most days."

God, I've been such a bitch to him. He grew up poor when I was given everything a kid could possibly imagine in my own kingdom. And he never knew his father until…until my mother passed away. He was eight so that means it was just after she was shot.

I open my mouth to tell him that I'm sorry, but this doesn't change the fact he lied to me, but he stops me.

"Let me finish." He clears his throat and runs a hand through his hair. The same color as my father's. I can't believe I didn't notice it before. He looks so much like him. "We rarely saw Giovanni through the years except for the summers when he came to take me for a week at his farm. Your stepmother hated me in her guts, and I had a feeling something wasn't right, but I didn't want to ask because I didn't want my mother to lose her monthly checks. Although she never used the cash, it put her mind at ease knowing she could save them for college."

"Is she…" I don't know how to say it. Whenever someone speaks of their parents, my mind immediately goes to death. That's what they did to me. Lucifer's father. My father.

"She's alive. I've told her about you, and she'd love to meet you in case you ever forgive me. But I'm not done with the story, and we have only two minutes. Lucifer connected the dots long before Giovanni whipped the crap out of me at my birthday. Lucifer brought me an aloe vera plant to put on my cuts so they wouldn't get infected. I stayed longer than a week that summer until my wounds healed, and then Giovanni escorted me back to my mother and told her that was the last time I stepped foot near my sister. That's how I found out he was my father."

"Oh God." I bite my lip.

"When Lucifer's family moved to New York after the massacre, he reached out to me and we became friends. We went to the same college, and when he took over the reins of Visconti's business, I decided to stay by his side and help him transform his rotten family into something better."

"Well, that explains a lot." I scratch my temple. My head falls into my hands as I try to comprehend all of this and make something of it. I'm a firm believer in second chances. Or I was. Am I? I'm so confused. I know what my mother would have done. She would've welcomed Marcel into the family with open arms, even if he was my father's illegitimate child. The fruit of his betrayal.

I know my parents were married for seven years before my mother conceived me. She once told me she wished upon a shooting star for me, and that's why she named me Stella. Because I was her lucky star. My grandfather was constantly pressuring Giovanni into having an heir before he passed away. My guess is he never recognized Marcel as his own because he truly loved my mother until her last breath.

"Listen, you have to trust me if you want to get out of here." He cuts my flow of thought.

"Why would you stand one minute for Lucifer, then Giovanni, and betray them both the next?"

"It's complicated." He sighs. He probably sees my untrusting stare because he explains, "A week after you got kidnapped and delivered to Lucifer, Giovanni contacted me. I was as surprised as you were that he was alive, but he quickly explained to me that he doesn't want this life for you, and that I need to remove you from Lucifer."

All these mobsters protecting me, and yet I still got kidnapped. Twice. Someone is clearly doing an awful job.

"Giovanni Morelli isn't a man you say no to. At least if you want to keep your head. I didn't mean to betray Lucifer, but I knew he was lying to you about his engagement, so I made my choice to stay alive." He gives me an apologetic half-smile. "There's a war coming, Stells. A big one. Because of you. I'll always choose Lucifer's side, but blood runs thicker where my sister is concerned. I'm not letting you become a casualty in the fight for power." He looks at his watch. "Now would be our time to go."

"But I'm in my nightgown." I look at my silk attire, just now realizing I'm screwing this up.

"I have a car waiting for us. No one is going to see you. Come on." He gives me a hand. I hesitate before I take it.

"Is Lucifer going to be in that car or waiting for us in Rosehill? Did he make you do this?" My heart flutters in my chest, that traitor.

"No," Marcel says hesitantly. He isn't sure if that's what I'm hoping for. Good. Because it's not.

I take a last look at my old home and the memories of my

old life. I'll keep them locked in a room inside my heart to serve as a reminder that I, too, survived in this massacre.

I take Marcel's hand, my only living relative where I'm concerned and the only one who actually made an effort to tell me the truth and ask me what I want. His gratitude for getting a second chance is written on his face. "Lead the way."

CHAPTER TWENTY-NINE

LUCIFER

"Started thinking you wouldn't show up." The smirk on Giovanni's face tells me he was expecting me earlier. I had to make excuses to the people from BFD Group after Stella ran away from her own fashion show. Couldn't let her hard work go to waste because of me.

I remember the first time I stood under the gold arch of Giovanni's door. The nine-year-old had just been torn away from his family yet didn't feel much sorrow. If anything he'd been a bit hopeful that he's been saved from his abusive father and uncle. After he saw the little blonde girl he had a feeling he made a new friend, and he didn't have many of them.

Pussy-whipped *from the very start*, is what Marcel told me after he saw the way Stella and I were. He was my second friend. I hope I'll see the traitor guarding his daddy's manor so I can kill him once and for all.

"So quiet." I break the silence of our stare down. "Like the grave you were supposed to be in."

I had a feeling after the massacre. Giovanni Morelli isn't

a man who gives up easily. He's cunning, ruthless, and smart as hell.

Once upon a time, I actually liked the motherfucker. Behind all the punishments and criticism he felt more like family than my real one because he liked me too. More than his stepsons, more than his second-in-command.

Right in this spot, eight years ago I heard him say the nicest thing that ever left his mouth. *Son, if we live through this, I'm fucking retiring. You have my permission to wed Stellina after her eighteenth birthday.*

He gave me permission to take his throne and his daughter a second before my family barged through the doors of his home. Our home. Hundreds of Visconti soldiers. Our bulletproof vests and AK-47s couldn't keep them down. I killed as many as possible before they captured me and took me to my real father.

There wasn't a doubt in my head that a single man could make it out of this room alive, but I should've known better. Giovanni Morelli isn't just any man.

"You've always had balls. I'll give you that, boy. Come for a bedtime story?"

I take a step inside and shut the door behind me. When I turn around, Giovanni has his don't-fuck-with-me smirk, although it's worn out by the wrinkles around his mouth. "Where is she, old man?"

"Running after the pussy as usual, I see." He chuckles.

"Don't play with me if you want to live to see your grandchildren."

He leans back in his leather chair. "If you were a tougher man, I'd be dead by now. Haven't I taught you anything or you just need a reminder?" He opens a drawer, and I glance at the whip inside it before he shuts it again.

I take the last steps to his desk and lean over it. "Still

trying to scare me off? That's a weak move. You're losing your touch."

His brows furrow. He knows I'm right. "This isn't a game, *Visconti*." He spits out the name I hate almost as much as he does. "I gave you a second chance to live your life. You had one task, only one. Yet you couldn't stay away from my daughter and had to drag her back into our world."

"I'm only going to repeat myself once. Where is she?" I pull out my gun, pointing it at his forehead. Giovanni doesn't waver. "I'm not leaving without Stella."

He raises from his chair, unaffected by the barrel of my gun following his moves, and he slaps a palm over the desk. "Sei un idiota! You started a war. For what? Love? I should've killed you when you were nine. Instead I gave you an opportunity, and this is how you repay me? By bringing every enemy of the Five Families to my little girl's doorstep."

"I was protecting her!" I growl in his face, smacking the desk. Losing my temper in front of the enemy. The worst mistake in the game of power. Giovanni taught me that but as it seems Stella Morelli is capable of making the strongest of men lose their mind.

"I've made peace with my decision. I have the means to fight anyone who comes for her. I won't let a single hair fall from her head." I regain my composure and step back from the table. "With all due respect, sir, I'll stop at nothing to get your daughter back. Even if that means escorting you back to the land of the dead myself."

Much to my surprise, Giovanni grins and sits back in his chair. "And what do you think she's going to become? Your mistress? You've become so blinded by your dreams of escaping this life that you skipped over the details, *son.*" I can count the times he called me that on one hand, and there's always a shit bomb following. "Your family is a joke among the mobsters. The Federoffs tricked you too easily, using my daughter to create a dent in your alliance with the Carters. Do you think Thomas Carter is going to let you walk out alive after disrespecting his daughter?" Giovanni's tone and stare are as serious as a heart attack. He motions for me to sit, and when I don't comply, he shakes his head. "Stubborn as a mule. If you want to live another day, you're going to sit tight and listen to me."

I nod, pretending to buy his show so I could give my guys some more time to clear the hallways before I come for Stella. They should give me the signal any minute now.

"While you were busy trying to wipe the blood off a world that's drenched in it, your enemies were plotting a system to demolish the remainder of your family. You see and hear a lot more when you're living in the shadows, and I've spent eight years hiding like a rat."

He stops, trying to hold down a cough, but it comes out anyway. I can't help but notice his hands trembling every now and then. The years have finally caught up with him.

Giovanni told me that in our world ruled by blood and sacrifice, love is a weakness we cannot afford, but if he didn't love me, I would've been dead by now. It's written in his fatherly advice hidden underneath vague threats. I'm compelled to give him one last chance to secure him a spot in our future life before I write him off completely.

"Sir"—I stare him down—"I've hurt your daughter, and I'll have my whole life to make it up to her, but I need you to listen very carefully to what I have to say." I stand up straight. I've given my guys enough time; they should be done by now. "I had to make a choice once, and I chose you. I've seen you at your weakest at your first wife's grave when you thought no one was following you. I know you've felt what we have once too. I'm giving you the same choice now.

You can have my back, and stay alive to see your grandchildren someday, or you can try to kill me and lose the life you just regained. Either way I'm taking what's mine, and I'm bulldozing anyone in the way."

There's a double tap on the door. Just in time.

"So what's it going to be? Because I have a woman waiting for me to save her, and I ain't wasting any more time."

Giovanni's gaze flicks to the door and back to me. It's been suspiciously quiet for the last few minutes. He must've had a feeling. "Come in," he shouts, trying me.

The door opens. A body of a man, one of his security detail, falls forward on the floor, blood trickling down from his gunshot wound onto the Persian rug.

"And so my path has been cleared." I stand up as Giovanni points his gun at my head. This time I'm the one grinning back at him, knowing I've outdone the teacher. He grits his jaw, realizing it, and I'm willing to bet a small fortune that he's somewhat proud.

Case in point: I am somehow still alive.

My guy shows up, the silencer of his gun pointed at Giovanni. "The hallways are clear, sir, but there's been some complications. A girl with Miss Morelli's description has been seen fleeing to the airport with what is most likely Marcel."

"*What?*" Both Giovanni and I say in unison.

"That's not all. I've gotten news from my guy at the Carters. They're gearing up."

"Told you, boy." Giovanni dares to chuckle, shaking his head. "The Russians played this whole thing out to let you two kill each other, but I haven't given up eight years of my life to let a fucking Federoff take what's mine."

"Then fight with me. I will give you whatever you want,

the Viscontis, the Carters, the Federoffs. All I want is Stella and some fucking peace."

"Now you're talking business." His conniving smile tells me he chose right.

Now where the fuck has that bastard taken my girl?

CHAPTER THIRTY

STELLA

Rosehill is Miami's little sister, prettier and posher. It attracts tourists and celebrities because of its clean beaches, exclusive nightclubs, and fine dining. The houses here are divided into two sections—pretty, neat, white-picket-fence type with a loving family eating dinner at a fixed hour every night, or huge, private, over-the-top mansions where the dinner is served by the staff, and it's usually organic bio kale salad for one because the other members of the family are either out spending what they have left of their divorce, or having brunch and mimosas at the other end of the world with clients or friends.

Obviously, I have no idea what the first one is like. Let me tell you about the second one, though…

Melanie Black's mansion is the epitome of rich. Her husband, Hyland, bought it for her when they got married. He promised her the world and whisked her away from her poor family that had to ask for a loan from him to make ends meet.

One time at the manor, Damien, Rosalie, and I were playing in the hallway when we heard a loud bang from their parents' room. Screaming and cursing followed, and Damien jumped up to cover Rosalie's ears, but he didn't know it should've been her eyes because seconds later a maid ran out the door, half-naked.

I try to forget about the other times for my friends' sake.

First lesson I learned from Aunt Melanie was never ever trust a man.

Second lesson was don't wait on anyone to give you the world. Claim it as yours and work your ass off so you will never be dependent.

Dependency of the prenup she signed is what keeps her married to Hyland even after he turned to his vices—cheap whores and expensive alcohol and drugs—when he couldn't fathom the fact his wife was better in the company's board room than him. She loves that company more than anything in the world.

With her fair skin, piercing green eyes, black bob and stone-cold façade, she is often perceived as a wicked witch. Flawless to a fault and immune to any emotion whatsoever.

She taught us that love is a deceit that messes with the mind to weaken it. I'm not saying she's right, but she isn't wrong either.

Until recent events I used to believe in love like religion. Her advice didn't have much of an impact on me, unlike Rosalie who guards her heart with a fire-breathing dragon and Damien who didn't think love was a necessity until he met Ivy.

Now I see all she wanted to do was protect her children from inevitable heartbreak. The only one who spared a minute to tell us the harsh truths about life.

The taxi stops in front of the iron gate with the B symbol for Black on it.

"Hey." Marcel gets out after me, and I give him a half-smile. "Don't be a stranger. I fucked up, but I never had much of a family. I'd like to get to know my sister someday."

I nod and hug him to hide the tears gathering in my lower eyelids. "Where are you going?" My voice is betraying me.

Marcel pulls away, the same tired look on his face as mine because we couldn't sleep on the airplane. "I'm going back to New York."

"To him?" It hurts too much to pronounce his name out loud.

"I told you, my loyalties lie with him."

"Please, don't tell him where I am."

"After I went through all this trouble to get you out?" He tries to lighten our goodbye with a chuckle. "Just be safe, okay? Keep a low profile for a while."

"Sure." I don't intend on doing anything that doesn't include my old bed and a blanket.

We exchange a polite smile before he drives away from the Gilded Age mansion. Passing around statues and fountains, I make my way to Rosalie's favorite rose garden. I pluck a single white rose and clean it from the thorns on my way to the entrance. It's our thing when I want something from Aunt Melanie.

I expect her to be surprised to see me, but it's me that stumbles and almost falls flat-faced on the floor when I step through the open doors of the dining room.

"Stella, my dear, are you all right?" Melanie's eyes widen, but it's not she who jumps up from her seat to help me. It's the gentleman that I just saw kissing her. I mean, *kissing her? Melanie Black, otherwise known as the Ice Queen.* She's sworn off men since, I don't know, forever?

Something is terribly wrong in this world.

"Here." The man offers me his hand and I take it

cautiously, "Let me help you." He leads me to a chair opposite of Melanie's.

"Thank you. I'm so clumsy." I try to mask my reaction, but Melanie throws me a knowing look.

Oh God, is this color on her porcelain cheeks?

This just turned a million times more awkward. And now I'm curious. A thrill shoots down my spine. I've forgotten how wanting to know the answers feels like. I've been too scared to ask the questions these past weeks.

"I didn't expect you, dear." She straightens up in her chair and flicks a crumb of bread off her black and white Chanel jacket. Fidgeting, that's a new development.

"Auntie"—I mask my smile—"you haven't introduced me to this gentleman." I turn my attention to the blond-haired man wrapped up in a navy shirt and white pants. Good energy radiates off his warm brown eyes and white smile.

I extend my hand to him, expecting a handshake, but he leans over the table and kisses it.

"I'm Stella Morelli." I slip my real last name by mistake, and Melanie and I exchange a look. She winks at me. *Winking*? Did I walk into an alternate universe?

"Nice to finally meet you, Ms. Morelli. Your godmother has told me so much about you." The man brings my attention back to him. "Matt Chandler."

"Has she?" I grin. It's about damn time. "I never thought I'd live to see the day when Melanie Black blushes. Thank you for this pleasure, Mr. Chandler."

"Please, just Matt." He chuckles. "And the pleasure is all mine." He sits back down and gives the ever redder Melanie a kiss on the cheek.

I'm torn between *ewww* and *awww*. "Tell me, how did this happen?"

Last I saw Aunt Melanie, she hated every male species

dead or alive, starting the list with Hyland Black. If she's still living in this mansion, that means he's still her husband, at least on paper. Not that I'm judging her for finding comfort in someone else.

As if reading my thoughts, she twists the wedding band around her finger, biting down on her bottom lip. "There isn't much to talk about. Tell me about you. What brings you here? I thought you'd be nose deep in work after the success of your fashion show."

My goodness, the fashion show! I totally forgot to give Raquel a call; she must have lost her mind when I ran away. My poor career has probably gone down the drain now, along with my contract with BFD Group.

"Umm, things got a little complicated. Can I stay with you for a while?" I swallow back the tears gathering in my eyelids and take a deep breath, aware of the two pairs of eyes focusing on me.

I can see Aunt Melanie's mama-bear instincts turning on. Sometimes family isn't about blood. Impending questions pile in her green eyes.

"Can you excuse us for a minute?" I ask Matt.

He nods and squeezes her hand, whispering something in her ear.

She waits until he's outside. "You can say anything in front of Matt, as long as you're comfortable, sweetheart. He's part of this family now."

I spit my water out on the Persian rug. *Say what now?*

Her brows furrow. "Don't look so shocked. Much to everyone's disbelief, I am capable of love, too."

My face heats up. "I'm sorry, I know you are, but Rosalie and Damien didn't give me a heads—"

She cuts me off with an icy stare. Now, that's more like her. "That's because they don't know yet."

Oh, I'm going to have a field day the next time I see them.

"Don't give me that look, little hellion. Don't you dare tell them before I do."

"I would never." I totally would. Can't wait to see their faces. "Now, about the situation..." There's no easing her into this. "Father is alive."

Melanie chokes on her bite of food, and I jump out of the chair to help her. She spits it out in a cloth napkin and takes a sip of wine before she looks back to me.

"How?" Her face is pale, as if she just saw a ghost.

"Apparently, no one looks for a dead man in his burned manor. Oh, and Lucifer is alive too. I got kidnapped nearly two months ago and delivered to his door by some Russian mob men who are starting a war over me now."

To her credit, she doesn't blink an eye while I tell her the whole story of the shitshow I've been through these months. She asks if I would feel comfortable sharing with Matt. I don't protest when she calls him back into the room. If she's sure enough in his loyalty, who am I to tell her who to trust.

"Over my dead body!" Chills crawl up my arms at her murderous tone. "If you think I'm cold to my children, wait to see what happens to the people who threaten them."

"I can arrange her transfer to LA. They'll never find her in my house." Matt shocks me when he offers his help.

"You'll meet his sons. They're good boys, nothing like that devil your father brought. Heath's in acting now but he used to be in the military, and—"

I cut her off. "Thank you both, but that's enough match-making for me. I'd rather stay home, if that's okay."

"I'm going to kill them and Chanel doesn't go with blood." She's dead serious. I wouldn't doubt she's already strategizing to make it stainless.

Matt takes her hand and places a kiss on it like he did

with me. "Let me make arrangements to double the security, and I'll find you when I'm ready, okay?" He leaves us, exiting through the doors.

Seeing Aunt Melanie looking after Matt with a mix of respect and love makes a beaming smile creep up on me. She's changed. It's not the stiff, straight posture and the poker face anymore. She carries herself to the other side of the table to get me some water like she's stepping on clouds, and a hint of a smile creeps up on her relaxed face.

Who would've known that a man from California would melt the Ice Queen?

She accompanies me to my room and helps me settle in. Everything is exactly the same as I left it years ago, not a speck of dust in sight.

"So, are you going to leave me hanging?" I ask as she tucks me in bed like I'm a kid again.

"If I tell you, you have to promise not to laugh." The woman who condemned love blushes again.

I chuckle, warmth blossoming in my chest, and I sneak a look at my wardrobe. Glittery *S*, *R*, and *D* letters hang on the doors. There's an *L* just like them hidden inside a music box my father gave Rosalie, and she gave to me when he passed away so I'd have something of his.

"Sweetheart?" Aunt Melanie strokes my cheek.

"No one will laugh at your happiness, Auntie." I answer her absentmindedly, staring at the wooden doors of the wardrobe. It seems the past follows me everywhere I go. I should burn it down tomorrow.

"I didn't want to blindside you like this, but Matt and I have been seeing each other since after the Halloween ball last year. He pursued me for quite some time before I gave in and granted him an hour of my time."

"How generous of you!" I tease.

She shakes her head and sighs. "It's odd, right? Maybe I'm just fooling myself."

Aunt Melanie not sure of something? This gets my attention.

"Stop it. It's amazing. You deserve someone strong enough to take the burden off your shoulders, but what about Hyland? The company?"

"I don't know. I'm"—a gracious smile lights up her face—"in love. For the first time in thirty years. And I'm a grandmother now. I want to spend some quality time with my family, including Matt. If that means I don't get to work in Hyland's company, then so be it."

Ah Dio, poor Ivy. She'll have the time of her life when she finds out her mother-in-law wants to spend more time with her.

"Enough about me. Get some rest, there's a big day ahead of you tomorrow."

"Huh?"

"Ivy's bachelorette. I thought that's why you came today? Damien is leaving for Vegas tonight, and I'm taking little Devora with me tomorrow."

A wave of guilt washes over me. This is the first time I've thought of my friends. It's only been me, me, me. I left Rosalie to plan my best friend's bachelorette on her own.

"I'll need a phone in the morning, Auntie." I try to sit up in the bed, but Melanie pushes me down.

"Don't worry about a thing, dear. Your godmother is always here to save the day. Now, get your beauty sleep."

It isn't long before I close my eyes, and tonight I sleep dreamlessly.

CHAPTER THIRTY-ONE

STELLA

Raquel shrieks on the phone pressed against my ear. "Tell me where you are or I'm going to kill you. Actually, you're dead either way, so you might as well save me the stalker time."

I chuckle, and Aunt Melanie's driver smiles at me from the rearview mirror on our way to the party. Apparently, he's never seen me scowl before, and he expressed his worry, asking if I was sick or something when I got into the car. I am, though not in the way he thinks. I'm sick of everyone's bullshit.

"Oh, so now you're laughing at me?" Raquel continues her rant. "You should be grateful I saved your ass and we still have a job. Well, the fact that both collections sold out the next day helped me, too, but I'm expecting a raise and a tropical vacation, expenses on the company."

"You got it. Somewhere far, far away."

"I know what you're trying to do, but you'll meet my wrath sooner or later. You're not getting rid of me that easily."

"I love you, too. Gotta go, babe. See you soon."

"Don't you dare hang up on…"

I tap the red button before she guilt-trips me into telling her my location. I'm not scared of her wrath. Okay, maybe just a teeny tiny bit. She's boarding the next flight to Madagascar whether she objects or not. I can't afford to let her end up between the bullets. Lord knows what's cooking up in New York or Sicily right now.

"We're here." The driver opens my door, and I realize we stopped a minute ago, but I didn't bother looking out the windows.

As soon as my heels hit the pavement, a blond, muscular man in nothing more than bunny ears, a bowtie, and a thong hands me a glass with pink liquid.

"Welcome to Ivy's Bachelorette Party. A complimentary *cock*tail." He winks at me, flashing a cute boyish smirk.

"Oh, no, she did not!" My worst fear has become a painful reality as a penis straw stares at me from the cocktail glass in my hands.

I snort out a laugh when another mostly naked guy runs outside, the words *Slap me!* written on his tight bottom cheeks.

"Oh, yes, she did!" Rosalie says from the other side of the yard.

Crap. I gulp down the *cock*tail when I see her power-walking in six-inch heels and bright-pink bikini, and I shove the glass at the man bunny, getting ready to flee, but it's too late; she's already reached us.

"I would've beaten your ass for ghosting me if I didn't think bruises and swimsuits don't go together. Speaking of which, why aren't you in a swimsuit?" She takes a shot from the other man bunny and tips it back before she makes the last step to me and hugs me, whispering, "I'm killing you for keeping the truth from me."

"Get in line." I titter.

There's pain in her voice when she leans in closer to my ear. "Mamma told me everything. I'm so sorry I didn't figure it out sooner."

"Don't worry, I'm home now," I whisper back, my voice shaking.

Rosalie squeezes me one last time and lets me go before taking two more shot glasses of tequila. "Enough with the feels, already. Cheers." The man bunny offers his hand with salt before we tip them back. Rosalie's eyes flash with mischief as I shove the piece of lime into my mouth. "Jesse, why don't you show my girl here what we do with people who don't follow the rules in cock world?"

"Did you just call it…"

"Gladly," Jesse says at the same time, smirking, and hands his ears to Rose.

My eyes widen as his arms wrap around me, and he throws me over his shoulder. "No, no! You're dead, Rose!" I shriek.

Rosalie yells after me. "Damien went to Vegas so I brought Vegas to Ivy. Ain't I the best sister-in-law or what?"

Jesse chuckles as he runs through the backyard, carrying me like I don't weigh a thing and in between my screams and Rosalie's booming laughter, I hear Ivy say, "Stells?" right before Jesse leaps off the ground and splashes us both into the pool.

When I emerge to the surface, Rosalie is leaning over the edge with the same devilish smirk her brother and mother have. "This is not a regular party. This is a cool party."

Another man bunny offers me a hand, grinning from the edge of the pool. I pretend to take it as I reach with the other hand for Rosie's ankle and pull it.

Her scream pierces everyone's ears as she stumbles and jumps over me into the pool.

"You bitch!" Her scream makes me topple over as she stumbles around the pool. I climb out of the pool before she actually drowns me in a catfight.

First person I see is Ivy, chatting up with Layla, her Bulgarian childhood friend, and some girls I've never seen. I sneak behind her and wrap her in a hug. She squeals when the wet fabric of my dress connects with her heated body, and she whips around. "Stells!"

Rosalie is next to follow, hugging me from behind and making the three of us fall forward. We roll on the grass and laugh until our bellies hurt, and for the first time in forever, I feel lighter than air. Turns out Ivy doesn't know most of the women here as they're Rosalie's friends from L.A. since we don't have many outside of our circle.

A few hours and a lot of pink drinks later, I find myself leaning in a chair, discussing this summer's fashion trends with a socialite from L.A. whose name I can't remember.

My eyes scan the crowd of women playing some bachelorette game and focus on a new person arriving late to the party.

"Tiana?" I have a hard time believing what I'm seeing. "What in the hell?" I jump up from my chair, leaving the socialite hanging as I run to Rosalie, who's having a dance-off with a bunny. I grab her by the arm. "What is *she* doing here?"

Rosie breaks eye contact with her opponent to see where I'm looking and yell in her direction, "Carter, get your ass here to meet the best designer in the world." She winks at me and says, "You're welcome!" As Jesse and some other guy lift Rosie off the ground and put her in the throne Ivy was just sitting at so they could give her a lap dance.

"Yay, woo-hoo," Ivy cheers when they bring Rose onto the stage. She's so drunk she joins them in the dancing, pretending to ride Rose's lap. Rosalie's friends are taking photos and videos of the scene as everyone else, including Ivy's colleagues from Masquerade, are busy dancing or playing penis-shaped Jell-O shots games with the rest of the boys.

No one seems to notice the rug being pulled from underneath my feet once again. Tiana Fucking Carter is staring at me from the other side of the yard. She nods to the door as if she wants me to follow her. Is this some joke?

I can't escape my past wherever I go. I just wanted a day without the reminder of how many people lied to me. A day with my girls who would never do that..

A feeling I don't often let get to me takes the reins in my alcohol-infused mind. White blinding rage lights my body up like a torch.

Hell to the no!

I get up from my chair, my shaky legs leading me toward the door where Tiana just exited, when an actress friend of Rosalie's vomits on the ground next to me. Gagging sounds and laughter come out of the girls near her. Thankfully, this will make my exit less noticeable.

It just occurs to me that for the first time in months, my reaction to a gut-punching moment wasn't vomit gathering in my throat. The corners of my mouth curl as I step on the other side of the door, prepared for a gun pointing at me, but what I see doesn't exactly make my Jackie Chan fantasies kick in.

Tiana's sitting on the ground against the wall, tugging the corners of her floral Dolce & Gabbana dress.

I wrap my arms around my middle, bracing myself for some kind of a trap. Even sitting she looks taller than me. I bet she can beat my ass too. She has those perfectly toned arms and sculpted body that suggests she does a three-times-a-week boxing class with New York's finest trainer and works her ass off in the gym the rest of the time. It's definitely a guess, not that I've internet-stalked her or anything. But you know, sometimes in fights it's not about the strength. It's about who's angrier and more desperate.

"He's the only reason my heart's beating, you know?" she says so softly I almost think I'm imagining.

"Lucifer?" Saying his name feels like a jab in the ribs.

She looks at me, and there's unshed tears in her eyes, balancing on her eyelids. "The guy that was with me at Lucifer's. Sebastian Federoff."

I blink twice, unable to comprehend what Sebastian Federoff has to do with everything.

She taps the ground next to her and sighs. "I thought you might be the only one to understand."

"To understand what?" I shorten the distance between us, but I decline her offer to sit. For all I know, I'm expecting a knife in my back any second now.

"Why I did it. I couldn't let you ruin everything I've protected for years."

"Are you drunk? How long have you been here?" I notice the slurring of her words, the redness in her eyes. I'm pretty sure she just arrived when I saw her.

She taps the ground again but looks me straight in the eyes this time. There's no menace there. Just simple pain. Something I'm accustomed to.

"Father will find us wherever we escape to. He's just going to kill Sebastian, I know it." When she gets the memo I won't be sitting next to her, she gives up. "Thomas loves me, you know. He just doesn't understand. He'd rather die than see me with our mortal enemy. But Sebastian is the air I breathe, the blood in my veins, the heart beating in my chest. He's everything but we can't be anything."

"Why are you telling me this?"

"Because I know you're the same to Luci, and he doesn't deserve to suffer like I do."

I finally give up and sit next to her. "He's still marrying you."

"Luci only agreed to this engagement to protect me. He let us meet in his house and covered for me whenever I needed him to. He never thought he'd see you again, but then Sebastian's family kidnapped you, and everything changed. You have to understand. My father would've wed me to someone else already if Luci hadn't stalled him."

"What's done is done, Tiana. He made his choice."

She surprises me when she rests her head on my shoulder. "He told me everything about you. I knew you'd understand what it's like having your life played out in front of your own eyes by someone else's desires. I even dreamed we could be friends." A little sigh falls out of her lips. "I don't have many."

There's a moment of silence as I can't bring myself to say anything. If I do, I might forgive her, and I'm not ready to let go of my anger, because what would I have then? Just a shattered heart and a broken soul.

In a few beats I manage to voice out the crucial question. "Are you still going through with the wedding?"

She lifts her head, wipes her tears with the back of her hand, and hugs her knees to her chest. "Nothing has changed. I just…"

I jump to my feet, the blood in my veins going from simmering to boiling in a second. "Then why did you come here? To find sympathy from the woman whose man you stole? To clear your conscience?"

She buries her head in her knees. "I know I'm an awful person. Sometimes I wish Sebastian would just kill him like Lucifer killed his father to protect you."

"*What?*" My question echoes in the empty hallway.

"You didn't know?" She sounds genuinely surprised. "I'm sorry, I didn't want to…"

I knew he did it but my part in all of this was new information.

"You did and you will. Want my forgiveness? Explain."

She relaxes a bit, letting go of her knees. "Luci's father found out you were alive and sent his soldiers after you. Luci, Sebastian, and I did a good job of handling them but in the end Angelo decided to finish the job himself. Luci did what he had to in order to keep you safe."

I swear I can hear her heels smacking into the shattered pieces of my heart like ornament balls.

"Oh, there you are!" Ivy's voice startles us, and we both get to wiping what's left of our tears just before she comes closer. Thankfully, she's too drunk to feel the waves of tension in the air. "I don't know you." She points to Tiana and chuckles. "Are you a friend of Stella's?" She tries to butt-smack me but she misses, and I catch her before she falls down on the floor.

She straightens up and smiles lazily, waiting for an answer. Tiana stands up from the floor, silent.

"If she doesn't marry Lou we could be," I mutter.

I understand her situation, I really do. And dammit, even now, I feel bad for her. But I'm only human. Everyone has put me on a pedestal as this pure, nice creature, but I've never been any of these things. I just make the choice every day when I wake up to be a better person than yesterday. Not today, though. Today, I'm jealous and I'm bitter, and I can't find it in myself to forgive when she's taking away the only thing I've wanted more than anything else in the world.

"*Whaaat?*" Ivy slurs, and I'm thankful for the booze because I don't have it in me to explain to anyone right now. "Never mind, I don't know most of the people at this party. Just grab a drink and ride a bunny. Or let a bunny ride you."

"Okay, now." I grab her by the shoulders and swivel her toward the bedrooms. "Time to get some beauty rest."

"Bye, girl." She waves to Tiana over her shoulder as I drag her along the hallway. "Oh, and thank you for coming."

CHAPTER THIRTY-TWO

LUCIFER

I knock on Damien Black's door like a fucking delivery guy or something. There's no sound from inside, so I repeat the motion, getting more impatient by the second. I knock a third time, harder and louder, my fists hurting with the need to smash through the glass door.

"Coming!" The low grumble of an angry woman's voice comes from inside, then I see Damien's woman, Ivy, marching toward the glass doors, a scowl on her face.

"Do you have a death wish?" she growls through gritted teeth, opening the door.

Leave it to Damien Black to find the hottest chick with the craziest temper.

"My only wish is to find Stella."

"Tough luck. You're dead to her. This time for real." Ivy tries to close the glass door in my face, but I push my foot stopping it.

"Ivonne, I'm not fucking around." Her jaw flexes when I use her real name. "I come in peace, but I won't hesitate to barge in and find her myself if you don't cooperate."

"Are you threatening me?" She narrows her eyes at me

and steps on my side of the door, straightening her spine. "I'll give you five seconds to leave my property before I call security."

"Lucifer, what the fuck are you doing here bothering my wife?" Damien's amused voice comes from behind me. I swivel around to see him locking an Aston Martin before aiming that billion-dollar-heir gait our way, carrying a Louis Vuitton luggage bag with the fucking careless smirk he left his mother's womb with.

"Fiancée," Ivy corrects him.

He drops the bags to the ground. "Keep saying shit like that, baby, and I'll haul your ass back to Vegas to change that real quick."

Ivy rolls her eyes, but the second he wraps her in a hug and lifts her off the ground, she melts in his hands.

"Not to be a killjoy, but I'm a man on a mission. Stella's location. Now."

Damien drops her to the ground carefully and swivels toward me with a glare that could give the scariest men on earth a run for their money.

"What have you done this time?" He doesn't know. I might have a chance at surviving this suicidal mission.

"Your *fiancée* can give you the deets later." I turn to face her. "Location. Now."

"Lower your voices, both of you. I'm nursing a headache from hell, and if you wake up my baby girl, I swear to God…" Just before she finishes her murder threat, a baby's piercing cry rings through the house. "Never mind." She charges toward me, flinging a fist at my face, but Damien catches her around the waist before it connects with my jaw.

"Calm down, baby." He restrains her, carrying her body kicking in the air toward the house. "Have you slept?"

"Barely two hours. I wanted my baby as soon as I woke

up, and I took her from Melanie, but she's having colic." Ivy actually whimpers at the end. It kind of makes me feel bad for waking her baby up. I can't even blame her for wanting to tear my eyes out. When Stella and I have a baby...

Whoa-whoa. Hold up. What?!

Am I fucking delusional now? I can't bring a baby into my cruel world. That's if Stella ever forgives me. Or if her father doesn't kill me before she does. Or if our enemies don't get to me first.

Damn, that's a lot of ifs.

"I'm sorry I left you." Damien cuts off my line of thought as he walks Ivy to the room she came from.

Fuck him, too, getting it all with the family and the happiness and the freedom.

"Go get our girl, and I'll be with you in a second. I caught some sleep on the flight, so she'll be with her dada while mommy's taking a nap." Damien's voice is soft when he opens the door for her, and she mouths the words *I love you* before she disappears inside.

Damien comes back to the door where I'm still standing. I was expecting a blow to the face or even a kick to the nuts, but all he grants me is a cold stare. In his eyes I can see the bullshit he just sold Ivy. He hasn't had a drop of sleep.

"I'm fucking tired of you breaking my sister's heart," he says matter-of-factly. I am still, eight years later, having a hard time believing he never saw Stella as anything more than a sister. But then again, Stella was mine from the moment I laid eyes on her.

He sighs, rubbing his palms over his tired eyes. "As it is, I know a thing or two about arranged marriages." He rubs his forehead. So the motherfucker knew all along. And yet he hasn't swung his fist my way once. Hope finds its way inside my lungs, filling me like the oxygen I breathe in. "The only reason I'm helping you is because Stella did the same for me. She's at my mother's," he says reluctantly. "But make no mistake, you hurt her again, and you're a goner. This is your last warning. Make things right or you won't live to see your arranged bride at the other end of the aisle." He actually does a better impression of a mobster than most of my Visconti cousins.

"Thank you." I nod, not feeling the usual hate I do toward him. "Apologize to your fiancée for me."

He glares at me. "Fuck off before I change my mind."

I chuckle, raising my hands and shaking my head. I make my way to Melanie's. Surprisingly, I don't have any trouble getting on the premises even with a load of security. A person would think the billionaire family would spend a little more on safety.

Rain is pouring like a waterfall while I contemplate my original plan of breaking in and kidnapping Stella as the ground sinks beneath my boots on my way through the court. I don't even know where I'm going.

"May I help you?" A woman's grave voice stops me in my tracks. A voice I can't forget no matter how much time has passed. The rain beats on the bare skin of my arms mercilessly as I swivel around to see Melanie Black standing under an open umbrella with a cigarette in the other hand. A cigarette that looks suspiciously a lot like a blunt before she hides it in her small hand. Flawless as ever, in her signature Coco Chanel style, not a straight black hair daring to curl from the humidity.

"I need to see Stella."

"Ah." Her lips twitch. "I was expecting you."

For a second there before she answered, I wondered whether she remembered me. The Ice Queen was a regular visitor at the manor, and she wasn't exactly known to be over-friendly. Yet, she had a soft spot for me. I don't know if it was because I was courting her favorite niece. Or because I was the only person who didn't look at her with pity when she caught her husband sneaking out of a different maid's room every morning. Nevertheless, she always brought gifts for me, too, when she came to visit, and it made Giovanni's stepsons furious.

"Beg your pardon?"

"Damn straight you should be begging." She drags her eyes from my muddy boots to my soaked T-shirt, and she gives me one of her rare smirks—the absolute exact one Damien was born with—when her eyes reach my face. I brush the curly strand of fallen hair from my face.

Melanie Black was also the last person I saw before I went to my own execution. I was out on a job for Giovanni in Rosehill, leaving on his private jet that had just landed Stella in Melanie's custody, and she was situated in a car on the other side of the airport. The rusty metal in my chest squeezed when I realized I'd never see Stella again as she was already traveling in another car. A single tear escaped me as I stopped before Melanie, who was waiting for instructions from me. For a second there her poker face changed into... hell, I don't know what...grief? Pity? She reached out to me and pulled me into her arms, hugging me tightly, like (I can only imagine) a mother would do. She gave me something I never knew.

"Listen to me, Lucifer. You and me, we're the same. We are the lone wolves of this world. The warriors. There's no one to fight our battles for us." She let me go and drew back. "So go there and fight. And win. Because when all of this is over, you have a prize to redeem. And she'll be waiting for you forever."

I wondered what she meant that we were the same, and

on the flight home I deciphered it. Melanie came from a poor family. She had the brains of a genius, the vintage look of a Hollywood actress, and she stood taller than any man I've seen in the manor. But inside, she was still the poor little girl whose parents gave her away for money, even if it was to secure her future. And maybe that's why she liked me. Because I was still that boy inside.

"I got it, sugar. Let's light that bitch up." A blond man shows up, breaking through my flashback moment in nothing but a pair of swimming trunks and an umbrella, waving a lighter in the air.

They were going to get high and it's barely noon. In the middle of a storm. How fucking romantic.

He stops when he sees me. "Who the hell are you?" His body is decent for a man looking in his sixties, judging by the gray hairs on his chest and the wrinkles on his face.

"Leave my premises before I have security escort you out," Melanie deadpans.

The blond dude steps in front of her protectively and crosses his arms. "You heard the lady."

"Glad to see you've missed me, Mel." I smirk. "You haven't introduced me to your pot friend."

Her face flames up as she glances between the two of us. Thankfully, she recovers quickly just as I start to fear she's having a heart attack or something.

"You lost the war, Lucifer. Admit defeat and back off gracefully before you cause my niece another ugly scene."

"I'm afraid this isn't going to happen." I shrug. Lightning splits the sky, and the rain intensifies. Water is dripping from my hair as my clothes stick to my skin, cold and uncomfortable. Just like Melanie's silent stare.

She snaps her fingers and opens her mouth, probably to yell for security, but before she can, the blond dude comes a step closer to me, now invading my personal space. "Boy, you disrespected my woman's request once, and she ain't gonna ask twice. I suggest you leave before I haul your ass outta here."

Despite the uneventful turn of events, a smile graces my lips. "You've found your warrior, ma'am." Melanie's lips tug at the corners. This is more emotion I've seen on her face in ten minutes than I have in ten years. "I'll see myself out but I'll be back."

The man raises a mocking eyebrow. "Is this a threat, Visconti?" Good. He knows who I am, and he isn't afraid to stand up for her.

"More like a promise." I salute him and the Ice Queen, whose kingdom is apparently melting, while I'm walking my way backward to the gates. "I've lost this battle, Mel, but the war is still up for grabs, and I have a prize to collect."

It might be my body freezing or my dimmed vision, but I think I see a smile rising on Mel's face as I exit through the door. Good Lord. There's someone on my side. Did hell just freeze over?

CHAPTER THIRTY-THREE

STELLA

I run my fingers through the soft petals of a yellow rose. The sun has finally forged its way through the angry clouds that dominated the entire morning. A couple rain drops slide from the velvet petals to my skin.

Raquel announces in the phone. "I need you back. Our partners are asking questions and making subtle threats. The assistant called to see if you got lost on the way to their office and briefly suggested you might get lost forever."

A tremble shakes my fingers, the water gathered in the center of the rose splashing.

"Don't worry. I'll be with you soon." I sigh, dropping my head back and closing my eyes. I take a deep breath, enjoying the rays of sunshine, fresh air, and the song of the birds before I have to return to polluted, noisy New York again.

"Promise me you'll come straight to me."

"Do I have anywhere else to go?" I catch myself mumbling out loud.

"There are rumors swirling around."

"What rumors?" I open my eyes too quickly, the sun blinding me. I squeeze them shut, expecting to hear the worst.

"Just get here as fast as you can, and everything will be back to normal soon," she says before we end the conversation.

If she knew how far from the truth that is... Nothing will be normal again. Nothing has ever been.

Even the refreshing smell of roses and freshly chopped grass can't stop the thoughts of my impending, doomed fate. Returning to New York is like signing my own death sentence. I might as well start writing my farewell letter right now.

There's the Federoffs lurking in one corner. Then there are the furious Carters on the other; though, I'm not sure if they want my head or Lucifer's. After that it's my father who by now must've torn his focus off his world-domination plans for a minute to realize I've been missing for two days. And then there's the biggest threat of them all. The one who broke my heart like none of my enemies' bullets could.

Happy thoughts Stell...

"Ahhh!" I shriek, opening my eyes when something wraps around me from behind. "Who are y—" My scream gets lost as a hand covers my mouth.

Hot breath coats my ear as it whispers with a painfully familiar voice, "Don't scream. It's me."

My eyes widen as I realize who's holding me hostage. The man that has never let me go.

He drops his hands, and I swivel around. "What are you doing here? How did you get past security?" I look around, seeing a security detail from the new company Matt called this afternoon walking around, patrolling the area around the mansion, far away from the rose garden and the maze.

Lucifer rounds the bench and stands in front of me, hiding the sun from my sight.

I'm speechless, mouth agape, as I stare at him. Tanned,

topless body, corded with muscles and tattoos stretching like a second skin. He's barefoot, in simple black sport shorts, his dark wavy hair ruffled, falling to his shoulders. A vision. An angel with the looks of a devil. I reach out to touch him to confirm that I'm not, indeed, going insane, but he grabs my hand before it connects with the bare skin of his abdominals and crouches at my feet.

"Princess, let me explain." His jaded eyes beg me. He doesn't look to have slept a minute since I left him. My instincts want me to pull him onto the grass and chase away his demons so he can close his eyes and rest, but the new voice in my head is clawing its way to the surface, making me turn my head to the right, avoiding his gaze.

"I don't want to see, hear, or have anything to do with you." I rise to my feet, folding my arms under my chest.

Lucifer grabs my calf before I have the chance to jump over him and escape. "You don't understand."

I twist my head around to make sure he sees the smile on my face. "Oh, but I do. Your fiancée made sure to let me in on the details." His astonished face makes me huff out a laugh. "Here's my early RSVP." I flip him off and pull my leg from his grip.

I manage to jump over his thigh and make a single step before he grabs me in his hands and twists me around. His face is so close to mine I can feel his breath sliding over my lips. "I called it off."

The audacity he has.

"A bit too late, don't you think?"

"We were never supposed to meet each other. I foolishly thought I could let you go and spent five years postponing the wedding before our paths collided again."

"So what now? You came here to profess your adoration for my persona as a farewell?"

"No, I came to tell you I'm keeping you, whatever it takes." His mouth crashes against mine, hot and desperate.

I love how sure he is of himself. The alpha male. The leader of the pack. Good thing he's in for a surprise.

I pull away, smirking. "You can't keep me if I don't want to be kept."

"Oh but I can." His arms sneak around me, and he hurls me on his shoulder. He slaps my butt and continues, "You know you will never love another man, princess. Spare us the excruciating time apart. Let me love you in the only way I know how."

A laugh escapes me. "You still don't get it, do you?"

"Get what?" he says as he jumps through a bush, looking around for the guards.

"Security!" I yell as loud as I can, and the two men behind his back twist their heads. They focus on us and start running, pulling out guns.

"Drop her or we'll shoot," one of the men says as Lucifer freezes and turns around slowly. I use the opportunity to jump back from his grip and almost land on my ass but somehow manage to keep my balance.

"Don't do this to me. To us. I'll always come back for you," Lucifer says, raising his hands in the air as the two men step in front of me, their guns pointing at his head.

"I'm done with men trying to control my life. I'm not your princess. I'm a queen, a monarch of my own fate." I blow him an air kiss as the men take his arms and twist them behind his back.

A ghost of a smile rises on his face. "You've always been my queen. And I will always be your mere servant."

The men take him by the arms, leading him toward the gates.

Watching him get taken away from me once again breaks the last remaining piece of my heart.

"Maybe we'll meet again in the next life."

"Don't count on it, mi amor. I'm coming for you in this one if I have to fight the whole world, including you."

His lazy grin stretches as he keeps watching me, even as the guards throw him handcuffed into a jeep and the impossible happens. I hear the shattered parts of my heart moving around and gluing together one by one. And dammit, not even Stella 2.0 can stop it. She doesn't even try.

CHAPTER THIRTY-FOUR

STELLA

"That little bitch sold us out," Raquel says as she wraps me in a warm embrace at the JFK arrivals.

"I'm happy to see you, too." I smile against her hair and take a sniff of her scent before I let her go. I've missed this so much. Just the two of us conquering the fashion world. "The assistant is keen on being a bitch, isn't she?" I ask, grabbing my small suitcase of belongings Aunt Melanie bought for me since she wouldn't let me out after Lucifer's breach.

"The one and only," Raquel squeaks out next to my ear and for a minute, I'm pretty sure I go deaf as the gazes of everyone in a thirty-feet perimeter turn our way. "I should've set up that goody-two-shoes with a man or a woman or whatever she's into. I could tell by her dirty glasses that she's in a desperate need of a good fuck."

She and I both, sis.

When we climb into a taxi, she fishes a small planner from her purse. "We have a meeting with the big bosses at four. You couldn't have picked a better day to arrive and save us."

"Jury's still out on that. If they're as pissed as the assistant said, we might get the boot either way." I sigh, looking out the window at Queens. Last time I arrived, I didn't have time to enjoy the view since Lucifer had me pressed against the door of the town car as he plunged inside me.

My face flames up in the window reflection.

It wasn't what I would've done, knowing there's a driver on the other side of the partition. That's what he did to me. He destroyed the last piece of innocence I had left, and without him I wouldn't have become the woman I am today.

My feelings are complicated. He tried to cage me like everyone else, yet he let me free.

I'd like to hate him, but my heart beats in his chest forever. Even if he dragged me down to hell with him, I'd burn in the fire as long as I was in his arms.

Raquel's chatter in the background slowly registers as we enter the Queens Midtown Tunnel. "...and the Insta-twins loved your designs so much they asked for a collaboration. Can you believe it?"

"That's great," I mumble, still looking out the window.

A hand presses against my thigh. "You weren't listening, were you?"

I turn to face her, the corners of my mouth twisting downward. "No, sorry."

"So how much of what I heard was true?" Her face is full of sympathy.

"Depends on the source."

"Just rumors, swirling around the models claiming to have witnessed a scandal."

I plaster a hand to my forehead as I sigh. "Better get used to it, huh? Nothing stays hidden in the spotlight."

"Not when you're dating an underground boss who's engaged to the highest-paid model of the year."

"Was. I was." I whimper, inwardly swearing at myself. This is not Stella 2.0 material. People can only change so much in three days.

"Damn, I could've sworn Lucifer looked pretty smitten."

"Can we change the subject?" I close my eyes, trying to stop the tears pushing from inside.

Silence falls upon us, something incredibly unusual for Raquel, and that's how I know she loves me as much as I love her. A few blocks more and the taxi comes to a halt in front of the apartment building in Mid-Manhattan. Seeing as Ivy's parents are still MIA, she let us use her old apartment.

Under the scorching hot water of the shower, it dawns on me what exactly I've been feeling since I stepped off the plane. Disappointment. Some part of me was expecting to see Lucifer make good on his promise to come back for me, despite everything. I make sure to take my sweet time drowning that feeling.

I have to get my head in the game for the meeting, seeing as my future is the only thing no one can take away from me if I work hard enough, which I haven't for the past few days. Raquel comes back with a bag of Japanese food from the restaurant at the corner, and we eat while rehearsing the story about my sudden disappearance, how much we value our partners, and other butt-kissing speeches that are going to grant us at least a consideration before they kick us to the curb.

A few hours later, as we climb into a taxi, I find my stomach twisting into knots even in the absence of my vomit reflex.

As we glide through the streets buzzing with traffic, I

come to the realization the tall buildings aren't as formidable as I thought they were. I used to be repulsed by the urbanization of it all as a person who lived around greenery and the beach all her life. Somewhere along the way, I got familiar with the absurdity of these streets. I mean, we just passed a homeless guy sitting against the wall of an office building that makes billions a year. This city sneaks up on you when you least expect it.

My eyebrows rise as the driver comes to a halt in front of the gates of a private property. "I didn't expect the meeting to be in a mansion," I tell Raquel, who's been going through my sketches and picking her favorites to be shown to the bosses.

She raises her head, and her eyes bulge. "Holy mother of Thor! What are we going to do?" She reaches for the handle tentatively.

"We're going to waltz inside like we own this beauty and blow their heads off." I practically push her out of the cab as I pay the driver. I take a deep breath and make the first step. We ring the bell and wait for a minute before a maid opens the door.

"Can I help you?" she asks with a tight smile.

Raquel shifts beside me. "We're here for the BFD Group meeting."

I kick her shoe. "Excuse our poor manners." I extend my hand. "Stella Morelli."

The maid gasps, staring at me. "There must be a mistake, I'm sorry." Her Italian accent is barely recognizable. She backs off, closing the door when a bulky man in a black tailored suit appears, sliding his hand onto the handle.

"I'll take the girls from here."

My gut stirs into tighter knots.

Raquel's the first to speak, ogling him like a steak,

ignoring the fact that there's an edge to his rough face that doesn't match the industry type. "We were starting to fear we got lost." She giggles. "We talked on the phone with your assistant, I presume, Mr...."

He leaves her question hanging in the air, staring at me like the maid did. I make a mental note to excuse myself to the powder room and check if there's something on my face.

"Anyways..." Raquel drawls, sounding frustrated that he completely ignored her presence, and I squeeze her hand, reminding her we're not here to mingle but to try to save our jobs.

"I'm sorry to keep you waiting, sir, but now that we've finally met, I can show you why we're worth the investment." I repeat my rehearsed line. He snaps like he was in a trance, blinking.

"I'm not the man you should be apologizing to. Follow me." He beckons us.

I sigh in relief because this was starting to take an awkward turn and give Raquel a pointed look to turn that frown around.

We step through the threshold into an all-gold designed foyer. It's intrusive, two golden warrior statues, dripping chandeliers, and a pyramid of gold bars in the center. The bells in my head ring: *money complex.*

The man who didn't introduce himself has a frown creasing his forehead, rushing us through the hallways. We stop in front of a door. "He's expecting you."

"Mr. Maurizio?" Raquel asks, her tone shaky.

This setting doesn't remind me anything of the interviews we've watched about Mr. Maurizio, the CEO of BFD Group. We haven't met him, but he seemed like a simple man, less of a show-off for all the billions he has.

The door swings open.

"Call me Hugo," a man with a thick Italian accent says behind a cloud of cigarette smoke and sunglasses. "We have a meeting and you're late. Get your pretty asses inside."

Raquel and I exchange looks that say the same thing. This is not the CEO. We've never seen this man.

The door clicks shut behind us, and we're left in a study similar to the foyer with gold-plated everything. There's another door at the other end of the room. Raquel clutches my hand, and I can feel the discomfort oozing out of her.

"Please…" Hugo gestures toward an oil green couch with a gold frame.

She looks at me as we take a seat, and I know what she's thinking. We didn't do our research beyond the most important figures in BFD, and we don't know any Hugos. From the Patek Philippe on his wrist and the Brioni suit, to the Cuban cigar between his fingers, this Hugo seems like the one calling the shots.

Maybe he's a silent investor? But why would he meet with us?

Dammit! I should've taken more time to do research instead of running after Lucifer.

"Can I just say how honored we are to be a part of BFD Group, sir." I break the uncomfortable silence when he sits on the opposite armchair. The smell of alcohol and stale air makes me scrunch my nose, and I quickly cover it with some babbling. "As I said to the man who greeted us, I'm so terribly sorry for my disappearance at the—"

A banging noise comes behind the wall to our left, startling me, and our heads swing in that direction.

Hugo turns back to us and says, "Is that why you think you're here?"

"Well, yes. Your assistant was pretty adamant that you—"

His deep, throaty laugh cuts me off. He shakes his head

and takes a sip from a crystal glass filled with brownish liquor. "You're here for an entirely different purpose, Miss Stellina. Do you mind if I call you that?" He smirks.

I shift in my seat. "I'd prefer just Stella."

"We could start by showing you the ideas for the new collection, perhaps, Mr...." Raquel leaves the question hanging as we still don't know his last name.

"Perhaps." He imitates her tone, sitting back, relaxed and avoiding the question.

It bugs me that I can't see where his eyes are looking because I can swear on everything holy that they're drilling a hole in me.

Raquel and I, both dive in to take the file with the sketches. I start taking out sketch after sketch and laying them in front of Hugo when the guy from before peeks through the door.

"Aldo?" Hugo raises an eyebrow, the cigar hanging loose from his lips.

That frown on Aldo's forehead is deeper now. "We have a problem, sir."

I look between the two men and notice a resemblance between them. Hugo shoos him away.

"We can come again if this is not a good time for you," Raquel offers. She's not oblivious to the odd tension in the air.

"You're not going anywhere." Hugo smirks and sits back in his chair, taking a sip. He gestures to one of my sketches as he swallows. "Mmm. This one. I like it. It would look good on my daughter-in-law."

"This is one of Stella's finest wedding dresses."

Hugo takes off his glasses and throws them on the table. "What do you think I am, an idiot?" He bangs the bottom of his glass on the sketch and the brownish liquor spills over it. "Oops." He chuckles, taking his glass back.

I grab a napkin from the table and lean over the table to try to save my drawing. As I lift it up, my eyes lift, too, and they meet Hugo's jaded gray gaze. I gasp, staggering back, my ass hitting the couch behind me.

I've seen this shade of gray twice in my life.

My fight-or-flight instinct makes me plaster my hand to my stomach. "I'm afraid I don't feel very well."

Raquel feels me as she quickly stands up, taking me with her, then shoves the other sketches back into the file. "You seem busy too. How about a reschedule?" We back off slowly toward the door, still facing Hugo.

Hugo stands up lazily from his chair, reaching somewhere behind him. "Did I not make myself clear?" He pulls out a gun and points it at me. "You are not going anywhere."

We come to a halt, dropping the files in our hands to the floor.

"Come, *Morelli*." Hugo spits out my name. "Don't make me force you." He moves his arm an inch, pointing his gun to Raquel's head. She squeaks and squeezes her eyes shut.

"Who are you and why are you doing this?" I raise my hands in front of my chest and start walking very slowly toward him.

"Stupida puttana!" He comes forward and grabs my wrist, jerking me toward him. "You've cost me everything. My reputation. Mi famiglia!"

He throws me onto the ground, stomping his foot on my stomach. "You were destined to die, and no one defies destiny." He points the gun at me, pressing harder with his foot. I cry out in pain. With my peripheral sight, I can see Raquel frozen like a statue where I left her. She isn't blinking.

I wish she'd close her eyes.

I do.

My heart rate eases its bang against my rib cage. You can only avoid death so much in your life. I've thought about it a lot, and I've made peace with it.

I only have one regret. That I didn't look for Lou earlier. Before he met Tiana, before I boarded that first plane to Rosehill. Things could've been so different.

A door opens with a bang, startling me and making me flick my eyes open.

"You're dead, motherfucker," a familiar voice threatens before I hear the cock of a gun.

My heartbeat accelerates as I see Lucifer pressing the barrel of his gun on the back of Hugo's head.

"Remove your dirty foot off of her," Lucifer commands.

Hugo chuckles darkly, pressing harder and making me whimper out of pain. "Make me."

"You're going to die a slow and painful death for that, *uncle*." There's so much determination behind Lou's words it makes me shiver.

I stare at his face, but he's not looking at me. His eyes are fixed on Hugo's head.

Aldo sneaks up unnoticed behind Lucifer, pressing a gun to Lucifer's back. "Let him go. We've got bigger problems."

"You're dead, too," Lucifer snarls. "I will burn this fucking family to the ground like I should have done a long time ago."

"Carter has ambushed us. Let my father go and fight for your family or die like a traitor." Aldo grunts. "We've lost several men outside. We've got to be moving. Their death is on your conscience, you know." He pushes the gun into Lucifer's back. He doesn't move an inch.

"Let. Her. Go," Lucifer commands. To my surprise Hugo

lowers the gun on me and removes his foot. He twists back faster than a man his age should be able to and elbows Lucifer in the nuts. Lou falls to his knees, his face reddening as both of the men make their escape through the door behind him.

"Tell me what to do." I crawl to him and take his face in my hands. He looks up to meet my eyes, and there's so much regret there. His face is starting to take a purple shade, his breathing ragged.

"I'll be fine. Raquel. I don't think she's breathing." He nods toward her.

I get up and run to her, ignoring the punishing pain in my stomach. "Raquel? Hey?" I wave my hand in front of her face. "I think she's in shock but she is breathing."

Lucifer is starting to recover as he tries to make his way toward me. I run to him and wrap my arms around him, squeezing him hard.

"I've missed you, princess." He rests his forehead on mine, our noses brushing.

"I love you," I hear myself whispering before I recklessly press my lips against his. He drinks me in like I'm the rain in his desert. He takes my cheek in his palm, angling my face, and his tongue dives in chasing mine.

A gunshot sounds from the hallway, interrupting us. The other door of the room swings open and another gunshot pierces our ears, along with Raquel's shrieking voice. "Oh! My! God!"

I turn around to see Aldo's body fall onto the floor next to her, bleeding out. The shot came from Marcel standing at the door, looking at Lucifer. "Figured you hate me enough already."

Lucifer nods. "Hugo must be close."

Marcel's jaw flexes. "On the kitchen floor."

Lucifer grabs my hand and squeezes hard as if I'm going to run away. "Let's go."

Marcel grabs Raquel by the arm, and the four of us run to the hallway, Lucifer leading us to the back exit. He halts when he notices the armed men with their backs to the exit.

"Too late. They've surrounded us. I called for backup," Marcel says.

There are shooting, grunting, and screaming sounds coming from the outside. This feels like all my worst nightmares of what I imagined went down in the Morelli manor all those years ago. My knees buckle as I slide to the floor, restraining the urge to vomit.

Lucifer kneels before me. "You're stronger than this, princess. Can you hold on a little bit more for me?"

Our gazes swing left as we see men coming inside the house. We turn to enter the room next to us, when we hear Thomas Carter's voice.

"And who do we have here?"

Lucifer turns around, under the doorframe, blocking it so I can't go out. "Back off," he says to me when I try to peek over his shoulder.

"No!" I wrap my arms around his middle from behind and hear a malicious laugh from the other side.

"Stella." Lucifer's voice is a warning that scares even me.

Two hands wrap behind me and pull me back. "Are you insane?!" Raquel squeaks in my ear.

Lucifer closes the door to the room, leaving him on the other side.

I writhe against Raquel's grip. "Let me go! I swear to God, if you don't let me go…"

A single gunshot pierces the air behind the door, and my heart stops. I push back the bile rising to my throat and focus the sudden urge of energy into getting away from her grip just as Marcel is done securing the windows so no one can enter through them.

"Lou!" I charge forward, swinging the door open. My eyes immediately focus on him beating up some guy on the floor, who is starting to give up and lose conscience.

The barrel of a gun appears on my side, Thomas Carter behind it. "I didn't want to do this. You felt like a daughter to me, Stellina." He says this with regret as it's clear that I'm already dead in his mind and by his hand.

His finger rests on the trigger.

A memory flashes in front of me.

Fifteen. Lucifer's curls vibrate with his laughter as he saddles up our horses for a ride to the beach. His warm naked chest pressing against my blouse as we make out on the sand, and I'm careful not to touch his first tattoo. The cliff is digging into my back, but the sweet pain in my intimate parts is much stronger.

Five. My father and my mother walk down the same beach. They're holding each of my hands, swinging me back and forth, laughing. One of my last and very few memories of my mother.

"Over my dead body, Carter." Lucifer's growl brings me back into the present as I see him shielding my body with his.

"That can be arranged." His finger presses the trigger. Lucifer falls on his knees in front of me. A noise pierces my ears, threatening to leave me deaf. I realize it's my screaming.

I tumble down, tears burning my cheeks, as I scream his name. Lucifer falls to the floor, his eyes glued to mine and his arm reaches out, trying to catch mine. A body wraps around me and pulls me back. I scream but no one seems to listen.

"Stella!" Marcel growls in my ear. The deafening sound of my heartbeat drowns him out. "Take care of him," he orders to someone and tries to lift me off the ground.

"No! He needs me. Let me go. He needs you." I writhe and scratch him but it's useless. Marcel is hard as steel, his grip strong over me as he drags me off the floor back to the room.

"Lucifer will come back from the dead to kill me himself if I don't save you. Stop fighting!"

"Let. Me. Go!" I roar like a wounded lioness, but it's too late; we're already in the room, and Marcel is guarding the door.

"This isn't your war. We're outnumbered. Stay back!" Marcel orders as my sobbing is growing stronger, and I curl on the floor, rocking back and forth.

Raquel sits next to me and wraps me in a hug.

"I am not losing Lucifer again," I cry out. She squeezes me harder, muffling my words.

"Shhh." She caresses my head. "You're not. He's strong. He'll pull through."

I pull back from her and look into her eyes. She avoids my gaze. She doesn't believe that either.

"But what if he doesn't?" The question hangs in the air for a minute, the three of us silent against the background of gunshots and crashing sounds.

When no one answers, I call out Marcel's name and wait to meet his blue gaze. "I need you to promise me something."

"What?"

"If he doesn't make it, let me die."

Raquel gasps, tears rolling down her cheeks.

"You're nuts," he barks out.

"I've lived once without him. I'm not doing it again. You might as well put me in the same grave because if Lucifer is going to hell, I'm going down with him."

"For Christ's sake, woman! I won't kill you."

"You won't have to. Just don't save me."

Marcel goes quiet as he stares into my eyes, searching for a sign of hesitation. When he doesn't find any, his head bobs in a barely noticeable nod.

Seems like I might get my fairy tale after all. It'll just be a different kind of ending.

CHAPTER THIRTY-FIVE

STELLA

I'm huddled in a corner, sobbing. Raquel is uncharacteristically quiet, switching between pacing the room and checking up on me. Marcel is pressed against the door, listening to the noises. They're slowly becoming quieter. A few minutes ago, a man's voice came out of the handheld transceiver on his belt. He told Marcel they've lost most of their men, which is the universal phrase for we're next.

Raquel had a minor breakdown, started crying and praying before she collected herself and continued with the pacing.

I didn't feel anything. There wasn't fear. There wasn't sadness. I just want everything to come to an end sooner so I can be with my love one way or another.

I can't help but wonder if that's what my stepbrothers felt like that night in the manor. I think about them every day. After the massacre, Aunt Melanie took me to church to pray for their souls. The preacher there said they'd found peace beside my stepmother. Aunt Melanie said she doesn't deserve it, but I think everyone deserves redemption. She wasn't born malicious after all; someone or something made her that way.

The preacher didn't say anything about my father, though. I thought that was because he didn't want to voice out what we all knew. He was a long way out of heaven, just not in the direction we thought.

And yet, I still prayed for him every day to find his peace. He's just my father. It's not like he was abusive to me; he gave me everything. He never truly loved another woman than my mother. He might have not been the best human being, but he tried to be the best father. I guess he could only do so much.

"Why is it so quiet?" Raquel's whisper sends chills crawling up my spine. She has a point. It's been too quiet for a while now.

Marcel picks up his handheld transceiver, bringing it to his mouth. "Talk to me, G. What is going on?"

The voice of the man on the other line comes in seconds later. "We've been surveying the house. Cameras show there's movement in the master bedroom. Otherwise, the house is empty. They've sprawled across the property, searching for the last of our men."

"How many?" The pain behind Marcel's voice must be tearing him to shreds.

"Twenty-two, sir. Only five got out alive."

"Christ!" Marcel sucks in a breath.

Another voice of a man comes in. "Sir, we've located a suspicious van parked near the property. We think it's the Federoffs."

"Motherfuckers," Marcel hisses. "Are they preparing for something?"

"Seems like they're just watching the show, sir."

Marcel drops the transceiver in his pocket and smacks the

wall. "Of course. That motherfucker set this whole thing up so they can watch us kill each other."

There's a burning sensation crawling up my veins. Fury clouding my mind. "So, this whole thing is because of Sebastian? Because he's jealous that he can't have Tiana?"

Marcel nods, rage inflaming his blue eyes.

All that power everyone's been saying I have finally erupts inside of me.

I grab one of the guns out of his holster. "I didn't kill Tiana when I had the chance, but this should hurt a little more." I drop the safety.

"Give me that." Marcel tries to take it away from me, but I hide it behind me before he can.

"I'll choke Sebastian to death if I have to, but that motherfucker is going down. No one touches my family."

The voice from the transceiver comes again. "Sir, I think it's best if you sneak out the house. Thomas Carter is still looking for you. They're in the living room."

"Copy that. Thank you, G."

Marcel opens the door slowly, Raquel and me behind his back. He scans the hallway and leads us out into a pool of blood on the floor. We sneak away, stepping over dead bodies. Raquel walks between Marcel and me, and her face color changes from white, to yellow, to green, as she carefully tries to avoid looking at the bodies. I, on the other hand, only feel relief as I try to recognize Lucifer's face in every one of them and fail.

We enter the kitchen area. Rough steps echo behind us. Marcel pushes us to the wall.

"Shhh," he whispers with a finger to his lips.

The steps start to subside when the three of us move our gazes from the door we came in to the bloody knife on the floor in front of us. Our eyes follow the blood trail, and I instantly regret it. There lies the body of Hugo, his belly sliced, guts spilling out.

Raquel grabs my arm, holding me for support as her lunch spills onto the floor. Bile rises to my throat, and I take a deep breath.

I can fight it—I chant in my mind as I breathe deeply in and out. The steps stop. A moment passes. Two. Marcel and I raise our guns, pointing at the door just as Thomas Carter and his soldiers enter.

"Well, well. What do we have here?" He smirks when he sees my trembling hands pointing the gun to his head. "I just want you to know, Stellina, this is nothing personal. It's a power game, and you're just a pawn. Lower your gun."

"Over my dead body," I spit out with anger I didn't even know I possessed. Well, I guess the apple doesn't fall far from the tree, right?

"That's what your boyfriend said before I put a bullet through his heart."

Without giving it much thought, I point the gun and pull the trigger.

"You fucking bitch!" he screams out as his shoulder goes slack. Not quite the organ I was targeting, but it'll do.

All of the guns point at me. Marcel and I have ours on Thomas.

"Take a knee or you're next." I make sure to aim better. "You're talking to a Morelli."

The smirk on Thomas's face turns to a full-blown smile. "I knew I shouldn't underestimate you."

Out of nowhere, the sound of an automatic firearm fills the air outside of the house, startling all of us.

"Where the fuck is my daughter?" Giovanni Morelli's furious growl makes us all turn to the door, a second before he knocks it down with his foot. Armed men spill into the house, pointing their guns left and right. My father walks in like he owns the house, an automatic firearm in his hands, yelling, "Stellina!"

I glance at Thomas Carter, his jaw on the floor, gun pointing down as he stares at my father. That's my opening.

Marcel seems to be one step ahead of me, as he pushes my hand down right before I pull the trigger and the bullet meant for Carter ricochets off the wooden flooring.

"Here, Daddy!" I call out, and the whole army of soldiers who are probably enough to guard one of our borders spills into the kitchen. Giovanni gives Thomas a hard stare until he notices me. He runs to me and lifts me into his embrace, kissing my cheeks and my head.

"Stellina! Never ever run away from me again." His voice doesn't waver for a second, which is why I'm so surprised when he whimpers in my ear so no one will hear the great boss of the underworld break. "I love you!"

His soldiers surround us, creating a human shield of strong bodies, bulletproof vests, and automatic guns.

"I'll be damned. Giovanni fucking Morelli!" Thomas Carter growls, seemingly astonished.

Daddy doesn't pay him any mind. He lets me down. "Are you injured? I'm going to kill them. Every one of them," he threatens as he searches my body with his eyes for any injuries.

"I'm fine, but Daddy…" He looks down, frowning at the gun I'm still clutching. I drop it to the ground as a tear slides down my cheek. "Lou. They shot him. I don't know where he is."

Daddy pinches his nose between his eyes as he takes a deep breath. "So help me, God, if he's…" He doesn't finish that sentence.

A deep, rich voice booms in the hallway like thunder announcing a storm. "Are you fucking insane?!"

Daddy and Marcel exchange narrow glances. Both of them turn to Raquel and me, whispering "Get under the table!"

We comply, squatting down. The house is dead silent, the noises outside stopped as well, as the only thing that can be heard are the footsteps of the mysterious man.

"Wasn't the Sicilian massacre enough for you?!" His question is rather a statement, hiding dark promises of blood behind it. "Someone is going to lose his head for this," he says simply.

A pair of feet shod in Tom Ford Black Alligator Boots that cost nearly fifteen thousand dollars steps into the room, not a speck of blood on them, despite the soaked hallway floor.

"Morelli," the newcomer states simply. He doesn't seem surprised by the revival of my father. Giovanni doesn't answer back; he simply nods his head in a greeting. "Welcome back," the man says, then proceeds to walk deeper into the kitchen. I can't see anything of him behind the bodies surrounding me, except his shoes.

Raquel's eyes are wide and wild. I take her hand. Everybody stays silent as the man reaches Hugo's body. He stops in front of it, and I can feel everyone in the room holding their breath for a minute, waiting for his response. Whoever that man is, everyone in this room, including two of the most powerful men in the underworld, fear him. There's power oozing out of him, clogging the room, making it hard to breathe.

"Hmm." He kicks Hugo's body, making his guts jostle. I have to suck in a deep breath and squeeze Raquel's hand hard to stop us from puking.

A man comes out of nowhere and instantly kneels down to the mysterious man in power, brushing his shoes with a handkerchief. When his shoes are squeaky clean again, he goes to stand between my father and Thomas.

The powerful man turns to Carter. "You'll answer to me for this."

This simple sentence is enough to make the mighty Thomas Carter's knees shake.

The Tom Fords turn in the direction of the exit. "Now, did Lucifer finally go home to hell?" There's a note of humor in his deep voice. My stomach decides it's the right moment to churn, swelling as the man's shoes turn my way. Dio! I hope he can't see me. Imagine what he's capable of if the mafia bosses are scared of him. What if he finds out I'm the apple of discord in this war?

Marcel speaks first. "We're not sure yet."

I can hear the smile on the mysterious guy as everyone holds their breath, once again waiting for the verdict.

"Good." That's the last thing he says with a positive note in his tone before he walks out of the house as fast as he came in.

It takes a minute after he leaves before everyone in the room collectively sucks in a breath of relief.

I'll be damned. I think we just met the king of the underworld.

CHAPTER THIRTY-SIX

STELLA

A few hours later...

*B*eep. Beep. Beep.
If my heartbeat had a speaker, it would've deafened us.

Beep. Beep. Beep.

But Lucifer's has. The sound is calm and slow, making mine beat twice as hard.

His eyes are closed, two doctors chattering, leaning over his body on the hospital bed in the middle of his bedroom, courtesy of my father with "the best doctors in New York" package.

They asked me if I needed any sedatives, but I don't. What I need is my heart to pull through beating for both of us as his is failing him.

I'm positive I could kill every one that brought this to him with my bare hands. I'll start with the one who shot him in the arm, but I won't miss his heart like he missed Lou's. Then the one who kneed him in the head, causing him to lose conscience. He won't be able to use his balls again. I'll finish off with the army of people who trampled over Lucifer's lifeless body on the ground, sending him straight into comatose. I'd like to tie them to the ground and let all of Daddy's purebred horses…

"There's nothing more we can do at this stage." The doctor's voice cuts off my train of murderous thoughts. She's talking to my father, whom I didn't notice coming in while I was busy plotting my revenge.

"The maid will show you to the dining room. It's past noon. You must be starving," Daddy tells them. The team seems familiar with him, which only proves there were at least three more people who knew of his survival before I did.

The two doctors and the nurse thank him and exit. Daddy sits on Lucifer's bed, back turned to me.

Beep. Beep. Beep.

The sound is bleeding into my ears now as silence falls over us. Every stroke hammering into my head.

The feeling of loss isn't foreign to me, but this time is different. My heart is no longer paper-thin. It's steel and it's strong. Lou and I. We're one and the same. Our hearts beat in the same rhythm. Our souls bleed the same blood. Come hell or high water, we'll walk through this together.

A ringing sound behind the doors splits the silence. Nina walks in, giving me a phone.

Daddy turns my way, an annoyed expression on his face. "Please take this outside. I need to pray for him."

Pray to what? The devil? 'Cause my God sure isn't going to listen to the person who murdered a dozen people a few hours ago. What kind of drugs are they feeding him because they could come in handy right about now?

The hallway is empty as Nina makes herself scarce.

"Hello?"

"Sweet baby Jesus! You scared the shit out of me." Damien's relieved voice comes from the phone.

"Why?"

"We just saw there was a gas leak at the Viscontis on the news and the house burned do... Oh!"

There's a rumble in the background, and I hear Ivy yelling like a warrior, "For the love of God, give me that!"

So they found out the official cover-up version. A gas leak caused the mansion to go up in flames and everybody inside to burn unrecognizable. Because another massacre on the news would've put everyone in danger. Or so at least that was what I overheard from Daddy's conversation with someone. My guess is the mysterious fifteen-grand-shoes man. By his mere presence, I could tell he can make everything he wishes to disappear.

Ivy roars on the phone. "Stells, if you're not dead already, I'm going to kill you. You almost gave me a heart attack."

"Why are you breathing so hard?"

Damien's laugh booms in the background. "She heard your voice all the way from the nursery, ran out, and literally climbed over me to get the phone. Bear-style, claws and everything."

Ivy huffs. "Don't pretend you don't like my claws, Mr. Playboy."

I clear my throat. "I'm fine, thanks for asking."

"What happened?" I knew Damien wouldn't believe this made-up story.

At the same time Ivy asks. "Why are you crying?"

And that's the difference between women and men. Best friends and brothers. The first thing a woman will always catch is your emotion, while men go straight to business.

"I can't talk about it on the phone," I answer both of them.

"It's Lucifer, isn't it?" Ivy speaks first.

"Have I told you how much I love you, babe?" My voice comes out as a whimper. Dammit, isn't crying my eyes out for hours enough?

"Is he?" Her question hangs in the air as both of them suck in a breath.

And there you go. Tears prickle on the corners of my eyes and roll down my heated cheeks as much as I try to stop them. I wipe them frantically. "He's in a coma."

Ivy lets out her breath first, and her voice shakes. "Oh, babe. Hang on. We're coming."

I sniff, snot falling from my nostrils like running water, mixing up with the tears. "What about Devora?"

"Oh God, Devora!" Ivy shrieks.

"Ouch!" Damien yelps. "You know you can just round the couch instead of running over me again, right?"

Ivy yells, distant in the background. "But where's the fun in that?"

Only my best friends could make me snort out a chuckle in this situation. "Did you two just leave Devora alone?" My stiff body relaxes under the unfamiliar sound.

I allow myself a moment of weakness. A moment where the pain and the tears mix with the love and the laughter and cause me to question my sanity.

Damien sighs. "We're the worst parents, aren't we?"

I thank the universe silently for my best friends and the way they make me feel alive even if just for a glimpse of a second with their weird, perfectly imperfect little family.

I beg God for forgiveness for the jealousy in my bones. Because I want what they have. I want to have someone to step over, and I want that someone to complain about me.

"Don't worry, that's why you've got me."

Damien is as serious as a heart attack now. "Hang tight, we'll be there as soon as possible. I love you, Stells."

He hangs up before I can tell him I love him, too, and I love Ivy, but more than all of them, I love baby Devora, and I want to live to see them. But most of all, I love Lucifer.

Selfish has never been a trait of mine, but it's starting to be. Because love is what I deserve. In life and in death.

A day later

I've been sitting in silence on the chair next to his bed for half an hour now, trying to figure out a way to start the conversation. I want to tell him so much, and I want to be mad at him for the next millennia.

"My dad apologized, Lou," I mumble. I don't think a right way to start a conversation with a comatose man will ever come, so I might as well start chronologically. "Can you believe it? Giovanni Morelli begging for someone's forgiveness! Do you think I should forgive him?"

The pulse on the monitor doesn't indicate any thoughts Lucifer might have on this, but I already know what he would've said.

On to the next matter of the day. "Maybe I should wait for you to wake up and find this on your own, but I'd rather prepare you. Giovanni's kind of settling into your townhouse. He's ordering around the staff, but don't worry. I didn't let him fire anyone. He brought his own people, too, though. He's in your study with Damien. Ivy's putting Devora to sleep in my bedroom. Rosalie will come when she has a break in her schedule too. It's kinda crowded." I look up to the ceiling, unable to meet Lucifer's closed eyes. Just in time for my point to drive home, some people start yelling in the hallway.

Stupidi, I want to burn this fucking house down with everyone in it. Oh God, what am I going to do with myself?

I sigh, reclining on the chair. "I miss the silence and loneliness we used to have. There was comfort in it." I close my eyes. "All these people make me anxious."

A minute of silence passes in this room as I hear the mumble and rumble going on in all other rooms. Finally, I muster the courage to open my eyes and bring my gaze from the ceiling to Lucifer. His scratched, patched, and utterly perfect face is the most serene I've seen him. I wonder if he's as calm as he looks. If he's found peace wherever he is or he's clawing his way back to me.

"I really miss you, Lou." My voice breaks, tears pushing for freedom. One rolls down and others follow behind it as I wipe them off with my thumbs. But they don't give up and they roll and they roll, just like my feelings are starting to spiral out of control.

"Do you think I should forgive you?" I whisper, partly hoping he will hear it. Because in my head he wakes up, and he begs for my forgiveness. But in reality he lies there, lips parted and no word coming out of them, only making my flow of tears stronger.

Thing is, I've already forgiven him. I didn't want to but it happened, long before the fight. What he did will come out of his ass, but I know whatever happens I will never ever leave him. I will torment him till death, but I won't let him die without me.

I grit my teeth as my tears are getting out of control and

the hiccups come. I growl in his face, "I'm angry at you, you know. You hurt me."

He doesn't move, and it only makes me angrier. Anything, literally anything will be better than silence. I jump to my feet and start pacing the room. It's as dark as a cave in here. It reminds me of us.

I try to calm myself, but I can't. I come to a halt in front of his bed and throw my hands in the air. "I don't even give a fuck that you lied to me. No." I take a step farther and plant my fists on my hips. "How could you leave me in the dark again, hanging on the thread between life and death? Nothing can be simple with you, can it?"

My fingers instantly tangle around locks of hair and pull on it, awaiting for one of his comebacks. For a sign of life, a ragged breath.

A simple *no* would do it.

I plop in the chair and throw my head back, sighing.

I wait and I wait and nothing but silence.

CHAPTER THIRTY-SEVEN

LUCIFER

I came into this world like a bastard, and I always knew I'd die as one. But not today. No.

My old friend is waiting at the gate, his horns gleaming in the dark. His smile is familiar; I've met him before. But I don't take a step farther down the lava-coated path.

"I've got unfinished business," I tell him. He nods and backs off. But before he leaves, he turns around to face me one more time, and I can tell this is the last one. I might have sold my soul and done his job on Earth, but he's done granting me favors.

Good. I only need one more to make things right. And I'll walk through hell and back to get to her.

CHAPTER THIRTY-EIGHT

LUCIFER

It's warm in here. A ray of light pierces the darkness. Beeping sounds hammer through my head.

I blink, and it takes me a minute to realize I'm awake. Something warm is holding my hand, and I look down to see a female hand. I trace where it links to and find Stella asleep on a chair next to me. She's bent in a weird position, and it must be so uncomfortable. I let her hand go carefully and try to push up from the bed. It's harder than I thought and a pain I didn't register until now shoots through my body. My left shoulder stings, and I can't remember why. Looking around my body, I just now realize this strange beeping sound in the background isn't in my head, it's a machine I'm connected to with a thousand wires.

Sitting up in bed doesn't go very well, but I manage to do it half-assed. I use the hand that doesn't hurt as much to caress Stella's cheeks, trying to wake her up, because clearly I won't be able to stand-up and transfer her to the bed.

"Hey." I smile when her lashes flutter.

She stares at me, holding her breath like she's waiting for

me to vanish into thin air. The beeping sound intensifies as I look into her widened blue eyes. My heart rate is making quite an effort to embarrass me.

"You look uncomfortable, princess. Come here." I tap the bed beside me.

Her eyes almost bulge out. "Lou?" she whimpers, placing her hand over her mouth. A tear rolls down her cheek, and I wipe it. She shudders under my touch and jumps up from the chair. I'm expecting her to lie beside me or sit, but she launches forward, wrapping me in the roughest hug.

"Dio mio! Mi amore. You're alive."

"Why wouldn't I be?" I say, but it's muffled from her mighty grip on me. I notice she left my hurting arm out of the hug. My caring princess.

"Don't you remember?"

I shake my head, the motion making me dizzy.

"Wait, let me get the doctors."

Sometime later, after many examinations, one excruciatingly embarrassing shower with the help of the nurse, and the removal of a catheter, the doctors prescribe me physical therapy and leave us the fuck alone.

Stella sits on the chair near the bed this whole time, listening. The second they close the door, I look at her and tap my chest. There are no words needed; she immediately jumps up and lies beside me, carefully placing her head on my pec.

"Do you remember when I was thirteen and we had the worst flu season?" She looks up, her forehead creasing adorably. I nod, a soft smile rising on my face. "I was so sick they isolated the whole floor for my nanny and me. But you know what? I was the happiest sick thirteen-year-old because those nights when you came to hold me through the fever, I knew no one would catch us. We were free."

"You were always free, mi amor. I would've never let anyone cage you."

"I want to be free now, too, Lou," she whispers, looking down.

I bring her chin up to look me in the eyes. "Aren't you?"

"I'll never be free of you. You've always been the first and last thing on my mind each day no matter if I had you or I didn't."

Hearing her say those words makes me both the most miserable and the happiest bastard. I hold my breath, waiting for her verdict. My memories of the shooting may still be appearing in little glimpses, but I remember fully how I broke her heart.

Instead of kicking me in the nuts like I deserve or telling me to go to hell, which I just came back from, she smiles.

"Remember the night of June eighteenth?"

How could I possibly forget? The date of our first time and the last time I saw her is sealed in my mind like a stamp. She both healed and broke my soul that night.

"Remember what we talked about at sunrise?"

Vividly. "Refresh my memory."

"You told me you wanted a family. Promised me we would run away the second I turn eighteen. I told you I wanted to have a house of my own, one that is filled with laughter and love. With everything that the manor lacked."

I brush a fallen hair strand off her face. "You said you would've been content with a small one as long as it's filled to the brim with children and animals."

Silence falls over us as my heart counts the beats.

One. Two. Three.

I can't help but break it. "What changed?"

"Us," she whispers.

I raise her chin to look me in the eyes. "Princess, my looks and character might've evolved through all the shit I've been through, but my love for you will never change even after we're long dead." Her eyes wet, and I squeeze her tighter. "I will understand if you…" The words get stuck in my throat. I open my mouth again, but a different truth spills out of it. "No. You know what, fuck that shit. We were always meant to be. I won't let you spend the rest of your life without me, but I will spend mine paying for my sins by giving you everything you ever wanted. Because this is us. Fucked up, bruised and shattered. Rare, beautiful and fragile. A real fairy tale. One that legends are told about. Because we aren't a fucking book or a movie. We are here and now, and that's the only thing that matters."

I bend my neck, a piercing pain shooting through it, to kiss Stella when the first tear falls down. I find her lips, soft and hot, and take what has always been mine. Her first and her last kiss. She answers me by opening her mouth and sliding her hot tongue ever so slightly over mine. Her tears wet both our cheeks as I let her lead. With every swift movement and every harder and deeper push of her tongue, she's regaining the control over herself.

She whimpers, making my dick instantly hard. I take over, wrapping both arms around her body and pulling her to sit over me. She settles on my middle, carefully, but it's not enough. I want to feel all of her.

"Stop." She suddenly tears her mouth away from mine like a painful bandage. "You are still healing. I don't want to hurt you."

"But I want you." I snake my hands up her body and start unbuttoning the tight blue blouse she's wearing.

Blush creeps up her neck, spreading down her chest and up her cheeks. "Let me take care of you another way," she says as she gathers her blonde hair in a ponytail.

Oh shit. Fuck yes.

I grin like the Cheshire cat as she rolls down my boxers, my cock springing impatiently.

"Turn around." I grab her hip and show her which way I'm talking about. Her cheeks turn bright red as she throws one leg over my face. Her panties are damp as I roll them down.

Instead of starting timid like always, Stella dives in until the tip hits her throat. Her tongue does magical things to me as her mouth works me up and down, fast and deep. I almost forget her pussy is right in front of my face, dripping and waiting for me to drink her up like God's nectar. I swipe my tongue, and her little moan vibrating on my cock almost makes me come. Her pink lips mesmerize me like it's the first time I've seen a pussy, and I bury my face in it, licking and sucking.

We work on each other, synchronizing our movements, our sounds, until my torso is shaking beneath her hands, and she's clenching on my tongue.

"Fuck!" I roar into her pussy as I feel the sensations up my spine, but Stella suddenly stops, cutting me off.

She whips her head back to look straight into my eyes. "I want to live in Rosehill," she states.

I raise an eyebrow, barely containing myself from grabbing her neck and shoving her mouth over my cock so I can come.

"With you," she finishes, staring me down.

"You got it," I say faster than a Bugatti Veyron. At this point I'd agree to go to a Trolls concert with her, and I'd even dress as Poppy. Don't ask me how I know their names.

She wraps her hand around my shaft and squeezes, making me shudder in pleasure. "Promise me." She licks the tip of my cock.

"Dammit, woman!" I growl. Returning the favor I suck on her clit until she screams. "I promise I will do whatever I can." I push a finger into her dripping pussy and trace another one around her anus. "Now promise me this ass is mine."

She moans as I press onto it. "I promise I will do whatever I can," she echoes and slides her mouth down until her lips graze my balls.

A minute more of licking and sucking, and we both come into each other's mouths at the same time.

I fall back on the bed like lead, feeling both drained and recharged. Stella slides off the bed, wipes the corner of her mouth with her finger and licks it clean, making me growl.

"You little minx."

She shrugs, a satisfied, playful smile on her beautiful face. "All is fair in love and war."

"Come here." I pull her hand, and she lies in my embrace. "The war is over for us, princess. Only love from now on."

CHAPTER THIRTY-NINE

STELLA

S<u>ometime after that...</u>

"Wow." My words echo off the high ceiling of the house.

"I'll go get a mop because you're drooling all over the wooden floors." Ivy disappears from my side, chuckling. Ivy's steps bounce off the empty walls in the far end, where Damien is cooing Dev to sleep. Another pair of steps coming from behind stop just as a warm body presses against my back and wraps two hands around my belly.

"So?" Lucifer buries his mouth on the curve between my neck and shoulder, nibbling.

"I love it!" I squeak out like a rubber duck.

"I told you!" Damien shouts from the other side of the empty space that's going to be our living room.

I knew Lucifer was looking at estates in Rosehill after I found him sneaking into his office talking to someone twice.

Somehow (I call it magic) that phone number landed on my phone's keyboard, and the rest is history.

The estate agent is now walking and talking animatedly in her pencil suit, ushering us to move forward, eager to show us the master bedroom.

"How many rooms is it again?" I ask as Lucifer slowly walks behind me, guiding me through an oil green kitchen space, even fancier than Damien's. I twist my head to the side and whisper to his face. "I love it." He smiles against my cheek and plants a little kiss on it.

"Five bedrooms, two office rooms, four and a half baths and a guest house," the real estate lady says from the top of the stairs where she stopped, waiting for us.

"Perfect." I gasp, looking around the hallway.

Lucifer's hand lands on my butt as I climb the stairs before him, making me jump. He squeezes hard before I swat it away with a chuckle. He makes a barking sound, trying to bite my butt cheek. I run upstairs, breathlessly giggling. As soon as I walk into the master bedroom, I stop short, bracing the door frame, making Lucifer bump into me. We stumble forward into what I decide in a second is going to be our bedroom.

"It's soundproof as you requested," the agent says, looking mischievously at Lucifer. I glance at him, and he's looking at me, a sinister smile on his face. My cheeks flame up from the knowing look in his eyes. "You have a view to the horse stables on one side and the pool on the other. The attached bathroom has a bathtub. There's a sauna and a steam room down the hall." She continues blabbing while I zone out by the floor-to-ceiling window looking over the stables. Something white flashes from inside of it and I turn around, eyes wide.

"I might not be a knight by any meaning of the word, but

I sure as hell will do anything to give you your fairy tale. So there's your white horse, princess, because in this story you saved me."

My heart somersaults in my chest. This man knows me better than I know myself. I fell in love with this house the second we stepped through the gated doors, and as if it wasn't perfect enough, it's ten minutes away from Damien and Ivy's house, so we're basically neighbors. I wanted to live as close to them as possible, but I never told him that.

"My heart knows every beat of yours, princess." He smiles. "We'll take it," he says to the realtor.

When we're done, Lucifer quickly shoos Damien, Ivy, and her out, sending them on their merry way.

"So..." He twists around, a smirk on his face and mischief sparkling in his eyes. The devil I know. He stalks toward me with a predatory gait.

"So..." I feign innocence, looking up at the ceiling and trying to contain my grin from rising.

Lucifer stops in front of me, grabs my hip bones, and turns me around to face the kitchen counter. His hand sneaks up my spine and curls around the base of my hair. He pushes me forward until my cheek hits the cold counter. "A promise is a promise." His other hand traces the curve of my ass and sneaks under my skirt. My legs start shaking as he slowly traces his fingers through the inside of my thigh and over my damp panties.

My hands shoot to push down my panties, and they fall to the ground.

Lucifer chuckles darkly in my ear as his fingers find my clit. "Always impatient. That's my good girl."

"I don't want to be good." My hushed confession provokes a growl from the depths of his lungs. He pushes a finger inside of me, then another one.

"Tell me more." His voice is a command, his hands possessive, but I know the power lies with me. So I decide to tease him a bit more.

I entangle my hands behind me and undo his belt. "No one has ever touched me like you, my wolf." The button on his pants is next, and his cock springs out right into my hands.

"Yeah?" He bites my earlobe. One of his fingers transfers my juices from my pussy to my ass, making lazy circles around it.

For the past few weeks, we have been experimenting with different types of butt plugs, toys, and lubricants.

"I love to feel the way you expand me. My pussy's made to your mold." I stroke him hard and punishing, the way he likes it. We've grown so accustomed to each other's needs.

There's a squeeze and cold liquid drips down my ass. Lucifer carries it to my hole as I feel it warming me up.

"Very soon your ass will be too." He dips a finger inside my hole, working on me slowly, the way he knows I like it. His other hand is cupping my breast, playing with my sensitive nipple.

I redirect his cock to my pussy and dip the tip in. A moan escapes us both, and I push my butt back taking him all in. He doesn't expect it, and his fingers push deep inside my ass at the same time, making me whip my head back and groan. "I want to be full of you all the time and everywhere."

That makes him groan, and he slides the fingers of his other hand in my mouth. I suck on them like a lollipop.

"Yes, my greedy girl. More." He growls, thrusting his cock and fingers deep into both my openings, and I bite and suck the life out of his middle finger. "If I had three cocks, baby, I would give them all to you, and you would gladly make them soaking wet."

I shiver at the thought of having me full on all sides of him. What a pleasure that would be.

He slides his fingers out of my mouth, carrying my saliva down to my puckered nipples.

Lost in the train of dirty, nasty thoughts, I don't realize I'm on the verge of coming until I say, "You make me your queen when you know I'll gladly be your slave," and his hand wraps around my throat. My whole body trembles with the convulsions of the orgasm as my pussy clenches for dear life around his cock.

He growls and before the last wave of the orgasm crashes in me, he moves his cock and slides it between my ass cheeks, wetting it with my arousal and the lube. Slowly, he pushes the tip first and then inch by inch sinks into my ass.

"I told you I'll get all your firsts." He licks the soft spot between my shoulder and my neck and whispers in my ear. "Make no mistake, princess. I'll be your last, too."

His fingers push into my pussy, and he fills me to the brim again.

A moan escapes me as my thighs tremble under him with an unknown feeling. I've come a lot of times when he fucked my pussy and had a finger up my ass, but I've never felt the way I'm feeling now. The little burn slowly decreases as the butterflies in my stomach and pussy multiply. His tempo increases until I'm all stretched out for him and warm and dripping on his fingers.

He slides his fingers out of me and to my clit. Our moans and groans echo off the ceilings of our new home, making me shoot to the top even faster.

"Our home," I say out loud as I stare into the countertop under me.

"I know." Lucifer growls sinking to my deepest point and

suddenly out of nowhere, my skin prickles. My clit swells, pulsating under the pressure of his moving fingers.

"I'm coming," I scream out as stars roll behind my eyes. The sensations erupt all at once like fireworks exploding in every cell of mine.

Lucifer's roar is enough to deafen the whole neighborhood as he pumps inside me two more times and stills in the deepest point.

Waves of pleasure crash into me, synchronizing with his shakes as he fills me with his release. Spurts of energy trickle up my veins into my brain, and Lucifer falls onto my back as if I drained the soul out of him.

"I love you, Lou, but did you eat a whale?" My words are muffled as he's pressing my cheek hard to the counter.

He chuckles in my ear, and it's the first time I've heard this sound. Like the world doesn't weigh on his shoulders—even though there's serious danger of him crushing mine—and he's free at last.

The biggest smile rises on my face as I realize it's true. He is. We are. Now that father took his organization back, we have our own home and businesses, and we're truly free for the first time in our lives.

Lucifer peels off me reluctantly. "I'll get a cloth."

He comes back a second later and cleans me up with the biggest grin I've ever seen.

"Could you be any more smug?" I roll my eyes and drop down like a sack of potatoes. Who cares if we're buck naked and it's cold and we're on the floor? We're fucking free.

My head can't wrap around the idea.

"Why wouldn't I be?" Lucifer lies down next to me. "I have the brightest star to myself." He looks at me and pushes my chin up to look to the ceiling.

I gasp as I realize I never saw the glass ceiling right

above our heads. Millions of stars sparkle like diamonds in the night sky right above us, and it makes my heart swell when I realize this is not by accident. Lucifer made this—in the kitchen, my favorite place—for me.

"I love you, Lou." I huddle into him as he keeps his eyes on me while I stare at the twinkling stars.

"Why do you call me, Lou? You're the only one who's ever called me that." He nuzzles my neck.

"Lou means wolf in Haitian-French creole."

His brows furrow.

"Everyone called you a lone wolf at the manor, and they weren't entirely wrong."

He pulls me until I'm on top of him, and he wraps his arms around me. My ear is pressed against his heart, listening to every beat like it's a musical masterpiece, and I smile when it skips as he says, "You know wolfs mate for life. I've loved you since the first day, and my heart has never strayed for a second. I'd do anything to protect you, even if it means stripping my own skin down to keep you warm."

"I'll always follow you, my Lou."

"And I'll always protect our pack, my princess."

EPILOGUE

STELLA

I hate being blindfolded. Usually. Okay, maybe these days not so much.

Fine. I love it. Lou turned it into a kink of mine.

Maybe I should see a therapist about it but *bleh*. What would Freud say if my taste turned out to be a little rough and perverted?

I don't care.

I left my past in the, well…past. I've got a future to build, and one I might say is quite bright, judging by the offers coming in day and night for my designs. I had to get Raquel's assistant an assistant.

I haven't thrown up since I stood up to my father. Maybe the therapist was right and I had held onto some unresolved feelings. Or maybe I'm the most comfortable I've been in my life. Whatever it is, I know my demons are defeated for now and hopefully forever.

Family is something that, too, pops up in my mind often, to be honest. Not my immediate one. My future one.

Especially when I feel the pressure of the man I look

forward to creating it with, against my ass. Which, to be frank, is quite often too.

No shame there.

A rock under my foot that makes me trip, slices through my train of thoughts.

"Ugh! Are we there yet?" I tap impatiently on his forearm, the one he's using to guide me forward. Or backward. I don't know anymore because I lost track of any direction after we stepped out of the airplane. Or rather after he carried me off the airplane because I was blindfolded. Again.

"You do realize Ivy's gonna kill me? I have to be on maid-of-honor duty."

"I'm pretty sure Damien will have her too busy to notice."

I roll my eyes, but Lucifer can't see it. I warned them not to sleep with each other on the night before their wedding, but they just laughed at my face. Said they did everything backward, and they will continue the tradition. Assholes. Both of them.

"Just so you know, I'm honoring the tradition on our wedding," I huff out.

"Whoa, slow down. Let me see if I can tolerate you long enough first." He laughs. At me. He's fucking laughing at me.

"Well, I know someone who did, but, oh wait, you killed him… Ahh!" I scream when he picks me up and throws me over his shoulder with a growl. "Let me down, you caveman!" I scream through laughter.

"Can you keep your pretty mouth shut for a minute more before I lose my shit and make it busy." He slaps my ass on his shoulder.

"Screw you." I huff in frustration.

"Oh, you will." I can hear the smile in his statement. I wonder what the bodyguards think of this exchange. Lucifer never lets me go out without them anymore. I would've protested, but I know he's too scared for me and after everything that happened, I'm not sure I'm quite ready to roam the streets alone again.

His pace suddenly slows down, and his feet sink while he walks like we're on a moving bridge or something.

"Where—"

"Thirty seconds, princess." He cuts me off.

True to his word, a couple steps after the ground normalizes again, he lets me down on the floor. There's a creak, like a door is opening, and he takes my hand.

My foot bumps into something, and Lucifer says, "Careful with the doorstep."

A-ha! So my instincts are right again.

"Come on, I'm dying of curiosity," I whine. "At least tell me where we are."

"Canada."

"Canada?" I shriek.

Lucifer laughs and takes me a few steps inside until he stops me.

"Open," he says, and I pull up the blindfold like it's choking me and I'm dying for a breath.

Mmm, choking. Another ki— My train of thoughts is lost as my eyes focus on the view in front of me.

"Wow." My mouth falls open as I stare at a gray wolf staring back at me on the other side of the glass. He or she is standing still and calm in the middle of what looks like a forest or a sanctuary of some kind. It holds my gaze captive just like Lou does, provoking feelings of love and protectiveness inside me. I only tear my gaze away when a brown wolf shows up on the right and comes toward us. It stops right in front of the glass separating us and lies down on the ground.

Lucifer is gone, a lit fireplace on a wooden wall in his place in the reflection of the glass. The wolf doesn't look me in the eyes like the other one did, but it looks down around my legs. I turn around to see what he's staring at, and my knees buckle. I have to grab the first thing next to me—a wooden chair—to steady myself. Lucifer is right behind me, kneeling on one knee, a black velvet box opened in his hand. Inside a pink heart-shaped diamond sparkles from the lowlights of the lamps in the cabin.

Tears gather in the corners of my eyelids as I stare at Lucifer's calm eyes. The silence in the cabin is deafening as we both stand still, staring at each other. He opens his mouth and closes it. I feel like I'm stuck in a dream, which are mostly good ones since we started living together, too afraid to say anything so I don't wake up.

A beat passes before Lucifer opens his mouth again. "I still can't understand if all of this is real and not the fairy tales I used to read to you, because I'm the most unworthy bastard in this world, and yet I have the privilege to be in your presence. Somehow, I even managed to strike one hell of a deal with the devil to make sure you'll be mine forever."

I fall on my knees in front of him, one hand plastered to my mouth and the other on my heart. My ears ring with the scream of the word *yes*, but my lips can't make a sound.

Sweat breaks on Lucifer's forehead as he looks down at the ring. "For the longest time I thought my heart died with my mother on my birth. Then I selfishly took yours when you offered it, and I broke it so many times that I was afraid I killed it too. But bruised and shattered and turned to dust, it never stopped. It kept me alive. It's only fair if I give you mine in return so I searched the darkest depths for what was gone, but it turned out I never actually lost it. It was always with you.

"So what I'm trying and failing to say is…" He takes the ring in his fist and then takes my hand, placing it on his chest. "Here, take mine." He silently slips the ring over my finger, smiling as we both gaze into each other's eyes, a flashback of our first meeting.

A moment of silence passes.

One. Two. Three.

His smile slowly falls, reminding me I never actually said the word out loud. I launch at him like a wild animal at its prey, knocking him down to the floor, burying myself, my feelings, and everything I own into a kiss that grows into something more.

We make love all night on the plush rug in front of the fireplace with the wolves howling behind the glass of the cabin. He came inside me and let me crawl up inside his soul, so I could light a fire and make a home out of it.

UCIFER

At twilight we board the plane back to Rosehill where the preparation for Ivy and Damien's wedding is in full-force.

Stella didn't technically say *yes* to my proposal, but she kept screaming it for all the wild animals to hear throughout the night while I was buried inside her. And I didn't technically ask her, I just took what's mine.

Renting the wooden cabin at the wolf sanctuary in Canada was one of my best ideas, short of making this woman my wife and having her birth a litter of my babies.

The latter she doesn't know yet, but I've decided to tackle one beast at a time.

Speaking of beasts, Devora pierces my left ear, screaming and crying at the same time in Stella's embrace.

"Maybe you should take her." Stella holds the baby in front of me, mischief sparkling in her blues. That little minx. She's testing me, but she doesn't know a father is the only job I've ever wanted. Besides being *her* husband.

"Gladly." I smirk back at her, and take the little hellraiser. Devora cools off in my arms, looking me straight in the eyes. I can see the rebel in her even now. I glance at Damien motherfucking Black at the other side of the table, the happiest bastard in this hall right now, just in time to see Ivy smashing his face into the cake.

I can't help but feel a little bit sorry for the fucker. He's got his hands full with these two. But come to think about it, all the best people are hellions, so he might have just gotten it right.

I know I did.

I look to my side and Stella's gone. Instantly, I scan the full hall, while rocking Devora back and forth. It takes me a minute to notice half the ladies at the party are gone.

The wedding isn't as big and posh as I thought it'd be. Maybe people do change, I think to myself as I look at Damien, who's now being taken as a hostage, with hands tied and blindfolded to the middle of the room on a single chair.

Suddenly, the music stops and starts again with a dramatic entrance of a dozen ladies dressed in lace and tulle bodysuits. A grin rises to my face as I notice Stella's among them, left of Ivy, who's in the middle in front of Damien. Ivy takes his blindfold off as the music starts and she dances her tail off for five minutes, bringing one hell-of-a-performance and making me realize why Damien is a goner. As if he wasn't smitten enough, he melts to puddle when she straddles him at the end of the mix, and they stay on the chair fullblown making out for two minutes in front of all their friends and relatives without an ounce of shame until someone breaks them off.

I'm pretty sure two more minutes, and he would've fucked her in front of all of us too.

Maybe we could be friends, after all.

A bit later the two of them take Devora from me and dance their first dance as a married couple with her. Then they leave her to sleep with Melanie, who's at the table with the same man I saw in the rain, and they take off somewhere, probably to finish what they started.

Stella and Rosalie, Damien's sister who participated in the dance, too, show up and sit at the table. I just turn around to give Stella a kiss when Rosalie's scream interrupts the whole table.

"That motherfucker!" She's red like a cartoon character but red is her color. From what I've seen from our few encounters, Rosalie has the mouth of a sailor but keeps the perfect image of a socialite. Make no mistake, though she looks as blond, thin, and fragile as a Victoria's Secret model, she certainly has the claws of a mountain lion and the temper of one.

"Who?" Stella's curious nature gets the best of her, and she lets me go sit next to Rosalie.

"That Australian piece of shit!"

Stella looks over Rosalie's shoulder to her phone screen.

"Wow. He's blasting you all over social media."

"I know!" Rosalie shrieks. "Did you see he went on a rant about the nepotism in Hollywood the second they announced that I'll be his co-star? I mean who does that? We'll be working together for months, the least he could do is save his opinion to himself. I've worked so hard to get this role."

"*I won't hesitate to strangle you on Monday.* Seriously Rose?" Stella laughs as she reads what Rosalie posted. "You even tagged him."

"Wait, he just uploaded something." Rosalie opens his profile. "*Can you even reach my neck?* Asshole!"

She's in need of a good fuck if you ask me.

Speaking of fucks, I take Stella's hand and silently lead her out of the hall, leaving Rosalie to deal with her social media drama.

As soon as we're in our room, I plaster Stella against the wall and press behind her. "You love testing me, don't you?"

She purrs innocently. "I don't know what you're talking about."

Yeah, right.

"Let me refresh your memory." I press my dick between her cheeks. She moans in response.

I raise her skirt, surprised to find there's no panties under it. "You're a naughty girl, aren't you?" I slap her ass and slide a finger over her pussy. "You wanna know if I'm ready for a baby, huh?" She's already drenched, making me want to drive home into her faster. "'Cause I am. Let's see if you'll chicken out of this one." My thumb slides to her opening, and I pull her head back to whisper in her ear, "And I brought the whipped cream."

THE END

ACKNOWLEDGMENTS

First, I want to thank myself. This book has been three years in the making. I wrote the first draft by the time I published the first edition of Bad Boys Bring Heaven (Oct 15th, 2020, phew, how the time flies.) I've lost several members of my family since, have been through depression, suicidal thoughts, I was in a reality TV show – the Bulgarian version of The Bachelor, and I got engaged (not to the Bachelor, lol.) Safe to say that I went through hell and heaven along with Stella and Lucifer. There is only one thing that stayed a constant in those years and that was the fact that no matter how happy or hurt I was, I could always go back to Rosehill. My safe haven. I hope these characters bring the same feeling to you.

Second, I want to thank my loved ones for sharing the stories of their struggles with Bulimia Nervosa through me. Their wish is to stay anonymous. I love you. I see you. You got this!

I want to thank all my beta readers, friends and followers for supporting me. I couldn't do it without you.

Thank you to my editor, Lia Fairchild, who is the most patient person in the world, to my proofreading team—SistersGetLit, and to my cover designer—Books and Moods. Without you I'd be lost.

The biggest thanks go out to all my readers for taking a chance on me. I know life is busy and there are so many books to choose from but you picked up mine and that makes me the most grateful person on this planet.

If I may have another minute of your life, please consider leaving **an honest review** on Amazon or Goodreads. It helps indie authors like me a lot!

I hope you enjoyed Stella and Lucifer's story. Rosalie is next and it's promising to be a wild enemies-to-lovers story of a stubborn heiress and Hollywood's golden boy. Stay tuned!

Xoxo, Leah

ABOUT THE AUTHOR

Leah K Plamm has a degree in Business and Entrepreneurship which comes in handy with her current professions—romance books writer and social media influencer (both of which give her mother a heart attack.) Her books contain a mix of contemporary, dark, suspenseful elements with a sense of humor, and you can always count on her to bring the spicy.
She's an avid reader, a passionate Swiftie, and she was a contestant on the Bulgarian version of the Bachelor. Most often you'll find her travelling the world, shooting books and lifestyle vlogs, or playing with her dogs.

You can find her on Instagram (@leahkplamm) or TikTok (@leahkplamm)

Get all the details about future releases here:
Website: www.leahkplamm.com
Goodreads (Leah K. Plamm)

Printed in Great Britain
by Amazon